The KING of the TREES
BOOK FIVE

THE DOWNS

The KING of the TREES
BOOK FIVE

THE DOWNS

WILLIAM D. BURT

WINEPRESS WP PUBLISHING

WinePress Publishing (PO Box 428, Enumclaw, WA 98022) functions only as book publisher. As such, the ultimate design, content, editorial accuracy, and views expressed or implied in this work are those of the author.

Cover and chapter illustrations by Terri L. Lahr.
Text illustrations by Becky Miller.

Scripture references marked NASB are taken from the New American Standard Bible, © 1960, 1963, 1968, 1971, 1972, 1973, 1975, 1977 by The Lockman Foundation. Used by permission.

ISBN 1-57921-797-4
Library of Congress Catalog Card Number: 2005904151

"He was oppressed and He was afflicted, yet He did not open His mouth; like a lamb that is led to slaughter, and like a sheep that is silent before its shearers, so He did not open His mouth."

(Isaiah 53:7, NASB)

CONTENTS

PROLOGUE

How I screamed and thrashed when the bloody knife clipped my ears! Father held me down until it was all over. "I am sorry," he said, though his eyes betrayed as much fear as sorrow. "When we found you, the Gray Death had stolen your memory. You mustn't go out until your ears and head wound have healed. If anyone should ask, you are an orphaned *flatlander*."

Acceptance came hard in Swyndon for a flatlander with scarred ears. Whispers followed me everywhere, even onto the Downs, where I pastured Father's sheep. He and Mother never had any children, so when a young fugitive from the Gray Death wandered bleeding into town, they were happy to take me into their home and love me as their own. Love me they did, though I didn't belong.

The life of a shepherdess is a lonely one, but I was content. My sheep accepted me, scarred ears and all. The Gadabout accepted me, too. He didn't visit often, but his presence was always a comfort, both to my sheep and to me. And then there was the Boar.

To me, he will always be "the Boy." He had a name, but everyone in the village called him "the Boar." He earned the nickname. We were pasturing our flocks one morning when the biggest hog I'd ever seen came rampaging through the sheep, slashing left and right with his wicked tusks. As our animals scattered, the beast came for me and tore my shepherd's crook out of my shaking hand.

Then the Boy appeared at my side. With his spear in one hand and his staff in the other, he brought that boar to its knees, but not before it had gashed his legs. Ignoring his bloody wounds, the Boy drove his spear through the hog's back and into its heart.

After that, the Boy fussed over me as if I were one of his own sheep. He didn't mind my scars, either, though I always wore my hair long to cover my ears. Still, one look at my face, and anyone could see I was an outsider. The Boy didn't care what I was.

At the first hint of the Gray Death, he always sent me with my flocks back to the upland pastures. He often followed us to be sure we didn't stray or lose our way. The afternoon sun casts a deceptive light on the Downs that can easily confuse the unwary.

"Off you go!" he would say, twirling his shepherd's crook over his head ever so playfully. "You can't stay here, else the Gray Death will catch you. You're much too young for a sheepshun."

Nobody, I have since learned, is too young for a sheepshun. I am so thankful no more sheep must needlessly die for the lost.

In my dreams, the Gray Death would call to me from across the Downs with the mournful hissing of wind-rippling grasses. Some days, I would stand alone at the breathing boundary between fog and sun, longing to fling myself into that cool, gray sea my friends so feared. I feared it, too, for it awakened in me dim memories of life before the Clipping, when I knew only the Cold.

"The Cold?" you ask. "Do you mean the cold of a winter's day when the bleak hills huddle against wind-whipped hail and sleet? Or do you mean the cold of a stone floor on bare flesh when the fire has gone as dead as old bones buried under the bitter sod?"

"No," I answer. "I mean the Cold that pierces soul and spirit like a thrice-frozen spear of sea ice. I mean the Cold that can sap the life-heat and living breath out of a body in seconds and leave her a solid lump of frozen flesh, senseless as a stone. *The* Cold."

Still, as a shepherd snatches a lamb's leg from the mouth of a ravening wolf, I salvaged one memory from the Cold: *Melina*.

My name is Melina.

CHAPTER 1

FAERY RINGS

CRASH! A heavy crock filled with bread dough toppled off the kitchen counter and shattered on the floor. Gwynneth had barely brushed the bowl with her elbow. Letting out a forlorn sigh, she gathered her work shift about her knees, knelt on the cold tiles and began picking up the pieces.

"Princess Gwynneth!" her mother Marlis scolded her. "What in the name of Elgathel has gotten into you? You've had your head in the trees all month. That's the third bowl you've broken this week, and now you have ruined the dough, too. I asked you to help me with the baking, but you're only making matters worse. Whatever will I do with you, child? You really must pull yourself together by tomorrow, or you'll be in no shape for the wedding."

Marlis and Gwynneth were filling in for Cook, who was making a few last-minute purchases at the Beechtown spring market. The other royal servants had also been busy day and night cleaning, preparing meals, sewing wedding garments and writing formal invitations. Gwynneth had done her best to stay out of the way.

"I'm sorry, Mother," she said, and tears tickled her cheeks. Ordinarily, she was as nimble and quick-witted as her brother Elwyn and sister Meghan, but lately, she had been leaving a broad swath of

11

destruction in her wake. And she was moody. One minute she was in tears; the next, in laughter. Even Timothy was finding excuses to avoid his betrothed. That didn't improve her temper. If only their wedding plans hadn't gone so disastrously awry!

First, Grandfather Gannon and his sister Glenna had insisted on attending, even if they had to climb gnarly old Lightleaf and ride a peevish griffin. That meant the wedding would have to wait until spring had stirred the torsil trees into leaf. (Timothy's parents knew nothing of Lucambra or of torsil travel. For their sake, a second ceremony would be held in the Beechtown chapel.)

The annual All-comers Griffin Race had further delayed the wedding. Setting out from the Hallowfast, griffin riders from all over Lucambra flew thirty miles down the rugged seacoast to Spider Snag, a dead spruce whose snaggly crown resembled a spider. After rounding the snag, the contestants flew back to the Tower of the Tree, circling it three times before crossing the finish line.

Gwynneth had handily won the race riding Windsong, her father's mount. Timothy and Smallpaw had come in a close second. Unfortunately, in whipping around the Hallowfast on his final turn, Windsong had sucked Gwynneth's wedding gown right out of her bedroom window. Catching on Smallpaw's claws, the dress was torn to tatters and dragged through the mud before Gwynneth could rescue it. Her mother spent an entire month sewing another.

Then there were the rings. Redwing son of Whitewing, king of the sorca, had promised to forge the wedding bands from griffin-delved gold. However, Timothy and Gwynneth had forgotten to send along their ring sizes, so the bands had come back too large. Resizing them had held up the wedding another precious month.

Marlis's green eyes twinkled as she wiped the tears from her daughter's face. "Now don't fret," she said. "Let's not spoil this special day over broken pottery and spilt dough. We still have plenty of flour and yeast, so I can whip up a new batch of bread in a blink. Now be a dear and finish helping me clean up this mess. Then you can fetch me another crock from the pantry outside."

While Marlis scraped dough off the floor, Gwynneth swept up the remaining shards of crockery. Hurrying out the door, she promptly collided with her father, who was carrying an armload of firewood into the kitchen. Rolin and the firewood went flying.

"Father! Are you all right?" Gwynneth anxiously asked as she helped him to his feet. Wearing a homespun tunic, Lucambra's king appeared shaken but unhurt. His mane of chestnut hair was festooned with lichen, moss and mistletoe from the firewood.

"I'm fine," he grunted, brushing himself off. Under his breath he added, "I knew I should have gone deer hunting with Timothy in the Brynnmors this morning. Some days it just doesn't pay to get out of bed, and this is shaping up to be one of those days."

Marlis rushed out of the kitchen to help Gwynneth collect the scattered sticks of wood. The queen caught Gwynneth's eye and when the king's back was turned, she pointed out the green sprigs hitchhiking in his hair. Mother and daughter snickered.

Rolin's head swiveled and he planted his fists on his hips. "How dare you make sport of me?" he demanded in a mock display of regal spleen. "I could have you locked up in the dungeon, or tossed into a dragon's den, or turned into toads, or—or—"

"We don't have a dungeon, and the dragon is dead, Father," Gwynneth reminded him. How she loved fencing with the king!

Folding her arms, the queen leveled a cool look at Rolin from under hooded eyes. "Toads can't prepare your supper, either! If you were forced to fend for yourself, you wouldn't last a week. As I recall, burnt porridge with curdled sour milk is your specialty."

The king feigned a wounded air. "You always like my oatcakes! Besides, you must know that when mistletoe catches in the king's hair, any maiden who comes into his presence must kiss him."

Marlis and Gwynneth dutifully pecked him on the cheek. Grinning, Rolin said, "That's more like it!" He waved a finger underneath Gwynneth's nose. "Speaking of porridge, the next time we have oatmeal for breakfast, you had better watch your back!"

The three broke into laughter. A week earlier, Gwynneth had used a serving spoon to catapult a steaming glob of sticky oatmeal smack into the back of her father's head. This opening shot led to a flurry of others as Bembor, Marlis, Elwyn and Meghan joined in the oatmeal war. Cook later remarked on seeing the empty kettle,

"You all must have been hungry this morning." In truth, most of his mush had decorated the dining room walls and floor. Gwynneth was still combing oatmeal out of her hair. Her great-grandfather Bembor had to go a step further and cut off part of his white beard.

Once the firewood was neatly stacked in the kitchen, Rolin went off to split more. Meanwhile, Gwynneth was helping her mother mix and knead out another batch of bread dough. It was hot working next to the roaring, wood-fired stove; Gwynneth was constantly mopping the sweat from her forehead with her apron.

"Why don't you cool off outside while the dough rises?" Marlis suggested. "The fresh spring air will do you good. When you're feeling better, you can come back and help me shape the loaves. Oh, and watch for mushrooms growing in the grass, won't you? After all the rain we've had, they'll be popping up everywhere."

"Thank you, Mum!" Gwynneth said. She fled out the door.

Clattering down the Hallowfast's winding stone stairs, she threw open the door and ran outside. "I'm going to be married tomorrow!" she cried to the cloud-strewn sky. She spun on the grass, arms outstretched and blond hair flying. Rings, dress, food, guests—at last everything was prepared. Still, a nagging doubt niggled at the back of her mind. The doubt erupted into full-blown panic. She and Timothy had yet to choose their troth-tree!

Not many years earlier, Lucambrians had taken their life-trees from ordinary forest saplings as substitutes for the Tree of trees that once grew on the Isle of Luralin. Now that the Tree had come to abide with them, Lucambrians planted its seedlings as sythan-ars. Gwynneth had her own life-tree. So did her brother and sister. As a Thalmosian, Timothy didn't need one. Still, he had planted a river birch beside his parents' humble home near Beechtown.

The troth-tree, on the other hand, was a symbolic sythan-ar. Uprooting a wild tree sapling, a betrothed couple would replant it beside the Hallowfast to signify their new life together. The bread dough would simply have to wait until a troth-tree was found.

Reeling with dizziness, Gwynneth collapsed into the grass and rolled onto her back. She was gazing up at the sky's spinning blue-white bowl when a feathered head and neck swam into view.

"Hmph!" growled Ironwing. "You will never get off the ground by twirling around with your arms stuck out like tree limbs. Try running forward and flapping your arms. Since you haven't got any feathers, I suppose you won't ever fly the way we griffins do."

"You're such a silly old sorc!" said Gwynneth cheerfully as she jumped up. Then she lightly scratched Ironwing's head and neck feathers. Purring with pleasure, he nuzzled against her cheek.

"Would you mind doing an errand for me?" she asked him.

Ironwing groaned, and his neck and tail sagged. "I should have known. Whenever you scratch my head, you want some favor or another in return. What is it this time? Do you wish me to fly to the Willowah Mountains and bring you back a glory stone for your wedding ring, or slay you a dragon, or fetch you some fresh venison? The local deer are filling out quite nicely this spring."

"No, thank you," Gwynneth replied. "I want your help in finding Timothy. He went away early this morning, and I haven't seen his shadow since. I think he went hunting in the mountains."

"Oh," said the sorc. "That's all? Why didn't you say so in the first place?" Ironwing spread his magnificent eagle's wings and leapt into the air. Climbing in lazy spirals over the Hallowfast, he shrank to a dark speck floating over the Lucambrian landscape.

The griffin returned minutes later with Timothy on his back. Carrying a bow and quiver of arrows, the Thalmosian hopped off and embraced Gwynneth. "What was so important that you had to send Lucambra's grumpiest griffin after me?" he teasingly asked her. "I was stalking a fat buck when Ironwing showed up."

"Just like a man—hunting on the day before his wedding!" she retorted. While she explained to Timothy the urgent necessity of finding a troth-tree, Ironwing lashed his tail in exasperation.

"I'll never understand these quaint two-legged courtship rituals," he said. "This pressing of lips together, wrapping of arms, planting of trees, exchanging of rings—what is it all for? Why not just bite each other as we sorcs do and be done with it? It's a wonder your earthbound race has survived for as long as it has."

Gwynneth tried to keep a straight face. "We have survived, my dear griffin, for the very reason that we *don't* bite each other!"

With a chuckle, Timothy asked her, "Where shall we begin our troth-tree search—in Lucambra or in some other torsil world?"

Climbing onto Ironwing's back, Gwynneth said, "Hop on! I think I know just where we might find plenty of tree seedlings."

Several hours later, Ironwing was flying the betrothed couple back from Thalmos—and Gwynneth had her troth-tree. As she had suspected, the amenthil Rosewand had spawned a small forest of offspring beside Cottonwood Creek. After some debate, Gwynneth and Timothy had settled on a sapling called Sweetspeech. She was so named for the sweet blossom scent of her kind that opens mortal ears to comprehend the speech of all living creatures.

As the Hallowfast came into sight, Gwynneth noticed hundreds of dark-green halos pockmarking the meadows below. The bands of lusher grass ranged from a foot to many yards in width. Marlis had been right. Recent spring rains had brought out the mushrooms!

Gwynneth smiled to herself. She had yet to introduce Timothy to the joys of picking and preparing wild mushrooms. Whenever those delicacies sprouted in field or forest, Lucambrians would drop whatever else they were doing and harvest the bounty.

Spiraling to earth, Ironwing landed near one of the rings. After thanking the sorc and sending him on his way, Gwynneth dragged a puzzled Timothy to the grassy circle's rich green margin.

"People often pass by these rings without noticing them," she explained. Parting some tufts of grass, she uncovered a cluster of wiry-stemmed, thimble-capped tan mushrooms. With a squeal of delight, she plucked and smelled them, relishing their tangy odor. They would go well in some scrambled Thalmosian chicken eggs. Early on, her father had taught her how to mingle the savory flavors of mushrooms and eggs in a variety of scrumptious dishes.

She presented the dainty fungi to Timothy, who sniffed them suspiciously before holding them at arm's length. "Toadstools!" he pronounced. "Will your people bring bunches of these things instead of flowers to our wedding? They smell absolutely horrid."

"No, they won't," Gwynneth told him. "And no, they don't. You're just not used to mushroomy odors. This fungus is one of my favorites. We call it the 'faery-ring mushroom,' or 'bay-bonnet.'"

"What do faeries have to do with fungi?" Timothy asked her.

"Legend has it that when the faeries dance, they leave behind these grassy circles. Supposedly, if mortals like us step into such a ring, they may be captured and whisked away to the faeries' kingdom. It's all poppycock, of course." Gwynneth ambled inside the ring and out again several times without apparent ill effect.

"There, you see?" she said, waving her hand. "Those old tales are nothing but nonsense. Elwyn doesn't believe in faeries, either. Bembor does, but he says it's the mushrooms that make these rings, not the 'tylwyth teg.' All sorts of mushrooms—even some poisonous kinds—grow in circles, but bay-bonnets are the most common."

"Tylwyth teg?" asked Timothy.

"That means 'the fair folk' in the Lucambrian tongue."

With a disgusted grimace, Timothy handed the bay-bonnets back to Gwynneth. "How do you know these aren't toadstools?"

Gwynneth grinned at him. She would make a true Lucambrian out of him yet! "For one thing, they're too small for toads to sit on," she quipped. "For another, we just *know*, the way you know the difference between a fir and a pine. Besides, I have been eating bay-bonnets since I was a little girl. I'd recognize them anywhere."

Timothy was aghast. "You're actually going to *eat* them?"

Laughing, Gwynneth said, "Of course I am going to eat them—and you are going to help me! If you want to marry a Lucambrian, you must learn to like mushrooms. I hope to gather enough to make a nice bay-bonnet omelet, so be a prince and start picking."

"No thanks," said Timothy, his lip curling. "I'm not touching those things. Toadstools can give you warts. Besides, someone needs to plant our troth-tree before its roots dry out." Kissing Gwynneth, he picked up Sweetspeech and headed toward the Hallowfast.

"Superstitious Thalmosian!" Gwynneth playfully called after him. For the next hour, she hopscotched from ring to ring, filling the pockets of her shift to overflowing with the fragrant bay-bonnets. Weary but elated, she made her way back to the tower.

After making sure Timothy had properly planted Sweetspeech, she tramped up the stairs to the kitchen. Having just finished the baking, a disheveled Marlis greeted her with a stormy glare.

Gwynneth apologized and told her mother about Sweetspeech. Then she emptied her pockets, piling the mushrooms on a table.

Marlis's frown softened. "Bay-bonnets! I'll fry them up in some eggs for our breakfast. And I'm glad you and Timothy finally found a troth-tree. My tree, Spirelight, will be glad of the company. Now run upstairs and try on your wedding gown one more time, to make sure it fits. I don't want to be making alterations at the last minute! On your way up, please stop off at the dining hall and tell Wendell the steward we will need more wine for our guests."

Protesting that she had tried on the dress five times already, Gwynneth headed up the stairs, naming the rooms on either side as she went. "Bedroom, storeroom, armory, scullery, *dining hall*."

After visiting with the talkative steward, who predicted warm weather for the wedding, Gwynneth trudged up the remaining steps to her room. She resented the long climb to her cramped quarters, when her brother and sister enjoyed more spacious lodgings many floors below. At least the endless stairs and great height discouraged annoying suitors and other unwelcome visitors.

At last she opened a door engraved with trees and griffins. The designs were copied from Rolin's old wooden box, which had met a splintery end between a hungry yeg's jaws. The batwolf's petrified body now graced one of the Hallowfast's many garden paths.

Stepping inside, Gwynneth decided her bedroom was more cozy than cramped. Besides, her window offered a magnificent view of the Brynnmor Mountains. On clear days, Mt. Golgunthor's smoking cone was plainly visible through the Gap of Gwylnos.

In one corner of the room stood her bow and arrows; in another, her lightstaff; in a third, a blowpipe and darts, and in the fourth, a digging stick for prying mushrooms out of the sod. Her bed occupied the center of the floor, and on the bed lay her wedding gown, a vision of white satin trimmed with green and gold lace.

After shrugging on the dress, Gwynneth appraised herself in a mirror hanging on the wall opposite the bed. At almost eighteen, she was already taller than her mother, with Marlis's luxuriant blond hair, pert nose and winsome smile. However, her high, clear forehead, narrow jaw and long fingers were all Rolin's.

Gwynneth removed the gown and laid it back on the bed. Then from a shelf she took down a few keepsakes: Winona's gold ring and dog-eared diary; three of the Tree's charred cones Rolin had brought back from Luralin; some dried starflowers from the Golden Wood; one of Whitewing's neck feathers; and a marsh dragon's eggshell. After the honeymoon, she would finish packing her few belongings to take to the valley of Liriassa, where she and Prince Timothy would be making their home as newlyweds.

Prince Timothy. What a grand title for a grand bridegroom! With that thought, Gwynneth lay back on her bed and fell asleep.

When she awoke, darkness had crept into the room, though her staff still shone bravely in its corner. Yawning like a sleepy griffin, she went to her window and looked out on the world.

Working by torchlight, hundreds of Lucambrians were toiling like ants to prepare the grounds for the outdoor ceremony. Gwynneth was turning away from the window when a gleam caught her eye. Beyond the glow of flaring torches, where the meadows lay steeped in shadow, a circle of stars bobbed above the grass. Gwynneth's heart skipped a beat. Had the tylwyth teg come out to dance? That night, she dreamt wicked faeries had kidnapped Timothy.

At dawn, she bounded out of bed. Trumpets were ringing, the birds were singing, and she was to be wed! She spent the morning surrounded by a bevy of seamstresses, perfumers and beauticians. When her mother brought in a looking glass, Gwynneth hardly recognized herself. A poised and elegant queen gazed back at her from the mirror. Like her great-grandmother Winona, she wore a circlet of purest white hemmonsil flowers in her hair.

She had asked her father to perform the ceremony. Rolin had reminded her that since Gaelathane enjoyed weddings, He might show up to bless hers. That suited Gwynneth to a stitch. Whenever Gaelathane appeared, His loving presence left a glow of great gladness on everyone's face. Rolin frequently described how the King of the Trees had taken part in his coronation ceremony.

Gwynneth prayed with her parents in the throne room. Then they went downstairs and opened the door. A sea of faces gawked back at them. Gwynneth gasped. She had no idea so many guests had been invited. In truth, most had invited themselves. No true Lucambrian likes to miss a wedding, especially a royal wedding!

Gwynneth ducked back inside while Timothy accompanied her parents to the front of the gathering. Next, a flurry of flutes and harps, trumpets and tambourines struck up the rousing Lucambrian wedding march. Smoothing down her gown and taking up her bouquet of starflowers, Gwynneth propelled herself through the door. Elwyn stood by to escort her to the wedding platform.

After they had mounted the dais stairs, Elwyn handed Gwynneth to Timothy and took his place as best man beside the groom. Looking every inch a Lucambrian scout and staff-bearer, Timothy wore a splendid green outfit under his full-length cloak.

Tears came to Gwynneth's eyes as she recalled first meeting the son of Garth. The Thalmosians were invading Lucambra, and Timothy had just borne the brunt of the Lucambrian council's fury. Hounded over plain and under hill by General Gorn's army, Timothy and Gwynneth had shared their first kiss in Gwilym's Gorge.

As maid of honor, Gwynneth's sister held the bouquet for her. Now grown tall and fair, Meghan wore violets in her flaxen hair.

Resplendent in his royal crown and robes, King Rolin beamed at the nervous couple. Under his guidance, vows and rings were exchanged. Next came the Cloaking Oath, an ancient Lucambrian wedding ritual revived by Rolin himself. Embracing Gwynneth, Timothy drew his cloak closely about her trembling shoulders.

"Within this cloak of mine, I thee wed," he said, his eyes holding hers with love's intensity. "It shall warm thee against life's deadly chills; it shall shield thee when dangers assail; it shall comfort thee in the midst of sorrow and loneliness. My cloak is now thy cloak, and in it shall our two hearts become entwined as one."

King Rolin then blessed the couple in Gaelathane's name. Still wrapped in Timothy's cloak, the two kissed. Finally, they faced their family and friends. Through tears of joy, Gwynneth saw her mother waving. Beside Marlis stood her brother Scanlon and his wife, Medwyn, recently arrived from the Golden Wood with a party of other worldwalkers. Bembor and his brother Marlon were tossing oak leaves into the air, another Lucambrian wedding custom.

Grandfather Emmer was grinning, while Aunt Mycena stepped out a lively jig. The brothers Opio and Gemmio raised their hands in salute. Sigarth and Skoglund, the royal huntsmen, were scanning the sky and the crowd for signs of trouble. Larkin scowled.

Grandfather Gannon was supporting his red-haired sister, who had apparently fainted (again) at the sight of a sorc. Gannon had blindfolded her before their flight to the tower on Windsong's back, but she had insisted on removing the cloth before the wedding.

Griffins were everywhere. Some prowled among the onlookers or lay on the grass preening themselves. Others wheeled high overhead, clicking and clacking their congratulations. Windsong and Ironwing lounged near the platform, waiting to take the newlyweds to the Willowah Mountains for a sunny honeymoon.

Laughing and crying, Gwynneth and Timothy descended the platform stairs and swept through the cheering throng. Near the back, Gwynneth caught sight of an old man clad in sheepskins.

What is he doing here? she thought. *Lucambrians don't keep sheep.* She was dismissing those fleeting thoughts when the shepherd's penetrating gaze fell upon her from beneath bushy brows, reminding Gwynneth of the autumn sun setting through clouds.

At the tower, she and Timothy tied a ribbon around their troth-tree's trunk to commemorate the occasion. Next, the two rushed upstairs to change into their traveling clothes. Then they went outside to greet their guests. Gwynneth was chatting with Bembor when she recalled the odd lights she had seen the night before.

Excusing herself, she tracked back and forth across the meadow until she found a faery ring within the line of sight from her bedroom window. The grass blades in the dark green circle looked undisturbed. If the fabled tylwyth teg had danced there from dusk until dawn, they were light-footed creatures indeed!

Gwynneth laughed at herself. She must have seen some children playing with torches. Stepping into the ring, she glanced around to be certain no one was watching. Timothy caught her eye and waved. She waved back. Then she strolled out of the faery ring.

Fear gripped Gwynneth's heart with frigid fingers. Her parents, Timothy and all the wedding guests had vanished in a gray mist.

CHAPTER 2

OWEN SON OF TADWYN

Now where did that dratted sheep get to?" Owen son of Tadwyn laid aside his wooden panpipes and counted his flock again. For nearly half of his fourteen years, he had herded his father's sheep, and he knew them all by name. His favorites were Floppy, a ewe with a droopy left ear; Snapper, a black-faced ram famous for nipping people's legs; Tramp, a frisky yearling; and Gappy, a mellow ram with two missing front teeth.

This afternoon, however, it was the ancient ewe, Tabitha, that was missing. Blind in one eye, Tabitha often became separated from the rest of the flock. Despite Tabitha's infirmity, Owen loved the docile old sheep, who liked being scratched behind the ears.

Owen squinted up at the sky through his locks of long, curly hair, bleached blond by the sun. He had less than an hour to lead the flock back to safe pastures near the village. Tabitha would have to wait. He couldn't risk the whole flock for just one sheep, and a decrepit one at that. He couldn't risk his own life, either. Too many villagers had already disappeared on the unforgiving Downs.

Hoisting his shepherd's crooked staff, he clucked his tongue and urged his charges into a trot, whacking stragglers on the rump. Then he ran alongside the sheep, whistling and shouting to keep them together. Veering away, they headed toward a fifteen-foot welving ring, but Owen skillfully deflected them around the grassy circle. He was careful not to stumble across its dark green border himself. "There's no sense in saving the sheep but losing the shepherd," his father Tadwyn was always fond of saying.

Long years before Owen's birth, a thick forest had covered the Downs. Evil spirits were rumored to inhabit the Greatwood, as it was called, snatching away any man or sheep foolish enough to enter. Every afternoon, an engulfing fog flowed from the wood, cloaking the countryside until dawn. The villagers shut their houses and penned up their sheep against the "Gray Death."

In those days, Owen's hilltop village was known as "Swandel," or "Dell of the Swans." It was so named for the birds living in a nearby hollow on Landon Lake. Owen had often visited the lake to skip rocks and toss breadcrumbs to the swans. Now he shunned the place for the terror it still held for him, especially on bleak wintery nights when death stalked the star-glinting ice.

Fearing the eerie Greatwood and its forbidding fogs, the villagers had cut it down, piled its trees in a huge heap and burned them. No green thing ever grew afterwards on that scorched and barren scald in the earth. Perversely, the dense fogs continued.

Soon after the Great Burning, tall grasses sprang up to hide the tree stumps, creating a rolling green prairie dubbed "the Downs." Among those fresh green blades emerged the welving rings, or "welt-rings." These circular bands of darker, thicker grass appeared mid-spring and grew outward until winter's first snows. Though most of the rings were only a few paces across, Owen had once measured a monster that spanned a good eighty yards.

With the welving rings' arrival, sheep began disappearing again, along with shepherds and shepherdesses, too. At night, a thick darkness flowed from out of the rings, devouring all flesh in its path and surrounding the town. To ward off this evil, the villagers set torches around their hilltop, lighting them at dusk. It was then the village was renamed "Swyndon," or "Deceiving Downs."

Nobody knew what caused the circles, but everyone knew the peril they held. Step across that lush green boundary, and you dared not step out again until late fall. Some of the rings were harmless, but since all looked alike, the villagers avoided the circles like the plague, even if it meant traveling miles out of their way.

Every spring, Owen lost a few sheep to the welving rings. Some of the witless animals hankered after the circles' luxuriant grass, while others wandered in by accident. Keeping track of the rings was nearly impossible, since they were constantly expanding, merging with one another or even disappearing altogether. Above all, Owen feared the "broken" rings that were missing sections. A shepherd could blithely lead his flock through one of these spaces, not realizing where he was going until it was too late.

Some of the villagers had tried to stifle the welving rings by tossing hay and straw over them. This trick had worked until the circles grew out from under the mulch, leaving the heaped fodder to rot, untouched and untouchable. Hundreds of such lonely haystacks still dotted the Downs, forlorn as the bleak fog, slowly sinking into the earth like so many lumpy scarecrows. Some in the village swore those straw heaps walked the Downs after dark.

In rambling fashion, Owen and his flock reached Lone Oak Hill, a smaller version of nearby Swyndon Hill. Letting his sheep graze freely along the hill's flanks, Owen began climbing. Behind him, a smoky haze was already obscuring the Downs. He and his flock had left the lowland pastures just in time, for as the saying went in Swyndon, "Whatever the fog touches, it takes." Those who made a habit of ignoring that pithy warning sometimes returned at eventide without their flocks, if they returned at all.

At the top, Owen found the tree for which the hill was named, a broad and ancient oak that had escaped the Great Burning. He was glad for its spreading boughs and thick foliage. Many an afternoon and evening he had spent sheltering in its shade, playing his panpipes or writing in his journal while the flocks browsed.

He sat back against the oak's furrowed trunk and soaked up the sunny spring day. The sweet scents of heather and clover and sheep-cropped meadow grass filled the air. Having outworn his welcome, Winter had packed his icy bags and was grudgingly retreating to the mountains. Owen was ever so glad to see him go.

He gazed up at the soaring swallows that nipped the heels of heaven's fleecy flocks. Tending sheep left Owen plenty of time for daydreaming—and for playing his panpipes. He put them to his lips and blew, knowing their breathy notes would lead his sheep back to him. He hoped Tabitha would also hear the soothing pipes and rejoin the flock before the deadly fog found her.

He hadn't been playing five minutes when a series of sharper notes harmonized with his. He stopped and listened, hearing a trilling in the leaves above him. Then a ball of fluff flew down to perch on his shoulder, and he laughed. His sparrow was back.

Nearly a year earlier, the Downs had taken Owen's dearest friend, Melina daughter of Mahilka. The two had spent many hours tending sheep together and discussing their dreams of leaving Swyndon for the wide world outside. Then on a sultry summer's eve, Melina's flock had straggled back to Swyndon Hill without her. Light-footed Melina of the golden hair and ready laugh was gone forever, leaving Owen to watch his flock alone. Only the sheep heard his bitter weeping, for after Melina's sheepshun, village law forbade even her parents to speak of her again. Sometimes Owen tarried by her house on his way home in the evenings, just to remember.

About a month after Melina had disappeared, Owen was sitting under his tree on Lone Oak Hill when a commotion broke out in the foliage. A small but doughty song sparrow was raising a racket from an overhanging branch. Before Owen could shoo the brown bird away, it flew off, only to alight at his feet. By darts and dashes, it lured him partway down the hill, where he found Callie, one of his ewes, tangled in a thorn bush. He cut the sheep free with his knife and sent her back to graze. When he returned to the oak, the sparrow followed him and perched quietly on a limb, where she listened to him read from his journal and play his panpipes.

From that day on, the bird was always waiting for him whenever he visited Lone Oak Hill. She would sit on a branch and listen with cocked head as he played his pipes or read aloud. Sometimes she would even perch on his shoulder. Often she would lull him to sleep with her twittering birdsong. Owen supposed the sparrow had hidden her nest somewhere in the oak, but he never saw it. If she was like the other songbirds, she had already raised her young that spring and was waiting to fly south for the winter.

Autumn arrived with its mellow golden afternoons and crisp nights. On Owen's hill, the oak's lobed leaves were blushing crimson and its acorns were dropping. Then one afternoon, Sparrow failed to appear. Thinking she was busy foraging for food, Owen scattered some breadcrumbs among the musty fallen leaves and left. The next day when he climbed the hill, his cheerful feathered companion was missing again, and the breadcrumbs lay uneaten. Putting aside his panpipes, he hearkened to the sleepy voices of the world around him. Knitted into the mournful death rattle of withered oak leaves ran a thread of soft, anguished chirping.

Leaping down the hill, Owen found Sparrow caught in the selfsame thorn bush that had ensnared Callie. The plucky bird appeared listless, and her dark eyes were dull. To his surprise, she did not struggle or try to fly away when he approached. Grasping her trembling body in his fingers, he freed her from the bush.

"You can fly home now," he told her, but she sat shivering in his hands. Placing her in the shepherd's purse where he kept his journal and meager lunch, he set out for Swyndon with his flock.

The Gadabout met him at the foot of the hill. Dressed in sheepskins, the mysterious old shepherd bore a staff in one hand and a bag in the other. Nobody knew where or how the Gadabout lived, but the Gray Death did not touch him. Lacking his own sheep, he looked after wayward animals belonging to others. The villagers welcomed him only when he came singing out of the evening mists, bearing some lost or injured sheep on his shoulders.

"What do you have there in your satchel?" the Gadabout asked him. Owen had an uneasy sense the old man already knew.

Reluctantly, Owen brought out the sparrow. As the Gadabout bent over the ailing bird, some of his shaggy locks fell aside, exposing a row of white scars ringing his forehead. Cupping the bird in his hands, the shepherd pointed out a dark patch on her breast where a thorn had pierced her and broken off inside. With sure fingers, he gently teased out the long, wicked barb and held it up, his hand tinged scarlet with the sparrow's fresh blood.

"I have some experience with thorns," he said. "They can leave terrible wounds. She'll heal up nicely now, but it will take time. Until she has regained her strength and is ready to fly again, you must nurse her back to health. Make certain she gets plenty of food and clean water." Then he handed the bird back to Owen.

"What do sparrows like to eat?" Owen asked. However, the Gadabout had moved on, and quickly, too, for an old man.

Each morning for a month, Owen placed the sparrow in his pocket and took her with him as he herded sheep on the Downs, feeding her breadcrumbs and grubs and bugs. At night, he put her in a box with a dish of water and another of breadcrumbs. He always left the box beside his open bedroom window for fresh air.

November's slate-gray skies were threatening snow when Owen awoke one morning to an empty box. Sparrow had flown, taking his heart with her. He rushed to the window, hoping to catch a glimpse of the lively brown ball of feathers, but she was gone. No doubt she had fled with her kind to sunnier southern lands.

"Good-bye, little sparrow!" Owen cried to the sky. "I shall miss you! Meet me at the oak tree next spring, if you can."

And so she had. For the next few days, the sparrow continued to visit Owen on Lone Oak Hill, listening to him play the panpipes or read from his diary. Owen then enjoyed a happiness and contentment he had not known since Melina's bloody sheepshun.

One morning after Tabitha's disappearance, Owen's father took him aside. A gray-bearded, balding man built like a barrel, Tadwyn gruffly told his son, "Lead the sheep up that hill of yours and leave them to graze. Then search the grasslands where you last saw Tabby. Your eyes are sharper than mine, and you know her tracks better than I; maybe I have missed something. Just don't go too far. I'd rather lose a sheep than lose you, boy. We don't need another sheepshun. Remember what happened to poor Melina."

Owen did, all too well. A sparrow's thorn pierced his heart with the bitter pang of love lost. As he left, he glimpsed a small brown form flitting out of the rowan tree that stood in the yard. After letting the flock out of the sheep pen, he led the bleating animals through the palisade of unlit hilltop torches and down the slope.

As he waded into the deep, dew-spangled grasses of the Downs, crooked-winged killdeers flittered away from their hidden nests with plaintive cries. Savoring the sweet, early-morning air, Owen stationed his flock at the base of Lone Oak Hill. The grazing sheep would work their way to the top and rest in the oak's shade when the sun grew hot. Owen climbed the hill alone and looked for his sparrow. He found her perched on a limb just above his head.

"Good morning, Sparrow!" he said. "I cannot linger here with you today, for my father has sent me away on an errand. Watch over my flock while I am gone, won't you? Oh, and I brought you some breakfast." From his shepherd's purse he took a crust. Breaking it up, he scattered the crumbs across the moist earth.

To his surprise, Sparrow did not immediately alight to feed on the morsels. Instead, she let out a strident cry and fluttered off a few yards. With a sigh, Owen shouldered his staff and followed her to the foot of the hill, where she sat on a rock, waiting.

As Owen approached, the sparrow flew off again and landed on a distant stump. In this leapfrog fashion, she led him southward into the desolate Graylands, breeding grounds of the treacherous Gray Death. Enticed by the Graylands' lush grasses, hundreds of sheep had come to grief there, and not a few shepherds, too.

He stopped at noon to rest and have a bite of bread and cheese. While he ate, Sparrow pecked up his lunch crumbs. Afterwards, she took him farther south. His uneasiness grew with every step. When the Gray Death came calling, he wanted to be sitting on Lone Oak Hill. "In for an inch, in for a mile," he muttered.

Finally, the sinking sun told him he had to turn back, Tabitha or no Tabitha. He was trotting north through the thick grasses when damp gray mist-curtains soundlessly surrounded him. He stopped, disoriented. Without the sun to guide him, he could not tell which way home lay. "Sparrow!" he called. "Sparrow! Where are you?" No familiar *chirp* replied from out of the muffling fog.

He hurried blindly onward, hoping to break free of the swirling haze. Then a honeysuckle-like scent stole into his nostrils, and he heard singing. Rapturous voices were blending in a swelling chorus that rushed by him like an unseen flock of doves.

As in a dream, the fog melted away, and Owen found himself in a dense wood. Where grasses had waved, towering trees raised their leafy arms. Owen rubbed his eyes. Where was he? Such mighty trees had not darkened the Downs since the Great Burning.

Then beating wings brushed his cheek and a familiar brown form dropped to his shoulder. Sparrow had returned! Owen sobbed with relief. Surely the bird would know the way out of this mysterious wood—unless she was an enchantress in disguise.

Following his feathered guide, he made off through the forest. Presently, he heard a faint bleating. Not waiting for the sparrow, he rushed through the trees toward the sound's source.

At last, he came upon a crude log corral holding ten or twelve bedraggled sheep. He recognized many of them, for Swyndon's shepherds cut distinctive notches in their sheep's ears as proof of ownership. Then one of the older ewes pushed her way to Owen's side of the corral. She raised her head pleadingly in a familiar scratching pose. One milky blue eye stared blindly up at him.

Tabitha! That clinched it. Someone had been rustling Swyndon's sheep, and Owen was going to take them back. He circled the pen until he found a rickety gate. Untying the rope that secured the gate, he was about to open it when he heard a shout.

"You there! What are you doing? Leave that gate shut!"

Owen spun around. A hulking stranger wearing a sheepskin coat and a horrible scowl was bearing down on him. Without waiting for an explanation, the man lunged at Owen with a sword.

Owen had no time to think. Swinging his sturdy shepherd's crook, he brought it down with a whistling *whack* on his assailant's sword arm. The sword went flying. Before the rustler could regain his weapon, Owen cracked him soundly over the head with his staff. The man grunted and tottered back against the corral.

Owen ran. Behind him, the recovered rustler was blundering through the brush, shouting and cursing. Eventually, the sounds of pursuit died away. Alone at last in the dusky forest, Owen stopped to catch his breath. Sparrow was nowhere to be seen, and he didn't dare call out to her for fear of giving himself away.

He was lost.

CHAPTER 3

THE DEADWOOD

H ello! I'm over here! You can all come out now!"
Gwynneth shouted through the mist. Nobody
answered. *They're hiding from me,* she thought. *I'll bet that rascally brother of mine is behind this prank. Well, I won't let him spoil my wedding day!* Avoiding other faery rings in her path, she set out for the Hallowfast's dark bulk looming through the fog.

She stopped short. The "Hallowfast" turned out to be a grassy hill. More shrouded hills marched through the thickening mist. Sheep bleated in the distance. A creeping dread tingled up Gwynneth's spine. Neither hills nor sheep belonged by the tower.

Falling to her knees on the springy turf, she closed her eyes and prayed, "Gaelathane, I'm frightened! I don't know where I am. Please show me the way back to Timothy and the Hallowfast!"

When Gwynneth opened her eyes, she found the same fog and the same hills—and no Hallowfast. A lump lodged in her throat.

Then over the fog-bound silence wafted faraway lilting voices. Like the ringing of crystal bells they sang, bringing tears to Gwynneth's eyes. She was trying to make out the singers' words when a rich aroma stunned her senses. The world briefly blurred. When her eyes focused again, Gwynneth thought she must be dreaming.

31

Gone was the fog, and with it, the grassy hills. She was standing in a thick wood of lofty trees. Their smooth bark resembled a beech's, but their leaves were as long and sharply toothed as a chestnut's. Glowing with the setting sun, fragrant magnolia-like blossoms crowned the peculiar trees with pink-and-purple glory.

"Well, well. What have we here? You're coming with me!"

A grim-faced, shaggy man clad in soiled sheepskins was swiftly approaching. Before Gwynneth could flee, the stranger grabbed her by the back of the tunic and tossed her over his shoulder like a sack of Thalmosian potatoes. She kicked and squirmed, to no avail.

"Leave me alone, you beast!" she screamed as the man loped with her through the woods. Fighting back, she raked his face and neck with her fingernails, but he backhanded her so brutally that dark specks floated before her eyes. The specks merged, forming a black curtain that slid across her vision, and she knew no more.

When the curtain parted, Gwynneth was lying on the ground, her wrists and ankles bound with cords. Her head throbbed, and her cheek stung where the man had struck it. Stern tree-sentinels with muscular gray trunks rose on all sides. Cupping the sunset's dying wine, the trees' colossal blossoms flushed magenta before dusk drained them to the dregs. In the gathering gloom, murmuring tree-voices shared deep secrets of leaf and twig, root and bole.

Flames leapt. Like shambling bears, dark, hulking forms slunk in and out of the fire's yellow glare. One of the bears towered over Gwynneth, the features of its hairy face cloaked in shadow.

"She's awake!" the beast bellowed, and it dragged Gwynneth by the arm over to the fire. Struggling into a sitting position, she found eight pairs of cold, empty eyes staring back at her.

The bearlike creatures were actually men garbed in heavy, full-length sheepskins. Most were seated on log benches arranged in a rough circle around the fire. One of the beasts tossed a branch into the flames. The man Gwynneth recognized as her kidnapper released her wrist and pulled a gleaming knife from his belt. Gwynneth shrank back, but grabbing her fettered hands, he sliced off her bonds. Then he cut the cords binding her feet.

"What is your name?" he demanded in low tones.

Massaging her wrists and ankles, she said, "Gwynneth, if you must know. Who are you and these other men, and why did you bring me here against my will? What is this place, anyway?"

Mockingly bowing to Gwynneth, her captor swept his hand toward his companions. "We're the mutton-men!" he growled. Then he led the other skin-clad "bears" in a rollicking, raucous chant:

When clammy fog flows round about,
Then it's no good to scream and shout;
Fool! Flee the shadows whilst you may,
Ere dreaded Deadwood comes to stay!

Shun the Ghostwood! Fear the Deadwood!
Never shall you leave the Dreadwood!
Dancing dremlens snare the mind;
Look too long and you'll go blind!

When once the forest takes you in,
Abandon thoughts of friends or kin;
You're dead to them as they to you;
For strong the spell you can't undo!

Grim the Ghostwood! Drear the Deadwood!
Never shall you leave the Dreadwood!
Dancing dremlens snare the mind;
Look too long and you'll go blind!

Once we walked the world at will
And wandered over windy hill;
Touching, holding, feeling, tasting;
Spellbound, all these pleasures wasting!

Green the Ghostwood! Dark the Deadwood!
Never shall you leave the Dreadwood!
Dancing dremlens snare the mind;
Look too long and you'll go blind!

While seeing yet unseen we gawk;
We tread the earth, an unfelt flock;
Though speaking, yet unheard we rave;
We wraiths beyond the wretched grave!

Glum the Ghostwood! Dense the Deadwood!
Never shall you leave the Dreadwood!
Strike a touch-tree, if you dare;
Death will take you unaware!

What little Gwynneth understood of the men's dirge sent shudders through her. Yet, the names "Ghostwood," "Deadwood" and "Dreadwood" hardly befitted this inviting forest, which seemed to her anything but "grim," "drear," "dark" or "glum."

"What are you going to do with me?" she asked.

"That depends upon you," said her kidnapper darkly. "Likely you'll fetch our water and gather our wood. Women are in short supply here, so we'll keep you busier than a tick on a sheep's hide!" He and his friends winked at one another and guffawed.

As if to confirm the man's words, a young woman of about Gwynneth's age edged into the firelight. Also wearing skins, she was toting two water buckets hanging from either end of a pole slung across her bony shoulders. As the girl lowered her burdens, Gwynneth saw fear and wariness lurking behind her liquid eyes.

"Have a care there with the water, Mirrah," warned one of the mutton-men. He was rubbing a red, swollen lump on his head.

The buckets were just brushing the ground when Mirrah noticed the newcomer sitting in the shadows. The girl's eyes widened and she swung her body toward Gwynneth, dragging the buckets with her. One of them tipped over, spilling water into the fire. A cloud of hissing steam erupted and the flames died down.

"You little minx! Now look what you've done!" the sheepman shouted, and he lashed Mirrah's legs with a long switch. Mirrah cried out and staggered to one side, spilling the other bucket. Before the switch could land again, she darted into the darkness, the pole and empty buckets clattering and thumping after her.

"Don't be so hard on her, Dask," said a lean, long-faced mutton-man. "Just because that shepherd boy clobbered you on the head yesterday don't give you the right to tear into Mirrah like that. It's after dark, y' know, and she's got no light. Be reasonable, now."

Dask drew a long-sword and waved it in the man's face. "Be reasonable? Mirrah belongs to me, Hammel, and don't you never forget it! What I do with my property ain't none of your business. Just keep your nose out of my affairs, or I'll chop it clean off!"

"You've made your point, Dask," said Gwynneth's captor. "You're scaring our new guest. Now sit down and shut yer mouth!"

Dask sat, still glaring at his opponent. Avoiding his gaze, Hammel pulled a burning brand out of the fire and made off into the darkness. "If nobody else will look after her, I will!" he called over his shoulder. Dask spat but said nothing. Then grumbling under his breath, he got up and followed, sword still in hand.

Gwynneth glanced around the circle of mutton-men. Only six remained now, but the hard looks on their chiseled faces told her it was no good trying to escape. After witnessing Dask's cruel treatment of Mirrah, she wondered whether a quick death might be better than living at the whims of these heartless taskmasters.

As if reading her thoughts, one of the younger-looking sheepmen pointed at Gwynneth and said, "Can I have her, Wolf?"

Wolf the Kidnapper was studiously honing his knife on a stone. Gwynneth's heart hammered as she leaned forward to hear the man's answer. He smelled of sheep fat and woodsmoke.

"Naw," Wolf said without looking up. "Since I found her, she's mine, unless you want to fight me for her, Stubs." Stubs apparently didn't. Grabbing a firebrand, he slunk off into the darkness. Gwynneth wanted to blurt out that she was already married to one Timothy son of Garth, but she choked on her tongue.

Wolf held up his knife to the firelight and examined its edge. His four companions watched him with glittering eyes. "Time to leave now, lads," he told them. "Better check on the other fires. Can't have any of them dying out, can we? I'll tend to this one."

"May your fires never go out!" the other mutton-men muttered as they slouched into the woods. Gwynneth was left alone with Wolf. Thrusting his knife back into his belt, he stood menacingly over her. She bit her lip to keep from screaming. If only Timothy or Rolin would show up to rescue her from this animal!

Wolf pointed to the ring on her hand. "Married?" he asked.

The tension drained from Gwynneth's body, and she burst into tears. "Yes, but I've worn this ring less than a day!" she wailed. "It isn't fair! I should be celebrating with my husband, family and guests. Instead, I'm with you. How did I end up here, anyway?"

"Weren't you listening to our verses?" Wolf said. "The cursed fog found you, and now you're here to stay, just like the rest of us."

Warmed by the reviving fire, Wolf shed his bulky sheepskins. Underneath, he wore a greasy tunic of coarsely woven homespun wool. A bushy black beard to match his tousled hair spilled down his broad front and over the belt that held up his ragged trousers.

Gwynneth was even more confused. "But where is 'here'?"

The mutton-man fingered the welts on his face where Gwynneth had scratched him. "That depends on what you mean by 'here.' My men and I have lived in the Deadwood for years, yet even we ain't rightly sure where we are. We only know that anyone who wanders inside this place is as good as dead. We've survived here only by following the rules—and I make the rules." He scowled at her.

"Then what is the 'Ghostwood'?" Gwynneth asked him.

Wolf spat. "As nearly as I can reckon, most every tree in this wood grows in *two* spots—'here' and some other place that looks real but ain't. We call that other place 'the Ghostwood,' since nobody who lives there can see or hear us. We might as well be ghosts."

"If you dislike this place so much," said Gwynneth, "why don't you leave it? The trees can't go on forever, can they?"

Wolf jabbed his knife into the nearest trunk, and the tree groaned. "You're right; they don't, but their power is everywhere. There's no living in the Deadwood, but there's no living in the Ghostwood, either. If I let you go now, you'd come crawling back before dawn—if you lasted that long outside this firewatch."

Gwynneth's captor dropped his sheepskin coat over her. Hot and heavy, it stank of stale sweat and dried blood. Gwynneth was trying to wriggle out from under it when Wolf stiffly told her, "You'll want some covering. Nights are chilly in the Deadwood."

After throwing another stick of wood on the fire, he sat down beside Gwynneth. "You're lucky I'm the one who found you," he said. "Living in this forest brings out the worst in a man. It takes a strong arm—mine—to keep the others in line. You can't ever turn your back on them, day or night. One o' these fine mornings, I'll wake up with a dagger in my throat. I've lasted this long by keeping my eyes and ears open. You'd be wise to do the same."

"But why aren't there more women here?" Gwynneth asked.

Wolf gruffly replied, "They rarely survive for very long."

After seeing Dask whip Mirrah over spilling her water buckets, Gwynneth wasn't a bit surprised. She knew better than to say so.

"Besides," Wolf added, "most womenfolk stick close to home, away from the fog. Since we men work farther afield as farmers, woodcutters and sheepherders, the fog catches us more often."

"You're shepherds, then?" said Gwynneth. *What a foolish question, when these men have "shepherd" written all over them!*

Wolf grunted. "Many of us were. Oh, we still make a miserable livelihood from those brainless bleaters, but only when they wander into the woods. We keep a few of them alive for their wool, but most we butcher for their meat and hides. There ain't enough forage for a large flock in this forest, and besides, whenever the mutton runs out, we can always bring down a deer or two."

He grinned at her, his teeth gleaming white in the firelight. "I'm called 'Wolf' because I can kill anything that goes on two or four legs with my bare hands. I'm right handy with a knife, too."

Gwynneth swallowed a dry mouthful of fear. These dreadful mutton-men were nothing more than a pack of two-legged wolves disguised in sheep's pelts—and she was a defenseless lamb.

"You had better get some rest," Wolf said, standing. "Tomorrow, I'll put you with the flock. That's how we usually break in the new girls. It's easier than hauling water and wood. If you need me, I'll be watching the fire. We always keep the fires burning at night, even during the hottest summer months." He bent low over her, his head eclipsing the stars. "As you value your life, don't stray outside the firelight after dark! Otherwise, not even I can save you."

Shivering with cold and fright, Gwynneth pulled Wolf's sheepskin coat under her chin and watched him pile more sticks and branches on the crackling fire. Soon, flames were roaring high into the night sky, setting spidery shadows to dancing behind the stolid trees. Like one of his namesakes, Wolf prowled about the campsite, his eyes glowing alertly in the wavering firelight. Lulled by the leaping flames, Gwynneth fell into a dream-heavy sleep.

The sound of singing invaded that lurid land of nightmares. Silent black shapes lumbered through the woods at the boundary between light and shadow. Pulsing swarms of firefly-like lanterns

flirted with the slumbering trees. Wolf was huddled by the blazing
fire, turning his head this way and that like a vigilant bird of prey.
Closing her eyes, Gwynneth dreamt of Timothy and home.

When she awoke, the sun had crested the forested hills, and
songbirds were twittering in the trees. Throwing off the sheepskin
coat, she stood and looked about. Wolf was nowhere to be seen,
though Gwynneth had the prickly feeling someone was watching
her. A spitted haunch of mutton was roasting over the fire's dying
coals, giving off a savory aroma. Gwynneth's growling stomach
reminded her she hadn't eaten anything since her mother's bay-
bonnet omelet the day before. How much she missed home!

Just then, a twig snapped in the forest. Her heart thudding,
Gwynneth peered between the trees. She saw nothing. Then from
behind a smooth trunk stepped Mirrah. The sun burnished her long
hair to a glossy acorn brown that matched her doe eyes. She warily
stared at Gwynneth, who smiled and motioned to her. As demurely
as a hunted deer taking proffered food from a human hand, Mirrah
glided into the fireside clearing to join Gwynneth.

"Hello, Mirrah," said Gwynneth. "That's your name, isn't it?"

Swanlike, Mirrah's head slowly dipped and rose, and her lips
quivered. "It is," she softly replied. Tears streaked her hollow
cheeks. Gwynneth enfolded the weeping girl in her arms, feeling
her angular frame tremble like a frightened rabbit's.

"Everything will be all right now," she murmured into Mirrah's
ear. "You needn't be afraid any longer. Gaelathane is here."

"I've been so alone," sobbed Mirrah. "Last night, I took you for
a spirit. All the other women here have died. During the day, I stay
with the sheep until it's time to fetch wood and water for cooking
Dask's supper. At night, he often keeps me chained to a tree."

Gwynneth's fists clenched in anger. "I'll put a stop to that, if I
have to break off your chains with my bare hands!"

Mirrah shied away, her eyes full of terror. "No! You mustn't
interfere. Dask would strike you down without a second thought!
He's terribly strong, especially when he is in a jealous rage, and his
sword is sharper than splintered flint. I've seen him lop off many a
sheep's head with it, and many a man's, too. Wolf keeps him around

only because Dask can spot a sheep or a deer in the woods sooner than anyone else, and he's a swift runner, too."

"Be that as it may," said Gwynneth in a steely tone, "he is no match for the might of Gaelathane, King of the Trees."

"Who is Gaelathane?" Mirrah asked with a curious look.

"He—He's bigger than this whole world, and He made everything around us," Gwynneth replied. How could she describe the King of the Trees to one who had never met or known Him?

Mirrah's eyes saucered. "Do you mean He's a giant?"

"Oh, no. He's not a giant. He looks just like a man. Deep down inside, He's much more than a man." Seeing confusion spreading across Mirrah's face, Gwynneth changed the subject. "What are you doing here, anyway? Won't Dask come looking for you?"

Mirrah recoiled again. "N-not yet. He's still sleeping. Wolf sent me here to find you and make sure you have something to eat. Then you can help me look after the sheep." She removed the spitted mutton from the coals and laid it on one of the log benches. With a flint blade, she sheared off a slab of steaming meat and offered it to Gwynneth. The mutton was tough and stringy but flavorful, and Gwynneth eagerly devoured every last scrap.

After the two had eaten, Gwynneth followed Mirrah through the woods to a rough sheep pen constructed of peeled logs. Mirrah opened the gate and let the animals out to graze. The wooly creatures began browsing on brush, weeds and tree seedlings.

A scraggy ewe trotted up to nuzzle against Gwynneth's arm. The sheep's left eye resembled a cloudy blue marble. "Why, I do believe the poor thing is partially blind," Gwynneth exclaimed.

"Oh, that's just silly old Blue Eye," Mirrah remarked, and she scratched the sheep affectionately behind the ears. "She showed up in the Deadwood a few weeks ago. I'm afraid she's been starving ever since. Meadows are scarce in these parts, and it's useless foraging for food in the Ghostwood lands beyond the touch-trees. Thanks to the spell, we can't even drink the water over there."

"What is this 'spell' you speak of?" Gwynneth knew Gaelathane possessed the power to defeat any sort of sorcery. Yet, she felt strongly that the Deadwood was a place of blessing, not of bane.

Before Mirrah could reply, Dask came charging through the trees, his craggy face twisted with fury. Mirrah shrank back, but with a roar, Dask raised his fist and delivered a blow that sent her sprawling. Then he jerked the girl upright and shook her.

"Where have you been, you lazy wench?" he shouted. "I looked for my breakfast hours ago, and now I find you idling away your time! After I've beaten some sense into you, you're going to cook me a proper meal!" In Mirrah's pain-glazed eyes, Gwynneth saw her unspoken question answered: *Yes, I have tried to escape, but Dask always tracks me down, drags me back and thrashes me.*

Stabbing a finger at Blue Eye, Dask growled, "That one's your favorite, ain't it? I've warned you before about mooning over these stupid sheep. They're witless animals, not your pampered pets!"

Dask drew his sword and poised it above Blue Eye's back. Calmly chewing on a curly dock leaf, the ewe paid him no attention.

Mirrah's face turned a pasty white and tears streamed down her face. "Not Blue Eye!" she pleaded. "Please spare her life! I'll make all the breakfasts you want, and mutton pie for supper, too."

"You'd better, if you know what's good for you," Dask grunted. Reluctantly sheathing his sword, he grabbed Mirrah by the hair and was dragging her away when Gwynneth blocked his path.

"Leave her alone," she said. "Wolf sent her here with me to tend the sheep. You mustn't blame her for doing as she was told."

Dask's piggish eyes narrowed. "Step aside," he snarled. "You're new here, so I won't strike you down for your insolence. If *you* don't do as *you're* told, though, I may forget my manners!" Releasing Mirrah, he wheeled on Gwynneth in a half-crouch. She stood her ground. Then Dask uncoiled like a tightly wound steel spring.

His head and shoulder connected with Gwynneth's midriff, and she flew backward into a tree, striking her head. After she had blinked away the bright stars floating before her eyes, she received another stiff jolt: Dask, Mirrah and the Deadwood had all disappeared. Instead, Gwynneth and her tree stood amidst a different forest that teemed with birds and other wildlife. This wood sloped down to a sandy shore that in turn slid into an endless sea. Blue waves marched from the dim horizon toward the beach.

Gwynneth ran. At last she had escaped her captors! Somehow, her collision with the tree had ushered her into a land of such serene beauty that she was already forgetting Dask and his cruel sword. Tiring, she stopped to listen to the forest. To her surprise, she heard none of the gossipy chatter common to Lucambrian and Thalmosian woodlands. Here, every living creature sang or spoke only in praise of Gaelathane and of His wondrous works.

Moving on through the forest, she noticed her feet left no prints in the earth. Likewise, she seemed to glide past bushes and low-hanging tree limbs without so much as disturbing a leaf.

Presently, she smelled a soothing perfume drifting upon the wind. Then the woods suddenly ended in a snowy sea of fragrant, bell-shaped blossoms that lapped at the trees' feet. "Hemmonsils!" Gwynneth shouted—the very flowers she had worn on her wedding day! As she waded into the foamy field of nodding blooms, their melodic meadow-song of worship moved her to tears.

If you should here tread on this Tree-hallowed ground,
You must never forget how the King once was crowned;
With the blood of His wounds that His enemies wrought,
He did purchase a pardon that cannot be bought.

Wonder and weep at the love we now tell,
How the King spoke a word and the thunderbolt fell,
To cleave the dear Tree, once mighty and tall,
To take on His body the wrath due us all.

Wonder and weep at devotion so grand,
That it called for a sacrifice long ages planned;
When the Maker of worlds gave His life for a friend,
And for three days His foes rejoiced at His end.

Reviving, He lives and shall nevermore die,
While the Tree of His word shines in splendor on high,
To water His worlds with the blood of His gift,
That restored life to all by bridging the rift.

Wiping away her tears, Gwynneth reached down to pluck one of the hemmonsils. It slipped through her fingers. Again she tried to pick the blossom, and again it eluded her grasp. Frustrated, she swept her hand back and forth among the blooms, but they remained as unruffled as the Hallowfast's flags on a windless day.

Gwynneth broke into a clammy sweat. Maybe striking her head on the tree had clouded her vision—or killed her. Farther along, she came upon a fountain merrily gushing from a wine-red pool. She had rediscovered the Isle of Luralin! Hemmonsil flowers had softened the fire-scarred landscape, but the Glymmerin's healing waters still issued from the pool in four diverging streams, just as they had when the Tree had risen from the island years earlier.

Gwynneth sat down beside one of the streams and dabbled her aching feet in it, though she couldn't feel the water's cool, pleasant caress. When she withdrew her feet, they were still dry. If she had died in the aptly named "Deadwood," why was she haunting Luralin's "Ghostwood" instead of rejoicing in Gaelessa?

A hand fell upon her shoulder. "Your body is still alive."

"Gaelathane?" she said timidly.

"You have been much distracted of late with your wedding preparations," said the King. "I have missed our visits together."

Gwynneth hung her head in shame. Planning the wedding had left her little time for reflective moments in Gaelathane's presence. Ordinarily, most mornings found her sitting under her favorite linden tree, basking in the love of her Lord and Master.

"I am sorry," she said. "Now that You are here, though, would You terribly mind taking me home? I seem to be stranded on this island, and I do so want to return to Timothy and my family."

"Do not be afraid, My child," said Gaelathane. "I will make you at home wherever you fare. In the meantime, you must go back the way you came, by touching the tree that first brought you here. Take heart, for your work in Feirian has only just begun!"

"Feirian?" said Gwynneth. "Where is that?" However, when she looked behind her, the King of the Trees had vanished.

For the first time, she noticed an oily film clinging to the ground, the rocks, the water and the trees like a transparent second skin.

She guessed this shimmering veil was somehow cutting her off from her surroundings. Her stomach rumbled. Unable to eat or drink anything Luralin had to offer her, she would have to leave the island soon or risk perishing of thirst and starvation.

The sun was sinking into the Sea of El-marin as Gwynneth tramped back through the hemmonsil meadow. Standing at the forest's edge, she felt a wave of panic wash through her. How could she retrace her steps through the woods when she hadn't left any telltale signs of her passage? Now she realized what the mutton-men had meant when they sang, "Strike a touch-tree, if you dare; death will take you unaware!" Tears spilled from her burning eyes.

"Gaelathane!" she cried. "How can I find the correct tree?"

Even as the words left her mouth, she had her answer. Zigzagging through the forest, she began chopping trunks right and left with her hands. She might as well have been chopping air.

Giggling, she wondered what Timothy would say if he could see her sparring with the trees. She was about to pause for a rest when—*thunk!*—her hand met solid wood. She howled in pain.

Once her hand had stopped throbbing, she saw she had returned to the Deadwood. The sheep were corralled again. At each of the pen's four corners burned a torch that cast furtive shadows among the restless animals. Mirrah and Dask were gone.

The light was failing in a leaden sky when Gwynneth struck out through the forest, searching for a place to call home.

CHAPTER 4

FLATLANDERS

N ight had fallen. After drinking his fill from a stream, Owen wandered through ranks of smooth-barked trees until he found a dry, inviting fir grove. Collapsing on a springy bed of fragrant fir needles, he had drifted off to sleep when a chill jolted him awake. He was back at Landon Lake, spread-eagled on the ice. Frost filled his aching ears, deafening him to his heartbeat.

Countless pairs of red eyes were crowding around him in an inky darkness, burning him with an unbearably freezing fire. He cried out, but his throat made no sound. Suddenly, a bright light blazed in the forest, and the red eyes winked out. A tall, glowing man approached and beckoned to Owen, saying, "Follow me, and make haste! Death awaits lightless wanderers in this wood."

Owen willed his benumbed body to move. Stumbling along, he followed the shining stranger to a tree. "Touch the trunk," the man ordered. When Owen did, the foggy Downs surrounded him.

"You must return home," said the man, pointing through the mist. "Tomorrow, wayfarers from another land will visit your village, and your parents will take them in. Befriend these folk, for they shall need your help. Now my presence is required elsewhere."

"Wait!" Owen cried. "Who are you? What is your name?"

"I am Celembrose, your guardian," the man said, vanishing.

Owen rubbed his eyes. He must have been dreaming. Yet, Celembrose's voice had sounded so familiar. *You must return home.* Long ago, Owen had done so, stumbling frostbitten through the winter's wind to Swyndon Hill, where his father had found him on the ragged edge of death. But how had he escaped Landon Lake?

Cold, hungry and exhausted, he now jogged through the rustling grasses. A whispering darkness pursued him. He pushed onward until Swyndon's lights came into sight. Climbing the hill, he reached the top just ahead of the smoky blackness, which halted at the bristling ring of blazing, oil-soaked torches. Thirsty, he went to the village well and put his hand to the windlass handle.

The handle would not budge. Instead, Owen's hand passed through the crank—or was it the other way around? Now he was sure he was dreaming, though his nagging thirst felt all too real.

Tearing through the village to his house, he grabbed the door latch. It, too, slipped through his hand like a stick through water. He hurled his body against the door—and fell through it. After picking himself up, he examined the door. It was as whole and solid looking as the day his father had set it in the doorway.

Tadwyn was sitting in the kitchen, shaping a shepherd's staff with his knife. A kettle of his wife's savory mutton stew hung bubbling on a hook in the fireplace. Owen's mouth watered.

"Father," he rasped. "I found Tabitha! Rustlers took her, but she is still alive." Tadwyn paid him no mind. "Father!" Owen croaked more loudly. "I need some food and water!" Still Tadwyn did not look up. Owen threw himself on the thickset man, but his arms clutched only emptiness. A dry sob tore from his throat. He must be dead. Yet, how could a spirit feel hunger, thirst and fatigue?

From the laundering room came his mother's voice. "Tad, has Owen come home yet? It's nearly time for supper, you know."

"No, Gyrta, he hasn't," Owen's father called back. "I'm sure the lad will be along soon. He's likely visiting with some friends in the village. Now that I think of it, the sheep came in hours ago."

Owen burst into the laundering room. He found his mother bent over her washtub, scrubbing the dirt out of Tadwyn's tunics.

Owen sadly stared at her, knowing she couldn't see him. He tried to touch his mother's shoulder, but his hand slid through her.

Overcome with horror, he blundered through an outside wall into the torchlit night. After staggering back to the well, he tried turning the crank again. His hand grasped nothing but air. With a tortured groan, he flopped down beside the well and fell asleep.

Flowing *up* the hillside from the darkness below, the cold awoke him. It sapped the warmth from his body and the very light and heat from the torches. As the sky lightened, Owen hurried down the path leading to his house. Walking through the closed and barred front door, he found his parents huddled at the old oak dining table. It was set with three untouched bowls and spoons and a pitcher of water. Gyrta was weeping on Tadwyn's shoulder.

"I'm sure he's all right, dear," Tadwyn murmured. "The boy knows his way around the Downs. He'll come dragging in at any moment now. You'll see. Come, let's try to get some sleep."

Gyrta shook her dark-haired head. Owen was dismayed to see new lines furrowing her kindly face. "No," she moaned. "Don't lie to me. My boy is never coming back again. He's been taken, just like all the others. Oh, whatever will I do without my Owen?"

Burying her face in her hands, Gyrta began to weep again. Owen hovered over her, waving his arms. "I'm fine, Mother," he cried. "You just can't see me!" *Or feel me or hear me or touch me.* He shouted and made frightful faces at his parents until his throat was raw and his cheeks were sore. Hungrier and thirstier than ever, he yearned to ladle some of his mother's leftover stew into a bowl. Try as he might, however, he could neither lift the ladle out of the kettle nor budge any of the bowls from the table.

"Let me help you with that," said a high, clear voice.

Owen glanced up to see a firefly flitting around the room like a warm, glowing star. Forgetting his hunger and thirst, he stared at the light. He had never known a firefly to talk, but then he had never walked through walls and barred doors, either.

"Were you speaking to me?" he timidly asked the firefly.

"Yes, I was," it replied. "Do you wish me to help you or not?"

"Of course I do," Owen replied. "But . . . but who are you?"

"I am Athyrea," she replied. "Now please stand aside."

A hair-thin light beam shot from the star, illumining a silvery veil floating just above the tabletop. The beam bored a two-foot opening in the veil and played upon one of the bowls.

"You may touch the bowl now," said Athyrea. Reaching into the hole, Owen nudged the bowl. It felt solid enough. He picked it up along with a spoon. The hole shrank to a dot and disappeared.

As Owen brought the bowl to the fireplace, he heard a gasp behind him. Covering her mouth, Gyrta was pointing at the spot on the table where the bowl had lain. "It was just there!" she exclaimed. "It was there five minutes ago, and now it's gone!"

"What was just there?" asked Tadwyn.

"The third bowl—and the spoon is missing, too!"

Tadwyn scratched his bearded chin. "Now that's mighty peculiar. I do recollect as how you set the table with three bowls and spoons. Are you sure you didn't put away the third set?"

Owen's mother jumped up and backed away from the table, knocking over her chair. "It's him, Tad!" she cried. "It's Owen! His spirit is here. I can feel him in the room. Owen? Owen!"

Strident voices answered her from outside the house. "Flatlanders! We got flatlanders on the Downs! Flatlanders!"

Gyrta and Tadwyn rushed out of the house. *Flatlanders.* Owen had never met any of the reputedly flatfooted inhabitants of the far-off lowlands. Curious, he was about to run after his parents when Athyrea's voice stopped him. "Please stay here," she said. "You must eat to regain your strength after such an ordeal." The sliver of light reappeared and painted the pot of mutton stew.

"No!" Owen shouted. "I want to see my mother and father—I mean, I want them to hear and feel and see *me* again! Now turn that light thing of yours on me so I can go back to my old life."

"Much as though I would like to do so, I cannot," came the sad reply. "I have already gone beyond what is permitted of me. Please eat before the *porthyl* closes, for I must leave shortly."

Owen gathered that a "porthyl" was the opening or "portal" that had appeared in the shimmering shroud surrounding the kettle. Still grumbling, he thrust his hand through the hole and ladled his bowl full of stew. He managed to wolf down three helpings before the portal closed. Afterwards, he felt more like himself again.

Next, Athyrea opened a porthyl over the water pitcher, which Owen drained to the last drop. Refreshed, he thanked Athyrea and headed toward his bedroom for an early morning nap.

Forgetting his awkward condition, he launched himself through the air and belly-flopped onto his bed. Sinking through it, he fell heavily to the floor beneath. There he would have lain, too weary to get up again, were it not for the arrival of the flatlanders.

Half asleep, he heard the front door bang open. His parents spoke, and unfamiliar voices answered them. A couple of the voices drifted down the hallway and floated into Owen's room.

"It's not the finest place I have ever seen, but it's certainly cozier than Arlan and Elena's cave," a woman loudly remarked.

Scuttling out from under the bed, Owen rolled right through a pair of legs. A man and a woman were standing in the room—*his* room. Both wore bulging knapsacks, which they shrugged off and tossed on the bed—*his* bed—along with their hooded green cloaks. Underneath, the two were dressed in forest-green tunics and trousers, outlandish garb even by flatlander standards. Owen stared at the visitors' feet, which appeared to be no flatter than his own.

The man lay back on the bed and closed his eyes. "Just give me a moment's rest, Marlis," he said. "Then I'll be right as rain."

Frowning at her companion, Marlis shook her head, and a torrent of golden hair cascaded down her back. "Rolin, we can't sleep now. We just arrived," she said. "Let's ask around the village for Gwynneth. Surely someone here must have seen her recently."

"Only if she went through the same faery ring that we did."

"I'm sure ours was the correct one," said Marlis firmly. "Timothy saw Gwynneth near that ring just before she disappeared, and we found her footprints both inside and outside the circle."

"For our daughter's sake, I hope you're right," Rolin replied. "I only wish we had not waited so long before following her. Larkin and his loutish bunch of Thalmosian-haters were absolutely convinced Gwynneth had already left Timothy for a Lucambrian. They'll never rest until a 'true' Lucambrian sits on the throne."

"They have all the nerve, that lot!" Marlis agreed.

After retrieving a pair of luminous staffs they had propped against one wall, Rolin and Marlis left the room. Fuming, Owen ran through their bodies and into the kitchen, where his parents were talking with more flatlanders. One of them, a grandfatherly fellow, was patting Owen's weeping mother on the shoulder.

"There, there, Gyrta," the old man was saying. "I am sure your son will eventually turn up, and my great-granddaughter, too."

"Mother! Father!" Owen shouted. "Why are you doing this to me? How could you give my room to these flatlanders when I went missing just last night? I'm still alive, and I'm going to prove it!"

Owen huffed around the house, looking for Athyrea. He fully intended to capture the little vixen and compel her to open a boy-sized porthyl for him. Besides, the stew he'd eaten had only whetted his appetite for more, and he couldn't refill the water pitcher.

"Where are you, Athyrea?" he called as he poked his head through cupboard and closet doors. "I need your help again!" However, Athyrea was gone, and Owen could not coax her back.

Fortunately, Athyrea reappeared that evening. Thanks to the porthyls she made, Owen could empty the stew pot and refill the pitcher at the village well. Morning and evening, Athyrea visited him. Though he never thirsted or starved, his soul grew leaner by the day with loneliness. Living in his own private world, he longed for a smiling glance or the touch of a loving hand. Often he played his panpipes to amuse himself, although nobody but Athyrea in the house or village could hear those breathy, lilting notes.

In time, he grew to accept and even to like the flatlanders who had invaded his home. As it turned out, they were not flatlanders at all. They hailed from an entirely different world of their own.

Apparently, Rolin and Marlis's daughter Gwynneth had strayed into a welving ring, and the searchers had followed her into Clynnod, as Owen's land was known. How a welving ring could open from one world into another quite mystified Owen. Then one morning, he was helping himself through a porthyl to a mutton pie his mother had left cooling on the windowsill. In a flash, he came to see the grassy rings as porthyls of a subtler sort.

In any event, Owen could not rightly continue calling the visitors, "flatlanders." Instead, he settled upon "outringers," which seemed a more fitting name, though hardly flattering.

There were six in all. Owen liked white-bearded Bembor the best and often accompanied the old man on his leisurely morning walks. When Bembor spoke to "Gaelathane," Owen assumed this unseen personage inhabited yet another welving world.

Next in age came Marlis and Rolin. Their son, Elwyn, spent most of his time with Timothy, Gwynneth's new husband. That left Scanlon, Marlis's brother, a sharp-eyed, quick-tongued character who liked to skulk about the kitchen. Owen suspected Scanlon was stalking him until he caught the fellow filching a pie.

Their first night in Swyndon, the outringers gathered around the table, where Bembor explained how mushrooms—not faery feet—created the welving rings. Whether found in meadow or forest, the circles expanded each year like ripples on a pond until they met water, solid objects or dry ground. In his lifetime, Bembor had picked many a mushroom from such rings without mischief. He couldn't understand what made Gwynneth's ring different.

Owen had kicked over and stomped his share of the fungi. He was persuaded—as was everyone else in Swyndon—that mushrooms found growing in a welving ring were poisonous or bewitched—or both. No sheep or wild animals would touch them.

"Perhaps," Bembor mused, "when the tylwyth teg danced in that particular ring, they opened a passage between our worlds."

Marlis's face reddened. "Surely you don't believe such creatures exist, do you, Grandfather?" she said. "Anyway, Timothy saw Gwynneth step in and out of other faery rings without harm. Her trail may be growing cold, but we needn't climb out on a weak limb just because it is the only one handy, don't you agree?"

"I do," said Bembor. "Still, nearly all fables and myths contain some kernel of truth. I am not suggesting the tylwyth teg actually spirited Gwynneth away. However, we must not rule out any explanation that might bring us closer to tracking her down. Besides, call me a liar or an old fool if you like, but when I was a lad, I saw faeries dancing in the grass on a fine spring evening!"

Shock froze on the faces of the other outringers. Then they hastened to assure Bembor that he was neither fool nor liar. Nevertheless, Elwyn later let on he still thought faeries belonged in the children's nursery. Whenever the subject came up, he would loftily remind his listeners, "Make-believe little people will never show us which way Gwynneth went. We must find her ourselves."

Owen wondered whether Athyrea was a faery, and if so, whether she could lead his friends to Gwynneth. Since only he could see Athyrea, however, the outringers were still on their own.

As the weeks wore on without any sign of the missing young woman, the outringers began bickering among themselves. When his nerves became frayed, Owen would retreat outside, indifferent to rain, hail, lightning or wind. The elements in all their fury passed through him as if he were the Phantom Shepherd of Swyndon.

One evening, all six outringers burst through the door, their cloaks heaped with mushrooms they had picked in a welving ring. When the visitors insisted on cooking the white-capped fungi, Owen's parents were duly alarmed. After a lengthy argument, Tadwyn and Gyrta had fled the house in dismay, muttering dire and gruesome predictions about the fate of their foolish guests.

The next morning, Tadwyn was measuring out a plot of ground in which to bury the surely deceased "flatlanders" when one by one, they emerged from their sleeping quarters like hungry bears from their dens. Word quickly spread through Swyndon, and people began bringing over mushrooms for the strangers to sort out. Nodding and smiling, the villagers would marvel at the odd names given their finds. Edible or poisonous, their mushrooms somehow always ended up on the refuse pile with the potato peelings.

After another day's fruitless searching, Rolin and Marlis held a meeting in their room. Owen felt few misgivings about sitting in and listening. It was still his room, after all, even though he no longer slept there and never entered unless the door was open.

To Owen's surprise, the outringers began their discussion by bowing their heads, closing their eyes and talking to Bembor's "Gaelathane." After requesting wisdom and guidance in finding Gwynneth, they thanked Gaelathane for their host and hostess and asked Him to bless and comfort them. Marlis asked protection not only for her daughter, but also for Owen, wherever he was. Tears moistened Owen's eyes. Why should these gracious people care what became of a shepherd boy they had never met?

Once this reverent ritual was done, Rolin announced that he and Marlis were releasing their companions from further search duty. Those who wished to return home were free to leave.

When nobody moved toward the door, Owen cleared his throat. "Look here," he said. "This is still my bedroom, remember? I'm going to need it again soon—very soon. You'll see I'm right. And you can't stay here with my parents much longer. They already have their hands full caring for the animals and keeping up the house. Continue searching if you will, but it's time for you to move on to another house or a different village." Nobody paid him any attention, even when he hollered at each person in turn.

Timothy suggested that Gwynneth might already have found her way home and was waiting for them there. "In that case, my father would have come looking for us," Scanlon countered. He had marked the faery ring the outringers had used so Emmer would know the right one. The discussion next turned to the peculiar people of Swyndon, who locked their doors every night and kept torches burning brightly around their town until dawn.

"What do you think they're afraid of?" asked Marlis.

"I'm not sure," Rolin replied. "But I have a feeling that if we want to know what happened to Gwynneth, we'd better find out why the good folk of Swyndon keep their lights burning at night."

CHAPTER 5

THE SHEEPSHUN

The next day, Owen awoke to the sounds of shouting and horns blowing. Yawning, he crawled out of the kitchen corner where he usually slept. He could have made his bed anywhere—in the hall or fireplace, under the table, inside a wall or cupboard, beneath the woodpile—but the corner was cozy and kept him out of foot traffic. More than once, he had awakened to the unsettling sight of legs and feet plowing through his midsection. Though these collisions caused him not the slightest pain or injury, he still preferred to avoid them whenever possible. Crossing paths with "solid people" was simply too jarring and unnerving.

Fortunately, sounds passed through the veil separating Owen from the real world. Otherwise, he would be completely cut off from other people. Reading lips was an art he had never mastered.

Owen's parents were talking in low tones. "You know we are supposed to supply a sheep today, Tad," Gyrta was saying. "I have never had to do this before; which animal shall we offer?"

"I don't care," Tadwyn dully replied. "Give them Gappy."

"You should know better than that," his wife scolded him. "We have to pick the best for the . . . rites. Nothing else will do. Gappy is missing some front teeth. What about Nimble? She's healthy."

Tadwyn winced and his shoulders sagged. "Oh, very well," he muttered. "Nimble it is. I'll get her." He shuffled out the door.

Owen's blood turned to ice water in his veins. The commotion outside, his parents' argument—it all made perfect sense now. He had been too wrapped up in his own cares to give any thought to the old rituals. In his short life, he had watched many a sheepshun performed for other villagers, most recently for Melina. Each one scarred the heart. Owen had never dreamed his family's turn would come. He slipped through the wall to follow his grieving father.

Outside, the sun had hidden behind a fleece of heavy-bellied clouds. A chill wind was whipping over the hilltop, hissing through the roof thatching. Owen heard the creak of the well crank as someone hauled up the water bucket. Hungry sheep bleated beside huts and hovels. Closer at hand, Tadwyn had let himself into the sheep pen attached to the house. Speaking soft words, he was stroking the head of a handsome, pure white ewe. Tears coursed down his bearded cheeks as he tied a rope around the sheep's neck and led her out of the pen. Just down the path, five of the village elders waited, each wearing his black ceremonial robe and carrying his shepherd's staff. Horror and regret filled Owen's heart.

Nimble was his father's favorite ewe. Playful to a fault, she loved to chase Tadwyn through the tall grass. She was especially fond of climbing rocks and hills like a spry goat, earning her the nickname, "Nimble." Soon she would climb no more.

Owen returned to the house, where he found his puffy-eyed and aproned mother cooking a hearty breakfast of mutton and beans for her guests. Not for the first time, Owen wished he could comfort Gyrta somehow, but he realized it was useless to try.

After the outringers had cleaned their plates, Rolin stood and thanked Gyrta for her hospitality. "It is time for us to move along now," he told her. "Since we have yet to find Gwynneth, we must continue our search for her elsewhere. May Gaelathane reunite you with your own missing loved one and grant you His peace."

"Never again shall I find peace in this house," Gyrta declared. "My son is beyond all hope, beyond the reach even of your Gaelathane. I thank you for your kind words of sympathy, but I advise you to return home. If your wayward daughter walked the Downs after dark, she has gone where you cannot follow."

"Nonetheless, we must do what we can to find her," said Rolin. "In token of our gratitude, we wish to offer you this." From his tunic pocket, Rolin took a glassy, egg-shaped object and handed it to Gyrta. She gasped. The thing shone like a small moon in the dingy room. "Thank you! What is it?" she asked in one breath.

"It is a cone from the Tree of Life," Marlis said. "Gaelathane gave it to us just after Gwynneth disappeared. 'This is not yours to keep,' He told us. 'Give it to her who has suffered a similar loss.'"

Gazing upon the gift, Owen was reminded of Athyrea's light. He felt strangely warmed, as if the cone's rays had the power to penetrate the shimmering veil and pierce his very heart and soul.

Meanwhile, his mother had carefully placed the cone in a nook where part of a brick had fallen out of the fireplace. Turning to the outringers, she said, "I had thought all your talk of a 'Creator' and 'life everlasting' was just grass blowing in the wind. But now . . ."

"But now?" Marlis asked her.

"Now I don't know what to think." Like a bird taking wing, Gyrta whisked off her apron and hung it on a nail. "If this Gaelathane is as loving as you make Him out to be," she said, "why would He rob me of my only child? Why has He snatched so many others untimely from their families, leaving orphans, widows and widowers? Not only am I bereaved of Owen, but I am forbidden to speak of him after his sheepshun, for such is the law of my people. The day following their sheepshun, the *Teithliniau*—'the Taken Ones'—are forgotten like babies who have died a-birthing. Ah, woe is me!"

"What is a 'sheepshun'?" asked Timothy.

"At noon, you shall see," said Gyrta grimly. "For now, I must prepare myself and my home, for after sheepshun, the whole village will gather here to share a meal and mourn with us."

While Marlis helped Gyrta cut up lamb, parsnips, garlic, onions and potatoes for roasting, the other outringers cleaned the house from top to bottom. Scanlon swept; Rolin scrubbed the table and floors; Elwyn washed the windows; Bembor dusted and Timothy knocked the cobwebs from the ceiling and out of the corners.

Feeling more useless than a broken staff, Owen retreated to his room, where he pouted under the bed. He didn't like being left out, but he didn't like being "left in," either. He was about to become the invisible guest of honor at a solemn ceremony for the dead.

Just before the watery sun had ridden to its zenith in the sky, Tadwyn reappeared at the house to collect his wife and six guests. After packing up their few possessions, the outringers trooped through the door. Realizing his friends did not intend to return, Owen felt a mixture of relief and sorrow. The village would seem empty and quiet without the newcomers, but at least Owen's parents could at last have the house—and their grief—to themselves.

Owen followed his father and the others down the path until they met a gangling peasant arrayed in red robes. In his hands the *menestr* carried an ornately carved wooden box. Wordlessly, he led the band among Swyndon's thatched houses. Unspeaking and stone-faced, other villagers joined the mourners.

Now some two hundred strong, the silent procession straggled through the ring of soot-blackened torches and streamed over the brow of the hill. Dropping back, Owen heard the worried-looking outringers whispering nervously amongst themselves.

"What do you suppose is in that box?" Marlis asked Rolin.

"Your guess is as good as mine," he replied, shrugging.

"Maybe Owen's ashes are inside," Elwyn suggested.

"They haven't found the boy yet," Scanlon reminded him.

The throng converged on a twenty-foot welving ring, where the village elders waited with Nimble. Using stout ropes, four shepherds held the terrified sheep in check. Her eyes rolled and she frothed at the mouth as she struggled against the restraints. Tadwyn tried to calm the agitated animal with soothing words and caresses, but Nimble seemed to know what lay ahead of her.

From among the elders stepped an erect, clear-eyed man named Crowlyn. He raised his hand for silence. As he spoke, his long, white hair streamed in the moaning wind like frosted grass.

"People of Swyndon," he cried. "Hear me well, and let the wind lend wings to my words, that they may comfort those who have lost their loved one. Where walks Owen son of Tadwyn this hour?"

"He walks beyond the Downs," the other villagers intoned.
"What evil has befallen him, that we see him not?"
"He has been *teithlin*—he has been taken," came the answer.
"Has any man's hand here struck him down without cause?"
"Nay—he has been *teithlin*."
"Has he fled to the flatlands to live among a foreign people?"
"Nay—he has been *teithlin*."
"Shall he ever lead his flock into pastures of green again?"
"Nay—he has been *teithlin*."
"Shall he drink again at the stream that flows from the hill?"
"Nay—he has been *teithlin*."
"Will he ever return to us while the sun still shines?"
"Nay—he has been teithlin!"
Crowlyn then asked, "Who stands for the son of Tadwyn?"
Tadwyn raised high his shepherd's crook. "I will."
At this, a forest of clattering staffs rose to meet Tadwyn's, resembling a sea of reeds swaying before a bitter marsh wind. Owen added his own spectral staff to the tepee-tent of wooden rods.

Then the villagers chanted as one, "If there be wrong, if there be guilt, we lift up our rods, that blood might be spilt!"

Laying his staff on Nimble's back, Tadwyn said, "Take now our trespasses with you into the darkness. Let the eyes that never sleep be pleased to accept this offering and trouble us no more."

The menestr opened his box and removed an engraved silver chalice and a gold-hilted, curved knife. He handed both items to Crowlyn. The onlookers sighed. In turn, the elder gave the knife to Tadwyn, who held it up for all to see. A hush fell over the Downs. Tadwyn stroked Nimble's head, speaking softly while his knife hand strayed below her neck. Then he swiftly slit the ewe's throat. Marlis and the other outringers blanched and quickly turned their eyes away from the ghastly spectacle. Owen let his tears flow freely.

With a blubbering groan, Nimble sank to her knees. Crowlyn crouched at her side, holding his chalice under the sheep's gashed throat to catch her gushing lifeblood. The chalice overflowed.

Meanwhile, Tadwyn had returned the dripping knife to the menestr, who wiped it off with a clean white cloth and replaced it in the box. Picking up one of Nimble's slack restraining ropes, Tadwyn then circled the welving ring to the opposite side, where he began dragging the ewe's lifeless body into and across the ring.

Owen ached with the agony his unintended absence had brought upon his parents. He longed to help his father haul on the rope, though it would slip through his fingers like water. Besides, only one family member was allowed to stand for the *teithlin*.

Just as it crossed the ring's far border, Nimble's body vanished. The outringers gasped and Tadwyn bellowed, "'Ware the ropes!" as all four cords sang through the air after the sheep's carcass.

Rolin remarked to Elwyn, "I wish I knew what makes these rings work. They act just like torsils, yet only grass grows inside."

Overhearing him, Gyrta said, "Nobody knows why the welving rings grow or what strange magic works within them. If you walk inside one, there's no hope of walking out again safely until first frost. Every year, some poor soul becomes trapped in a ring and must stay there till winter, living on supplies we toss to him."

Tadwyn strode up and wiped his hands on the grass. "Last spring," he added, "a feller accidentally backed into a ring. He didn't want to spend the next six months there sitting in a tent, so we built a block and tackle over his circle with poles. When we lifted him out, he still disappeared, and so did our contraption."

"How very sad!" said Marlis.

"What will you do with the sheep's blood?" Bembor asked.

Tadwyn looked away. "It will be sprinkled on all of Swyndon's door frames and window sashes, to ward off our enemies."

"And who are those enemies?" Rolin pressed him.

Tadwyn's face twitched. "You're better off not knowing."

"But we must know," said Rolin. "This very hour, we are setting off across the southern Downs for the lowlands. We're certain that is the way Gwynneth must have taken. You have been a kind host, but we cannot delay any longer, or it may be too late to find her."

"You're already too late!" said Owen, waving his arms.

"You're already too late!" said Tadwyn. "The flatlands lie a long day's journey from here. To reach them, you must leave at dawn—no earlier and no later. You had better take a guide with you, too."

"Please don't trouble yourself further," said Marlis. "We have our own guide. Gaelathane knows the way, and He will help us."

Tadwyn's eyes narrowed and his beard bristled. "You don't know the risks! If you leave now, we'll be having a sheepshun for you, too." Shaking his head, he started hiking back up the hill.

Owen followed him. Tadwyn was right. Nobody of sound mind would venture into the Graylands after noon. The outringers had been warned. Owen should return home and help pasture the sheep. He stopped. *You fool! You can't look after the sheep anymore. You can't even look after yourself, much less your aging parents.*

He sat down on the grass and wept. What was he to do? Where was he to go? He already knew what awaited him at home that afternoon. Over cups of strong mullein tea, old men and women would retell their fond memories of Owen son of Tadwyn. "What a fine boy he was!" they would say. "He was always so good with the sheep. 'Tis a shame he was taken so young, and an only child, at that. Poor Tad and Gyrta. What will they do without him now?"

What indeed. After the villagers had left Owen's house, they would never bring up his name again. He would become a forlorn spirit, haunting his own home until his parents grew feeble and died, never knowing their son had been present all the while.

Owen made up his mind. So far, he had been unable to help the outringers as Celembrose had suggested, but at least he could tag along and try to keep them out of harm's way. Tromping back to the blood-smeared ring, he found his friends talking to Gaelathane again. When they opened their eyes, their determined gazes swung southward, across the hills and into the blue distance.

"To the lowlands and Gwynneth we go!" Rolin cried.

"To the lowlands and Gwynneth!" echoed his companions. The sun was burning through the clouds when six pairs of green-cloaked legs made off through the Downs' waving, waist-high grass.

Glancing up at the sun, Owen muttered, "You might as well say, 'To our deaths we go.'" Looking over his shoulder at Lone Oak Hill, he wondered what had become of his sparrow and whether he would ever see her again. Then he fell in behind the outringers.

CHAPTER 6

PRINCE PERCY

Gwynneth's heart beat wildly as she raced through the woods. Surrounded by silent trees cloaked in gloom, she had neither flint nor steel for kindling a fire. Worse yet, the trail leading to the firewatch was all but invisible in the dusk. Was she about to learn why the mutton-men so feared the darkness?

Then she spotted a yellow light gleaming through the trees, and hope surged in her heart. She made for the flickering glow, praying she would find fire and food waiting for her but not Dask.

A few bumps, scrapes and scratches later, she was sitting beside a crackling fire with Wolf. While she gnawed on a juicy mutton bone, he whittled an arrow out of a fragrant stick of sweet birch.

After Gwynneth had stripped the bone bare, Wolf asked, "Why were you in the woods so late? I warned you about the danger of leaving the firelight after dark. Were you trying to escape?"

"No, I was lost," Gwynneth replied, and she launched into her tale. When she had finished, Wolf simply nodded, as if visiting other worlds was a commonplace occurrence in the Deadwood.

"First," he said, "don't ever cross Dask. An hour ago, he was storming about the firewatch, threatening to cut your heart out. He won't rest until he has had his revenge. Watch your back!"

Just days ago, Gwynneth's father had spoken those same words of warning. However, she knew Dask had something far more deadly in mind than flinging spoonfuls of oatmeal mush at her.

"Second," Wolf went on, "you should avoid touching any of the trees in the Deadwood, 'specially the slick-barked ones."

"Why is that?" Gwynneth asked.

Wolf scowled, bringing out the scars and furrows in his face. "If you so much as brush against one o' them trees, you'll find yourself in a Ghostwood land. The only way back here is to touch the same tree again—if you can find it." He pointed his unfinished arrow at Gwynneth. "There's always the risk of gettin' lost. Don't forget to tie a rag or string to a tree before you touch it, so's you can find it again. Lose your head on the wrong side of a touch-tree, and you could end up deader than a poleaxed sheep."

"Do all the trees take you to the same place?" Gwynneth asked. It wouldn't do, she knew, to mention the Isle of Luralin by name.

Wolf shook his head. "In these parts, I've visited most of the trees, and they all go to different places. Because of the curse, you can look, but you can't touch. If you want to stay a spell in a Ghostwood world, you'd better bring your own vittles and water."

These trees are sounding more and more like torsils, thought Gwynneth. However, to make passage through a typical torsil, you had to climb the tree all the way to the top and then back down again. Great-grandfather Bembor even had an adage for it (as he did for nearly every quirk of nature): "Touch the top, then drop." Since these smooth-skinned forest giants looked nothing like torsils, perhaps they really were enchanted or accursed. But if so, why would one of the trees have taken her to the Blessed Isle?

Fireside sleep was claiming her when she noticed firefly lights flitting again in the treetops. The creatures' graceful flight filled her with delight. Yet, she had never known fireflies could sing.

Smothered under Wolf's sheepskin coat, Gwynneth awoke to a rhythmic *whick-whick* noise and the sweet scent of freshly peeled sticks. The fire had burned down to a pile of smoldering coals.

Wolf was whittling away on another arrow. A pile of shavings and finished shafts lay at his feet. Picking up the bow lying beside him, he fitted the arrow to the string, drew both back to his bearded cheek and sighted down the shaft with a practiced eye.

"Good morning!" Gwynneth said to him, throwing off the sheepskin. The cool morning air cleared the cobwebs from her head. In Lucambra, she rarely slept under the stars, since one never knew what might pop out of a torsil in the middle of the night.

The mutton-man grunted back and set his bow aside. "Rest well?" he asked brusquely without looking up at Gwynneth.

"I did," she replied. "Just before I fell asleep, I heard singing, and I saw some lights like fireflies swarming in the tops of these trees. The lights appeared the other night, too. What are they?"

"Dremlens," Wolf said. "Everyone knows fireflies can't sing."

When the mutton-man offered no further word of explanation, Gwynneth said, "You've made yourself a nice bow there. Do the arrows fly true? Mine usually veer off to one side or the other."

Wolf stopped whittling long enough to peer up at her from beneath his shaggy eyebrows and hair. "You shoot, do you?"

Gwynneth blushed. "Both my mother and I do. She's a better markswoman than I. We make our shafts of cedar and the heads of flint. Our bows are yew wood. We string them with deer sinew."

"This here's an ash bow," Wolf offered. "It's strung with the braided inner bark of basswoods." He sheathed his knife and stretched. "Time to rustle up some decent feathers for these arrows," he said. "I've already got obsidian for the points. Mind the fire while I'm gone." With that, the mutton-man melted into the forest.

Gwynneth felt terribly alone and frightened. Without Wolf's protection, she would make easy prey for Dask and the other mutton-men. After tossing some dry branches on the fire, she climbed into a cherry tree that overhung the firewatch. To her disappointment, most of the cherries were still green and hard. Wedged in a wide fork in the tree, she dozed off in the leafy green sunlight.

She awoke to the chattering of an angry squirrel. "Move along, two-legs! This is my tree!" it scolded her, twitching its furry tail.

Gwynneth reassured the nervous squirrel that she had no intention of raiding its cherry larder. The gabby creature then bent her ear for an hour with tidbits of forest news—where the sweetest nuts grew; who had the best nest, the most offspring and the biggest food cache in the woods; how to spot hawks, and the like.

When she could fit a word in, Gwynneth said, "You spend lots of time in the treetops. What are those firefly lights, anyway?"

All at once, the squirrel vanished with a flip of its tail. Then a wee, sharp voice spoke in Gwynneth's ear. "Hush! Don't move!"

Gwynneth looked for the voice's owner but saw no one. Then she shrank back. Dask was prowling the firewatch. With his sword, he poked at the fresh branches Gwynneth had thrown on the fire. Next, he began searching the clearing in ever-widening circles.

At last he stopped beneath the cherry tree and peered upward. Gwynneth held her breath and stayed very still, her heart racing. Suddenly, Dask's head snapped around and he froze in a listening pose. Sheathing his sword, he loped back into the forest.

Moments later, Wolf shambled into the clearing. Releasing her pent-up breath, Gwynneth was shinnying down the tree to meet him when a shout echoed through the woods. Wolf rushed into the trees, and Gwynneth followed him. Before long, they came upon Hammel and a blocky mutton-man missing his right ear. The two pointed at a touch-tree marked with a tuft of red wool.

"We've caught another bird in the grass," Hammel told Wolf. "He's not dressed anything like the other shepherds, though."

Wolf snorted. "Let's have a look." The three mutton-men touched the tree and disappeared. Not wishing to be left alone in the woods with Dask lurking nearby, Gwynneth did the same.

She found herself among the same foggy hills where she had first become lost. The Deadwood had vanished. Only the touch-tree remained, standing like a lonely lookout amidst the windswept meadows. Wolf's men were pointing and laughing at a gaudily dressed young man mincing along with a walking stick.

"Just our luck," Wolf groaned. "A fop in all his finery. Why is it mostly drunks, weaklings and ne'er-do-wells wander in here?"

"He looks to be about my size," said Hammel's companion. "That there's a fine cut of purple cloth he's wearing, I'll wager."

Hammel guffawed. "You've been staring at the dremlens too long, Pudger! You're as big around as a barrel, and he's skinnier than a rail. Besides, what man in his right mind would dress up like that fellow? He'll wish he hadn't showed up on our doorstep."

"And we will, too," said Wolf gloomily. "It's bad enough that he's come here on Feeding Day. We'll have to take him with us."

"What is that sweet smell?" Gwynneth put in. She had just caught the cloying scent of honeysuckles. Sniffing the air, she saw the wayfaring young man also crinkle his long, pointed nose. Suddenly, the gaudy stranger vanished, nose, walking stick and all.

In a flash, the Deadwood sprang up around Gwynneth and her companions. Smiling cruelly, Wolf drew his knife, while his men took up two cudgels they had left leaning against the touch-tree.

As a mournful, bleating cry warbled through the woods, Wolf raised a finger to his lips and motioned for Gwynneth, Hammel and Pudger to follow. Beyond a clump of vine maples, they found the purple-clothed dandy wailing like a lost lamb for its mother.

"Help! Help!" he was shouting. "Where am I? Somebody help me! I'm lost!" Relief flooded his features when he noticed Gwynneth and the mutton-men. He strode briskly toward them.

"Who are you and where are we?" he demanded imperiously.

Snickering, Pudger and Hammel elbowed each other. "You tell him, Wolf!" they said. "You tell him who's boss around here!"

"You have entered the Deadwood, your new home," said Wolf curtly. "We are your friends. You have nothing to fear from us."

Seeing the men's weapons, doubt and suspicion clouded the stranger's brown eyes. "I fear no one," he declared, clutching his staff in a white-knuckled grip. "You may call this disgustingly untidy forest 'home' if you wish, but I prefer my lowland palace."

He bowed to Gwynneth and said, "Even if your companions have refused me the courtesy of disclosing their names and origins, I personally have been better bred. Please allow me to introduce myself. I am Prince Percy, heir to the throne of all Clynnod. I trust my frank words did not offend your tender feminine sensibilities. Have these filthy, smelly shepherds mistreated you? If so, the ruffians will have to answer to me and to my father, His Majesty."

Pudger and Hammel stiffened, while Wolf's eyes glittered like dark, steely marbles. The air fairly crackled with tension.

"First, we are not shepherds," said Wolf evenly. "Second, after a few weeks with us, you will look and smell exactly as we do."

"You are kidnappers or brigands, then," stated Percy flatly. "I have heard the uplands are swarming with your lawless kind." His voice climbed an octave higher as he squeaked, "If you so much as touch me or this lady, I will see you all hanged from the tallest gibbet in the kingdom! Now show me the way out of this wood before I lose my patience and teach you some proper manners!"

If you will pardon my saying so, Wolf and his men were grinning wolfishly at the prince. Gwynneth gathered they were about to enjoy some sport at his expense. Unspeaking, they led him to their touch-tree and into his own world, where they took him to a high hill out of the fog's reach. Percy chafed every step of the way.

"Leave now if you wish, *princey*," Wolf told him, pointing across the prairie. "Go wherever you like, but you will find only ashes and death inside the Ghostwood. You'll be back—if you can find us, that is—and then you'll beg us to take you in as a slave."

"You presume too much, peasant!" Percy sniffed. "We shall never stoop to serving any man, especially the likes of you. And address us by our proper title, or you shall know our wrath!"

To Gwynneth's amusement, her captors clumsily bowed to the peevish prince. "Yes, Prince Percy!" they scornfully chorused. "At your service, Prince Percy! Whatever you say, Prince Percy!"

Percy turned as purple as his outlandish garb. Drawing himself up, he shrilled, "Churls! You mock me! Now you have left me no choice but to thrash every one of you until you cry for mercy!" With that, Prince Percy swung his walking stick at Wolf's head.

The Deadwood's chieftain easily caught the staff in mid-swing and broke it in half like an old bone. Then he seized the prince by the shoulders and pushed down, driving him into the ground as easily as a river boatman shoves his oar into the wet sand.

"Unhand me, you scum!" squealed the prince. "Unhand me, or I'll—urkh!" All that now remained of Percy above ground was his head, which nestled in the grass like a hairy, perspiring egg. The prince's eyes bulged with terror as he struggled in vain to free himself. Kneeling, Wolf lowered his face inches from Percy's.

"Allow me to introduce myself," Wolf growled. "I am Wolf. I eat boys like you for breakfast! You have trespassed upon *my* kingdom, where I am king, prince, judge and executioner. If you ever threaten me again, I'll flay you alive!" Wolf waved his knife between Percy's eyes, which practically popped out of their sockets.

"Take 'is ears and nose, Boss!" the other two men called out.

"Shut up, you boneheads!" Wolf snarled at them. "He's no good to us maimed! Besides, I need him to help us burn down this accursed forest." Turning back to Percy, he said, "Should I start carving on your pretty face now, or do we have an understanding?"

Percy nodded, his chin sinking into the dirt and popping out again. Thrusting his knife back into his belt, Wolf grabbed a fistful of Percy's dark hair and yanked him cleanly out of the ground.

Rubbing his head, Percy stood staring stupidly at his foe. He made a start at brushing himself off but found nothing to brush. His purple suit was as spotless as the day it was first tailored.

"How—how did you do that?" he stammered.

"Never you mind," Wolf said. "If you don't behave, I'll push you all the way under and leave you to rot. Now move along!"

Returning to the Deadwood, the party was traveling through the forest when Wolf brought everyone to a sudden halt. Ahead, a black, tarlike pool had drowned several leafless trees. Despite the balmy weather, a bitter chill drove deeply into Gwynneth's bones.

Herding his followers around the pool, Wolf said, "Steer clear of borwog holes like this one unless you want to be sucked in."

"What is a borwog hole?" Gwynneth asked him.

"You ask too many questions," he grunted. "Don't talk. Just walk. It's a long march to the Feeding Camp, and if I know this lazy lot, we'll have to start the fire again from tinder and sparks."

The late afternoon sun was bathing the forest with gold as the mutton-men led their captives farther into the woods. After fording a clear, cold stream, the company came upon a clearing strewn with rotting stumps and charred limbs. Beside one of several fire circles bleated a frightened sheep tethered to a stake with a rope.

Wolf cursed. "What did I tell you? Those good-for-nothings left us to build the fire and see to the sheep, too!" He kicked the half-burned branches back into the nearest fire circle and flicked a thumb at Hammel and Pudger. "Get to it, boys! While you're at it, put Mr. Fancy Pants here to work hauling firewood for you."

Percy's nose practically speared the sun with disdain. "What about *her*?" he said, pointing a manicured finger at Gwynneth.

So much for chivalry! thought Gwynneth sourly.

"She's going with me to Black Lake," said Wolf. "I'll need help with Tilly." Wiping his eyes, he untied the sheep's tether and handed Gwynneth the end of the rope. "If she balks, just yank on this," he told her. "We can't be late with the feeding, or we'll all pay. Now let's go." He headed across the clearing and into the woods beyond.

Gwynneth had never led a sheep before, since Lucambrians rarely kept livestock. She pulled on the tether, and Tilly trotted along behind her. Evidently, the sheep knew it was feeding time.

By now, the warm evening sunlight was lingering in the leafy aisles between the trees, though the air was cool. It grew colder still as Gwynneth tramped with Tilly and Wolf through miles of woodland. At length, dead and dying trees stood out among the green. Despite the sun's heat, frost lay thickly on the wilted grass, and Gwynneth's shivering breath made foggy plumes. Farther on, the trees' leaves hung shriveled and black on withered limbs.

Finally, the three came to the frozen threshold of a tarry lake. Like a foul canker, this vast, black borwog hole darkened the very sky above it and ate away at the earth beneath. A frostbitten deadness drummed against Gwynneth's ears, deafening her. Before her eyes, a leafless tree clinging to the shoreline toppled soundlessly into the lake and vanished without a ripple. It was a dismal scene.

Wolf took the rope from Gwynneth and knelt beside Tilly. He buried his face in her thick wool, his shoulders shaking with silent sobs. Then he woodenly coiled the rope and flung it into the lake. Instantly, the rope went taut, dragging Tilly toward the darkness.

CHAPTER 7

THE BORWOGS

As Black Lake swallowed up Tilly, Gwynneth went numb with shock and cold. She realized now what Wolf had meant by "the feeding." He was not feeding the sheep, but the lake—and she had been a party to his cruelty!

"You beast!" she screamed at him. "Why did you kill that poor, innocent sheep?" Ice throttled the words in her throat.

Wolf turned away from her muffled tirade, his back and shoulders hunched. Gwynneth trailed him as he plodded through the groves of dead trees. When he faced her again, his eyes were dark with sorrow, but his deep voice was firm and clear again.

"Where I come from," he said, "we sacrificed a sheep whenever someone disappeared while pasturing the flocks. Sometimes, those slaughtered sheep show up in the Deadwood, and we make good use of them. Our sacrifices here are meant to keep the borwogs at bay. The beasts seem to crave the warmth of living bodies, so we throw small animals into their holes to appease them. Once a month, we send a sheep into Black Lake, as I just did Tilly."

Gwynneth sniffed, "Well, I think your 'borwogs' or whatever you call them are no excuse for murdering a sheep." When Wolf ignored her, she asked, "What made that lake in the first place?"

"The best part of the Deadwood once stood there. In those days, that forest also grew near my home. When my people cut down and burned all the trees, a borwog hole opened in the forest here. The lake's been growing ever since, destroying everything in its path—trees, wild animals, people—and sheep, too."

Acting on a hunch, Gwynneth said, "You raised Tilly, then?"

"Yes," Wolf replied. "She was a bum lamb, a cripple at birth. I fed her gruel till she was old enough to graze. She was like a daughter to me." He hung his shaggy head. "I never had a wife or children. Let the others think you're my wife. Otherwise, they'd try to take you away from me. You wouldn't like that at all."

"If you loved Tilly, why not sacrifice another sheep?"

"That was Dask's doing," Wolf grunted. "He staked Tilly at the firewatch to get back at me because of you. He knows if I dared show any fondness for a sheep or other signs of weakness, the rest of the men would go for my throat. As I warned you before, Dask has a long memory and a longer sword, so beware of his treachery!"

Gwynneth nodded, at a loss for words. She patted the mutton-man's hairy arm. "Thank you for defending me!" she said, though she knew it was really Gaelathane Who was looking out for her.

Wolf actually smiled. "Come along, now," he told her. "We'd better head back before the lake erupts. We were late with Tilly."

Gwynneth hurried after him. "What do you mean by that?" she asked. "What difference does the time of sacrifice make?"

"If we're even a little late with an animal—as we were today— the borwogs will come looking for us," Wolf gravely replied.

As the sun dropped behind blushing peaks, its blazing shield cast long shadow-fingers across the dusky landscape. "Pretty mountains, ain't they?" Wolf said. "Some of my men once journeyed westward to seek their fortunes there, but they never returned."

Darkness fell like an ax, and a sickle moon rose, swimming in a sea of frothy clouds. Its sickly light fell upon a black river flowing north through the forest. Gwynneth stopped to gaze at the dark tide oozing toward her among the trees. A chill wind passed through her, deadening her hearing again. She was clawing at her ears when Wolf roughly pulled her away from the swelling river of tar.

"Keep moving!" he shouted in a distant, reedy voice. Then a black wind snatched up his next words and carried them away. Reading his lips by moonlight, Gwynneth caught one word: *Run*.

Run they did, as if a hundred dragons were breathing down their backs. Gwynneth willed her legs to slog through an invisible ocean of ice water that dampened all sounds except the thundering of her heart. At last, she spotted a cheery light shining through the trees. With a final sprint, she and Wolf burst into the clearing where they had left Hammel, Pudger and Prince Percy. Bonfires were blazing, their tall flames silently spearing the night.

Still chilled despite her exertions, Gwynneth threw herself trembling down on the ground. Hands picked her up and laid her next to a fire, where she slowly thawed. When she felt warmed enough to sit up, she found thirty or forty mutton-people huddled with their children around the fires, their arms waving and fingers fluttering. Mirrah was among them. Her movements were brisk and birdlike. Gwynneth was about to join her when all hands and arms froze in flight, and all eyes turned toward the dark forest.

The black tide had arrived, frosting the earth and shriveling the green grass. The friendly flames sank lower, and some of the men hastily tossed more sticks of wood on the fires. Red eyes pierced the darkness as squat, black bodies jostled into the shrinking circles of firelight. Borwogs. Thousands upon thousands of them.

Gwynneth screamed soundlessly. She screamed again, feeling her throat rattle, but she might as well have been a single snowflake whispering to the myriad frigid stars. The borwogs' eyes mocked her. *Scream till you are hoarse!* they said. *Only we can hear you.*

Was she going deaf? She beat on her ears, wincing at the pain. Then Percy staggered up, his red face contorting and mouth flapping. Gwynneth couldn't understand a word he was saying.

As the prince wildly hopped about in a fit of rage, the bystanders pointed at him and threw back their heads in silent, scornful laughter. Then they returned to waving their arms at each other.

Leaving Percy to his tantrum, Gwynneth scurried over to Mirrah, whose eyes lit up with recognition. The two girls embraced. Mirrah wept, her tears flowing from bruised and blackened eyes.

Gwynneth tried speaking to her friend, but again, her throat made no sounds. Mirrah's hands danced like a pair of hovering doves, yet Gwynneth could make no sense of the odd motions.

Years earlier, while visiting Beechtown, she had observed three urchins in the market square gesturing to one another. She had spoken to them, but like Mirrah, they couldn't hear her. Later, Rolin had explained that the children were deaf and were using Thalmosian sign language instead of speech to communicate.

This was different. How could so many hearing, speaking people become deaf and speechless overnight? Moreover, how had they learned sign language? Puzzling over these questions, Gwynneth flopped down on a pile of dried leaves and fell asleep. The borwogs' red eyes bored into her nightmarish dreams all that night.

When she awoke, a fine mist was sifting down from a troubled sky. Jumping up, she shook the water droplets off her tunic and glanced about. Mutton-people still lay sleeping around the fires, which had died down to smoking embers. To her relief, the borwogs had apparently returned to their lake during the night.

Percy was lying beside another of the campfires. The prince sat up, yawned daintily and stretched. His bloodshot eyes turned on Gwynneth, and he wrinkled his nose in supreme distaste.

Gwynneth suddenly became aware of her filthy garments and hair. She must look a fright! Blushing, she clumsily gestured to Percy that the borwogs were gone. Seeing his expression change from contempt to bafflement, she decided to try a different tack.

"GOOD MORNING!" she bellowed. "CAN YOU HEAR ME?"

Percy winced and covered his ears, while Gwynneth gasped. She could hear her own voice again! From all around came the groans of mutton-people jarred out of sleep. Birds chirped; frogs croaked in the underbrush; the dying fires sputtered in the mist.

"There's no need to shout," Percy grumbled. He yawned again. "What a perfectly dreadful night's sleep I have had. Don't these people believe in beds, sheets, blankets or pillows? Wake me when breakfast is served. I would like bacon, eggs, sausages and sweet rolls. Fry the eggs over easy, and don't break the yolks. Now I am going back to sleep, though I doubt I will rest well."

As Percy curled up again beside the fire, Gwynneth felt the urge to roust him out, preferably with a heavy stick. Knowing that Gaelathane wouldn't approve of her taking matters into her own hands—however richly Percy might deserve a drubbing—she shook off the temptation. Quietly, she made her way through clumps of slumbering men, women and children to the clearing's edge.

Although her father had taught her the finer points of tracking, Gwynneth found no footprints or other signs that a host of fell creatures had visited during the night. Except for a few broken twigs where she and Wolf had barreled through the trees, the forest lay undisturbed as it basked in the morning's gray light.

Gwynneth sat on a log and let her lonely tears mingle with the mist. When she could weep no more, she prayed, "Gaelathane, why did You bring me to this place with its mutton-people and borwogs and unreachable worlds-within-worlds? I want to go home to Timothy and my family. I'm sure they are worried about me. I am worried about them, too. Please let me see them again."

"Who are you talking to?"

Opening her eyes, Gwynneth found Mirrah curiously staring down at her. "I was just . . . praying to Gaelathane," she answered. "You remember Him; I told you about Him when we first met."

Mirrah peered this way and that through the forest. "I don't see anyone here except us two. And what is 'praying'?"

"Praying is when you talk to someone who is far greater than you are," Gwynneth explained. "You can't see Gaelathane, unless He reveals Himself to you. He always hears and answers our prayers. He's especially good at helping people like us in trouble."

Mirrah threw back her shoulders. "I don't need anyone's help. I can take care of myself." She brushed away a lock of hair. "You talk like someone the borwogs have touched. They can twist your mind and make you forget who you are and where you're from."

"My mind is perfectly fine," said Gwynneth. "Gaelathane does exist, and He loves you. But what *are* the borwogs, anyway?"

Mirrah shrugged. "We don't know. After dark, they come out of Black Lake and other holes. They hate the light. That's why we keep the fires burning at night. Borwogs don't move very fast, but they can steal the warmth out of a body from a distance. It's how they live, I suppose. Wolf says that when we burn the Deadwood, we'll have more pastureland for the sheep, and the 'wogs will go away. I hope so. I miss walking freely under the stars and moon."

Recalling her brush with the borwogs, Gwynneth shuddered. "Why build fires when heat attracts the beasts?" she asked.

Mirrah nervously glanced back at the camp, where the other mutton-people were stirring. "The heat draws them, all right, but the light drives them back into the shadows. This way, we can keep the creatures from attacking our sheep at night. We have fifteen firewatches like this one, with a firemaster for each."

"A firemaster?" asked Gwynneth.

"Yes. He's the one responsible for keeping the fires burning, night and day. Since he can't leave his firewatch, the rest of us bring him food and water. So long as all the fires are lit every evening, anyone passing through the woods after dusk can usually find safe refuge before the borwogs come looking for him."

"Supposing the fires go out," said Gwynneth. "What then?"

Mirrah grimaced. "That happened at this watch last month. Everyone fell asleep and let the fires die. The next day, we found twenty-nine adults and children, all frozen to death where they lay. If the firemaster had lived, we would have hanged him."

"Oh, dear," said Gwynneth. One reason Wolf had expected to find the ashes cold in the Feeding Camp was that the firemaster had died. "But why couldn't we hear each other last night?"

Mirrah turned her dark eyes on Gwynneth. "The 'wogs feed on sound, too. They draw it into themselves like the heat and light."

Someone shouted in the firewatch, and a panicked look came over Mirrah's face. Grabbing Gwynneth's hand, she pulled her to her feet and dragged her protesting toward the rough clearing.

"That was Dask!" said the servant girl. "I know his voice. He must be calling for me. If I don't come right away, he'll beat me."

When the girls stumbled into the firewatch, they found Dask and Prince Percy facing off. Dask was brandishing his sword. Blood was streaming from Percy's nose, and he looked terrified. The other mutton-people were silently watching from a respectful distance.

"So it's eggs and sausage you want, do you?" roared Dask, poking his sword at Percy's belly. "I'll give you eggs and sausage, you knock-kneed ninny! While you're at it, why don't you ask for dumplings, too? I'm sure we could whip some up for you." He waved his free arm toward the subdued spectators. "What do you say, mutton-mates? Are we the eggs-and-sausage type?" Averting their eyes, the others mutely shook their heads.

They're all as scared of Dask as Mirrah is, thought Gwynneth.

"You see?" Dask gloated. "They agree with me. Let me tell you what we serve in the Deadwood, you sniveling milksop! It's mutton for breakfast, mutton for lunch, and mutton for supper! And if you're very, very good, we might even share a bone or two with you!" Dask punctuated each word with a sword stab that came perilously close to puncturing Percy's scrawny, quivering neck.

Now Dask waved his sword like a conductor's baton. "I think it's time this fellow learned our Mutton Song, don't you, boys?

If you have a hankering for sweets or finest wine,
If you hang a kerchief 'round your neck before you dine;
If you like an egg or two for breakfast or for brunch,
Mutton every meal is all you're going to get to munch!

Mutton, mutton, mutton is the meat we love to gnaw,
Roast it, boil it, fry it, bake it—even serve it raw!
Morning, noon and night you'll eat it from a greasy plate;
Mutton is a dainty dish that soon you'll love to hate!

If you like your tableware of silver and of gold;
If you turn your nose up when your supper's growing cold;
If you find monotony in fare that oft repeats;
Mutton every meal is all you're going to get to eat!

Mutton, mutton, mutton is the meat we love to gnaw,
Roast it, boil it, fry it, bake it—even serve it raw!
Morning, noon and night you'll eat it from a greasy plate;
Mutton is a dainty dish that soon you'll love to hate!

76

Dask's sword tip tapped Percy's thin chest. "You have a lot of nerve, princey, barging into our forest dressed like a fine dandy and putting on airs. You're no better than the rest of us. In the Deadwood, we have only two kinds of men: the living and the dead. If you don't watch yourself, I can promise you'll end up dead!"

Whiiit! Twitching his sword, Dask sliced through Percy's purple tunic from top to bottom. With a few more twitches, the garment dropped off in tatters. Next came the trousers, leaving a very red Percy clad only in his pink floral undershirt and drawers. The onlookers pointed at him and burst out laughing.

"When my father hears of this indignity, he'll see you all hanged!" fumed the prince. "Do you hear me? Hanged! And I shall relish setting the nooses and pulling the trapdoor lever."

Everyone laughed again—except Dask. Up flashed the sword, leaving a thin, bloody trail on Percy's cheek. The prince gasped.

"There's the kind of talk that will get you staked out on the ground at night—without a fire!" snarled Dask. "It's time to teach you a lesson." He raised his sword to slash off one of Percy's ears.

"That's enough, Dask." Knife at the ready, Wolf strode up and stayed the mutton-man's hand. "You've had your fun. Now let the poor fellow go. We'll need his help when we torch this queer forest. Besides, one-eared, he can't rightly hear a sheep's bleat."

Grumbling, Dask sullenly stalked off to one of the fire circles, where his companions made way for him. Using his sword, he furiously hacked a hunk of meat from a side of roasting mutton.

Hammel found Percy a spare tunic and trousers. After dressing himself, the humiliated prince huddled beside a campfire. He was shivering, though Gwynneth suspected it was not from the cold.

"You're lucky he didn't slice your head clean off," Mirrah told the prince, wiping blood from his cheek. "A quick temper, that one has. He's always spoiling for a fight. Pudger lost an ear to him over a piece of meat two years ago. You had better mind your mouth, or next time, you may not have Wolf to defend you. Now hold still so's I can clean out this cut. You don't want it becoming infected."

Percy groaned and made hideous faces while Mirrah scrubbed the wound with a wet rag. Then she stanched the flow of blood with a pinch of brown powder she had taken from a purse in her pocket. The powder resembled the insides of a dried-up puffball. Gwynneth used puffball spores for the same purpose. Over that, Mirrah smeared a dollop of a honey-colored, sticky substance.

"Poplar pitch," she explained. Gwynneth approved. In the fall and winter, Lucambrians often collected cottonwood and other poplar buds, warming them before pressing out the fragrant "balm." This gluey substance sealed off wounds and hastened healing.

"That gash won't grow foul or breed worms now," Mirrah said. "You'll still have a scar. Don't tell Dask I did this. He'd kill me."

Percy nodded. Vanity and fear warred in his face. "Thank you," he said stiffly. "I am sure my nurse could have done no better. You would make a passable servant, with some instruction."

"Hah!" Mirrah's eyes flashed and she snapped her fingers under the prince's nose. "What makes you think I would *want* to be your servant, Mr. Hoity-toity? I pity the ones you already have!"

Leaving Prince Percy dazed and speechless, the two girls made off in search of a proper breakfast, giggling as they went. Gwynneth quickly sobered when she caught sight of Dask. He glared at her with a venomous look that said, *I haven't forgotten your impertinence. Just wait. When you least expect it, your turn will come!*

CHAPTER 8

THE GOLDEN CAVERN

By mid-afternoon, Owen and his friends had reached the Graylands. Already a mist-halo was crowning the sun with ghostly wisps and streamers. The mist spread and thickened, blotting out the sky and blurring the light of the outringers' shining rods. As an otherworldly singing floated through the perfumed fog, the grassy hills of the Downs faded. Owen and his companions stood among great trees glowing in the afternoon sun. Turning round and round, Owen realized he had returned to the phantom forest where he and the sparrow had found Tabitha.

"Hello! Who are *you*?" the outringers asked, staring *at* him instead of *through* him. Instantly, he felt naked and embarrassed.

"I am Owen son of Tadwyn," he said breathlessly. "Don't you remember me?" Inwardly, he kicked himself. Of course they wouldn't remember someone they had never seen or heard before!

Rolin brightened. "You're the boy who was lost?"

"That's right," Owen said. "Only I was never really lost."

Reaching out, he touched Elwyn's arm. "You *are* real!" he said. Evidently, Owen himself became real only inside this strange forest. "For many a day, I doubted my own senses. Yet here you all are—Bembor, Rolin, Marlis, Scanlon, Elwyn and Timothy."

"If you truly are Tadwyn and Gyrta's lost son, how could you possibly know our names?" Bembor demanded.

Instead of answering him, Owen bent down, picked up a stick and broke it in two. The satisfying *snick* of the snapping stick clinched it: He was still alive and not a spirit or a ghost after all!

Settling on a stump, he poured out his incredible tale. Afterwards, Rolin and Marlis recalled their visit to a place they called "Limbo," where they had become invisible as well. Unlike Owen, however, their bodies had remained solid and substantial.

"It sounds as if your 'Celembrose' might be an angel," said Marlis. "Few people ever see one this side of Gaelessa, you know."

"Maybe Athyrea is an angel, too," Timothy suggested.

"What are angels?" Owen asked.

"They are Gaelathane's servants," Marlis began. "Their chief task is to assist His adopted children whenever they call upon Him. Ordinarily you can't see angels, but they are everywhere, flying about on the King's business. Gaelathane is always ready to help us, but we often forget to ask until we are in real trouble or danger."

"What about Owen's sparrow?" said Elwyn. "I'll bet she's an angel in bird disguise. Can't angels take on any form they wish?"

"Who ever heard of a 'guardian sparrow'?" Rolin teased him.

Your Guardian, Owen's shining rescuer had called himself. Owen let his mind drift back to the shattered ice of Landon Lake. Strong arms had encircled his waist, pulling him out of those frigid waters. He had felt a rush of air, and his feet found solid ground. Shivering and dripping alone on the frozen shore, he had watched the swan he had freed flying off the lake—but who had freed him?

"Angels or not, I say he's made up this whole preposterous story," Scanlon said. "After all, he could have learned our names and much more besides simply by asking around the village."

"Not without his parents finding out!" Marlis countered. "Remember, all of Swyndon has been searching for this lost boy."

"Maybe he just ran away and wants to cover his tracks."

You asked for it! Owen thought, and he told the outringers how he had caught Scanlon pilfering a mince pie Gyrta had hidden in a cupboard. Gyrta had blamed the missing pie on "pixies," as she did the other foodstuffs that had mysteriously vanished after the flatlanders' arrival. Scanlon turned redder than a ripe strawberry.

"You should be ashamed of yourself," Marlis scolded him. "I hope you choked on that pie. You owe Gyrta an apology!"

Laughing, Rolin told Owen, "You have us at a disadvantage, young fellow. We know very little about you, but you know all about us! Now do you wish to throw in your lot with us pie-eating Greencloaks, or would you rather return home to your village?"

"My staff is your staff, as we say in Swyndon," Owen replied, and he extended his shepherd's crook to Rolin.

In turn, Rolin touched Owen's staff with his own clear, shining stick. "And my staff is yours as well," he said gravely. All the other outringers also pledged their staffs to Owen—even Scanlon.

"Your mother is a fine hostess," he told Owen with an impish grin. "I hope we can return to Swyndon and sample more of her cooking. Perhaps she would share some of her recipes with us!" Owen later learned that Scanlon had married a tree-nymph, who knew little about preparing meals suited to mortal palates.

Owen grinned back at him. "Mince pies are her specialty!" Noticing the shadows lengthening among the trees, he added, "We must hurry now. It is dangerous to stay in this forest after dark."

Collecting their knapsacks and various weapons, the outringers followed Owen through the woods. He was hoping the trees would run out before the light did, but the farther he and his companions hiked along, the thicker and gloomier the forest grew.

"Where are you taking us?" Rolin finally asked him.

Owen stopped and faced the outringers. "I don't know," he admitted. "I was sure we would have left this wood by now."

A fine guide I turned out to be, he reflected. He waited for Rolin to tell him so. To his surprise, the outringer merely nodded.

"Gaelathane will show us the way," he said.

I hope Gaelathane knows His way around this forest! Owen was thinking when a tiny star flew at his face. He ducked as it began to dart back and forth like a dog anxious for its master to follow.

"Athyrea?" he exclaimed. "Athyrea, is that you?" But the star had flown off into the forest again, where it circled, waiting.

Motioning for the outringers to join him, Owen tracked the spot of light as it dashed through the trees. Like the sparrow, the pixie-light would pause after each dash, quivering with eagerness or impatience until Owen and his friends could catch up to it.

Presently, the ground sloped down into a moist, steep-sided ravine. Twilight flowed into it like the rivulets Owen saw trickling over ferny stone outcroppings in the canyon walls. By staff light, the company trekked farther into the valley until their guide vanished among the shadows at the base of a sheer cliff face.

"Now where did she go?" Owen muttered to himself. Then he spotted a crescent of thicker gloom nestled beneath the cliff.

In greener days, a river had cascaded over the valley rim above that place. Thundering into the rock basin below, its pent-up waters had boiled back against the cliff, carving out a deep hollow in the living rock. Into this echoing cavern the tiny star had flown. After Owen and his friends entered, it immediately flew out again.

"What a cozy cave!" Marlis remarked. The floor was reasonably level, and there was plenty of room for everyone. While the outringers laid out their sleeping gear, Owen explored the chamber. To his disappointment, it dead-ended at the rear in ragged rock. There would be no escaping that way if enemies found the cave.

Then he heard a rustling noise. He had disturbed thousands of restless bats clinging to the ceiling and walls. With madly fluttering wings, the tiny creatures took flight, pouring out of the cave entry and fanning into the dusk. Owen was relieved to see them go.

After the last bat had left, a deadly chill crept into the cave, despite the departed sun's lingering warmth. The red-eyed shadow creatures had come calling, and Owen's back was to the rocks.

As their breath froze in clouds of glittering ice crystals, the brave Greencloaks pointed their crystal staffs at the burning eyes crowding into the cave. Six light beams shot into the darkness. When the outringers lowered their rods, however, the eyes returned.

Silence pounded at Owen's ears as an unbearable cold seeped into his bones like an icy fever, freezing his marrow. *Help me!* he tried to cry out, but the words froze in his frosty mouth. He felt only a rasping in his throat and the crackling of his ice-brittle hair.

Clawing at the stones behind him, he sought for a way out. Black specks were swimming before his eyes when his fingertips caught on a cold, thin cord. He pulled on it and fell forward through a gap in the rocks. His heart's pulse suddenly roared in his ears.

He could hear again.

Picking himself up, Owen saw he was in an immense cavern. Though only the dimmest dusk straggled through cracks in the lofty ceiling, the gold-pebbled walls and roof threw back that wan light in a blinding blaze. Owen wandered through the hall, marveling at the riches embedded in its rocks. Presently, he came across a stone cradle. In it lay the composed figure of a fresh-faced woman, her eyes closed as if in sleep. However, the flesh of her pallid cheek felt as cold and hard to his touch as polished marble.

As darkness dulled the cavern's light, Owen left the living corpse reposing in her stony tomb. Hurrying back the way he had come, he faced a solid wall of gold nuggets. How had he entered this place, and why hadn't he brought along a torch or an outringer's staff? A hard fist of fear gripped his heart. He had to find a way out.

Following the wall around, Owen came to a small square that was free of nuggets. A thin film of frost was forming on the exposed stone. In the gathering darkness, he patted the patch's surface with a blind man's splayed fingers. There. A shallow oval cavity had been undercut into the rock, creating a convenient handhold.

Gripping the undercut, Owen pulled up, and the entire blank section of stone swung grittily outward on unseen hinges. A blast of frigid air hit him in the face as he ducked through the opening and into the chilly cave. The stone slab grated shut behind him.

His friends lay on the cavern floor, stiff and cold, their staffs glowing beside them. Frost whiskered the outringers' eyebrows and lashes, while wisps of vapor curled from their nostrils. A few reddish eyes still lurked in the cave's mouth. More appeared as Owen checked the bodies for further signs of life. Icy needles pricked his bare skin and froze the very air in his laboring lungs.

Finding faint pulses in the outringers, he dragged them one by one to the cave's back wall. If only he could reopen the trapdoor, his friends might recover in the golden cavern. Using Bembor's bright staff, he searched the wall until he spotted the silvery glint of a braided metal wire. He gave it a good, hard tug. To his horror, something gave way above, and the cord came slithering down to the ground. Owen beat on the stubborn wall with his fists and then with the shining staff, but the hidden door refused to open.

"What am I to do now?" he cried. "Gaelathane of the outringers, please help us! Please save us from these creatures of the cold!"

Icy shadows were pressing into the cave when firefly lights appeared among them, driving the beasts back outside. Then a glowing waterfall of fiery diamonds silently spilled over the cave's mouth, creating a dazzling curtain of living light. Going to the front of the cave, Owen poked at the jeweled curtain, which smoothly flowed around his finger like water around a rock.

A current of air whispered over his hand, as if thousands of murmuring wings were beating in unison. Looking more closely, he saw that the "jewels" were not dropping to earth. Instead, they were rising and falling, falling and rising like gnats hovering over still water on a sultry summer's eve. The light-waterfall was alive.

Now a gnat-like buzzing was growing in his head. At length, his thawing ears identified the sounds as human voices. The outringers were talking to one other, and he could plainly hear them! Like half-frozen January robins warmed by the winter's sun, his friends were gradually reviving. Standing and moving stiffly about, they stretched their cold limbs and wiggled numb fingers.

"What are they?" Marlis was saying, pointing at the curtain.

"I have never seen the like of them in my life!" said Bembor.

"Whatever they are," Timothy said, "I hope they stick around until our red-eyed visitors leave for good. Those creatures gave me the creeping shivers—inside and out. We nearly froze to death! What are those beasts, that even lightstaffs cannot touch them?"

"Do you know, son of Tadwyn?" Rolin asked Owen.

Owen shook his head. Then his companions wanted to know why they had found themselves piled against the cave's back wall. Owen explained how he had fallen into the golden cave with its life-like corpse. Even after producing the silver cord, though, he failed to convince his friends of the great wealth he had discovered.

Bembor remarked, "As far as I know, gold naturally occurs only in isolated pockets and veins in solid rock. I have never heard of nuggets coating the walls of a cavern such as you have described. Perhaps you saw something else that resembled gold."

"It was real gold," said Owen stoutly. "Acres and acres of it!"

"Perhaps he is right," Rolin allowed. "His cave might have been gilded as a burial sepulcher for that woman he found."

Scanlon kicked at the rock. "This wall sounds solid enough to me. Maybe Owen was so cold he started imagining things. Visions often appear to frozen travelers lost in the ice and snow. Why, just now, I saw Medwyn as clear as clear can be, but she wasn't real."

Owen held up the broken wire. "I didn't dream this!" he said, and opening his shepherd's purse, he dropped the cord inside.

"The boy does have a point," said Marlis.

"Real or imagined, that cavern is closed to us now," said Rolin. "Our only way of escape is to leave the same way we came in." He planted himself by the quiet waterfall of luminous gems. "These lights remind me of the tiny angels Marlis and I saw in Lucambra-future when old Percel the hermit died and went to Gaelessa."

"Gaelessa? What kind of place is that?" Owen asked. Marlis had mentioned it earlier in the day when she was describing angels.

"It is Gaelathane's kingdom," Rolin replied. "The only way to reach that far-off, wondrous place is through the Tree of trees."

"Do you mean an oak?" Owen had spent many an hour sitting in his oak tree, watching his sheep and admiring the view from Lone Oak Hill. Sometimes he even talked to the tree, sensing it was more than mindless wood, leaves and sap. How he wished he could climb the Tree of trees to reach this land called Gaelessa!

"Oh, no," Marlis said. "It is much larger than any oak tree; it is bigger than any tree that has ever stood in any world that Gaelathane has created. There is none like it, nor will there ever be again. When Gaelathane's enemies slew the Tree, Gaelathane died, too—but not because He had to. He willingly sacrificed Himself for our forgiveness so that we could live forever with Him in Gaelessa, His home. Three days after He died, He came back to life and returned to Gaelessa, where He reigns as King of kings with the Tree of trees, never to die again. If we had perished in this cave today, the angels would have taken us directly to Gaelessa, too."

"And I could go there as well?" Owen asked breathlessly. It seemed too wonderful to be true, yet if a person really could live forever, such a gift would be worth all the sheep in Swyndon!

Marlis replied, "First, you must ask Gaelathane to forgive all your wrongs and make you His child. It's not difficult."

Confused, Owen stared at her, forgetting it was rude to gawk at someone who could see you. "But who *is* this Gaelathane?"

"He is the King of the Trees, the Ageless Creator of all that exists," Rolin said. "Before any world was, He had already lived an eternity. When the sun, moon and stars are no more, Gaelathane and His Tree will still be as young as the dawn and as old as time itself. With His own sword, Gaelathane cut our lightstaffs from the Tree of trees. Each one is priceless, for no ax or blade forged by the hand of man could ever sever the Tree's slightest twig."

"If Gaelathane is so mighty," said Owen, "why couldn't He have saved Melina from being taken on the Downs last year?"

"Who is Melina?" Bembor asked.

Owen didn't answer. He needed time to think. Stretching out on the ground, he pillowed his head on his hands. His thoughts strayed back to the golden cavern and the nameless woman lying forever locked in death's dreamless sleep. As in a trance, he saw the nuggets drop from the cave's walls and roof to bury the lifelike corpse in a mountain of gold. Then the heap flew apart and whirled in a cloud high into the cavern's shadowy recesses.

At dawn, Owen awoke to the ringing tones of voices sweetly singing in a strange tongue. As morning's first rosy light tiptoed into the cave entrance, the shining waterfall quietly vanished.

Then Owen's ears pricked up at another sound. Outside, someone was screaming for help like the town crier at sheepshun.

THINBARK

A fter a scanty breakfast of mutton and berries, Gwynneth and her companions set off for the next firewatch. As usual, Percy dawdled behind, grumbling about his aching legs and feet. Dask prodded the prince along at sword-point, bullying him every step of the way with insults and dire threats.

While Dask was busy tormenting Percy, Mirrah was free to chat with Gwynneth. The two girls talked gaily as they strode along the sun-splotched forest floor, their footfalls muffled by dead leaves. In morning's light, Gwynneth's troubles retreated behind the trees.

Mirrah taught her some of the gestures the mutton-people used for communicating with one another when borwogs were about. Gwynneth's clumsy attempts at mimicking the finger, hand and arm movements sent Mirrah into gales of laughter. Still, Gwynneth soon learned enough signs to converse haltingly with her friend.

As the days passed, Gwynneth became accustomed to the mutton-people's habit of sleeping in a different firewatch each night, to confuse the borwogs. She occupied her mornings with Mirrah watching the sheep. Usually by late afternoon, Wolf and his band of followers would stop by on their way to another firewatch, and the girls would join them. The two spent their evenings gathering firewood, tending the campfires, preparing meals and chatting with each other in "fireside sign language," as Gwynneth called it.

Gwynneth also trained herself to listen with half an ear for the sudden borwog-silence. One night, she heard instead a moaning and wailing close at hand. At first, she thought Mirrah was weeping in the woods, but the servant girl was curled up asleep by the fire.

On a hunch, Gwynneth edged closer to a lone touch-tree standing on the outskirts of the firewatch. Over the wailing, she heard words cutting through the smoky air like drawn swords.

"Oh! Oh! Oh! Whatever am I going to do? So many of my brothers and sisters lie slain upon the earth, and I shall be next! Oh, to think that I should live to see such a day. A dreadful death is my lot now, and who shall mourn my passing? Am I good for nothing more than to rot or burn? Help! Help! Can anybody hear me?"

Gwynneth cleared her throat. "I can hear you, whoever you are. You mustn't make such a racket. What is the matter?"

"What is the matter?! How can you ask such a question, two-legs? Just look around you. See how the mighty are fallen, every one a relative or friend of mine! All night long I must stand watching my loved ones burn, knowing my turn is soon to come! Oh me, oh my. Fire and ax, ax and fire. I am destined to become a heap of ashes. My fate is certain, for who can stay the bitter ax?"

In spite of herself, Gwynneth smiled. Since receiving the Gift, she had spoken with many a tree, but none had been as overwrought as this one. She reached out to pat its trunk but withdrew her hand, recalling what had happened the last time she had touched such a tree. Instead, she asked, "What is your name?"

"Thinbark," snuffled the tree, and then it began to cry. "You don't want to touch me, either! Nobody wants to touch me, because I'm the ugliest tree alive. She-trees need touching, just like everyone else. Otherwise, we grow all hollow in the middle. I'm feeling hollow already. Maybe I am better off as a smoking pile of cinders, forgetting and forgotten." Droplets of sticky sap rained down from the tree's leaves, dampening Gwynneth's hair and exposed skin.

"I don't think you are ugly," said Gwynneth. "People won't touch you because they know they'll end up someplace else if they do.

That's why the two-legs are chopping down your friends. They're afraid of you. In fact, they're afraid of this whole forest."

"I cannot imagine why!" said Thinbark indignantly. "We're just ordinary trees trying to add a ring or two of wood each year."

"Ordinary trees don't send a person into another world with the touch of a finger," Gwynneth retorted. Catching the frank stares of some mutton-people sitting at a nearby fire, she told Thinbark, "Oh, all right. If it will make you feel any better, I'll touch you." She laid a hand on the tree's trunk and felt it shiver with delight.

Instantly, she was standing by the bank of a rolling river. A log-laden barge was floating past, poled by gaily-dressed bargemen. *The Foamwater!* Upriver, Beechtown's slick slate roofs gleamed in the sun. Lucambra and home were only a torsil's climb away!

"Hello over there!" she called loudly to the rivermen, but they ignored her. Evidently, they were too far away to hear her voice. She picked up a stick to throw at the barge, but the stick wouldn't budge. She groaned. It was the Isle of Luralin all over again.

"You cannot touch or remove anything here," said Thinbark.

"Why not?" Gwynneth countered. She felt an argument coming on. She hated arguing with trees. For one thing, they were always so *right*. For another, they often rambled far afield at the drop of a leaf. Worst of all, most trees spoke so slowly and deliberately that Gwynneth tended to doze off while they were talking to her.

"You must be new here," replied the tree. "Only a *glynnie*, one of the People of the Glen, can break through the veil that separates their world from all others. Oh, how I wish I could pluck up my roots and flee to safety! You two-legs are fortunate; you can run away when ax or fire comes calling, while we trees cannot."

Gwynneth didn't bother to ask what a "glynnie" was, knowing the answer could take hours—if not days—and she had only seconds to catch the barge. In a peevish fit, she stuck out her tongue at Thinbark, rushed down the riverbank and dove into the water.

Swiftly running with cold spring snowmelt from the Tartellan Mountains, the Foamwater ordinarily froze the breath out of anyone foolhardy enough to test its waters at this time of year. Bracing herself for the shock, Gwynneth plunged into what felt like a vat of goose down. Fishes swam past and through her, but she was still warm and breathing air. A greenish stone lazily rolled along the muddy bottom, yet try as she might, she could not grasp it.

Realizing that even if she did catch up to the barge, the men could not help her—let alone see her—Gwynneth "swam" to the surface. Then she crawled out onto the bank, as dry as feathers.

Thinbark's leaves rustled. "What did I tell you? You cannot get out and you cannot get in. I have watched many a two-legs jump into that river, but nobody ever goes anywhere—except back to the Glynnion Wood. I would find your plight distinctly amusing if I were not so preoccupied with my own predicament. Now if you will excuse me, I must contemplate my impending demise."

The tree began to moan and weep as it had earlier, its branches waving and thrashing. Fuming, Gwynneth stood by with a mixture of sympathy and disgust. Then she stamped her foot—hard.

"Stop it!" she yelled. "Just stop it!"

Thinbark paused mid-sob. "What's wrong? What is it? Have your two-legged companions decided to chop me down now?"

Gwynneth stamped her foot again. "Shame on you!" she said. "Why are you upsetting yourself over something that may never happen? I was truly hoping to spare you the ax, but since you have already cut yourself down with your own words, why bother?"

"I am terribly sorry," said Thinbark humbly. "I don't blame you for disliking me and my weak-wooded ways." The tree began weeping afresh, showering Gwynneth with so much sap that she had to back away. Evidently, Thinbark needed comfort and reassurance, not scolding. Gwynneth knew just what to say to her.

"Hush now, dear tree; don't cry," she began in a soothing tone. "Everything is going to be all right. I will try to make sure nobody cuts you down. You should be safe as long as I'm around."

The sap-shower let up slightly. "Really? Do you mean that?"

"Of course I do. You must believe me! I wouldn't lie to you. Gaelathane hates lying. Now, in exchange, I need your help."

Before Gwynneth could utter another word, Thinbark's tears dried up. "My help? I'd be happy to do whatever I can to assist you, but how could a she-tree like me help a two-legs like you?"

90

"It's really quite simple," Gwynneth replied. "I want you to tell me just what you are. I have never seen your type of tree before."

Thinbark's leaves stirred at the question. "What am I? Why, in your tongue, I believe you would call me a 'purveyor-of-passage tree,' if I am not mistaken. I rarely am. Mistaken, that is."

A torsil! Of course! It all made sense now, except . . . "Every other tree of your tribe that I've known couldn't grant passage without my climbing it to the top. What makes you so different?"

Thinbark sniffed. "We are not like those other trees. Fortunately for you two-legs, touching any part of a 'purveyor' will show you the land that lies beyond. Otherwise, you would find our trunks and limbs too slippery to hold onto. Of course, if you did manage to reach my very top, you could climb right out of this world."

Touch-torsils! Mirrah had called them "touch-trees," which amounted to the same thing. Gaelathane must have created as many types of torsils as He had torsil worlds. Gwynneth wondered whether all touch-torsils were as thin skinned as Thinbark.

All of a sudden, Mirrah appeared beside the tree. Startled, Gwynneth screamed. "I'm sorry for surprising you," the servant girl said. "Wolf has been looking for you. He doesn't like his people sneaking off, just in case we all have to leave in a hurry. You never know when the borwogs might decide to overrun a firewatch."

"I wasn't sneaking!" Gwynneth snapped back. "I—I just wanted to get away for a bit, that's all." She knew better than to tell Mirrah she had actually been conversing with a touch-tree.

"Good-bye, two-legs," said Thinbark. "Remember your promise not to let anyone cut me down! And visit me again—soon."

Mirrah had already disappeared when Gwynneth clapped her hand on the touch-torsil's trunk. "I shall, and I—mmph!"

No sooner had she made passage than a callused hand stuffed a wad of greasy wool into her mouth. Then the hand dragged her roughly by the hair into the tree-whispering moonlight.

"Thought you'd play me for the fool, did you?" growled a deep voice. "Thought I'd forgotten you? Ha! Nobody gets the best of Dask, especially not some uppity, weak-witted wench! Now I'll be rid of you for good, you and this lazy, fumble-fingered trollop!"

Dask yanked his other fist, and Gwynneth heard a girlish yelp. The mutton-man was hauling Mirrah along by her hair, too. Clawing at his fingers, Mirrah whimpered in pain. "No! Please!" she pleaded, but Dask jerked her head again so viciously Gwynneth feared her friend's neck would snap. Then they bumpety-bump-bumped down a brushy slope. At the bottom, Dask began tying his captives to a thick-boled ash with coils of tough sheep sinews.

Mirrah was weeping hysterically as Dask cinched up the last knot. "That should do it," he grunted. "By the time the others find you down here, it will be too late. I can always say I caught you thievin' vittles from me. Wolf might make a fuss over you, but he knows his knife is no match for my long-sword. He won't pick a fight over the likes of you scum. Enjoy your last evening together! I knew those borwogs would come in handy one day."

Chortling, Dask stalked off into the moonleafed darkness. Now Gwynneth could hear only Mirrah's soft sobbing, the hooting of owls and the scuttling of night creatures through the shadows.

When Mirrah fell silent, Gwynneth called out to her, "Are you all right?" Hearing no answer, Gwynneth continued talking. "Dask must think he's quite clever, letting the borwogs do his dirty work for him. Supposing we are very, very quiet and don't move, would the beasts still find us in the dark down in this woodsy hollow?"

"They will find us," came the dull reply. "As long as we are alive, they will find us. The 'wogs can drain the warmth from a mouse or a mole hiding deep underground without ever touching it. That's why you will find plenty of frogs and lizards in this wood, but few warmblooded beasts except birds. They can fly away."

"Then we must escape while we can!" said Gwynneth. She would not surrender to her fate, not while another heart still beat on the tree's opposite side. She struggled to free herself from her bonds, but the sinews only cut more deeply into her flesh. Dask knew his knots all too well. Panic seized her as the crescent moon sank below the treetops, silhouetting them in silver. At last, only a bright moonsliver shone. Then darkness flooded the forest.

Mirrah screamed, a high, thin shriek that ripped the silken veil between sanity and madness. The scream choked off as an uncanny silence hammered at Gwynneth's ears. A few paces away, a night-devouring darkness was gathering. The borwogs had come.

Gwynneth tried to scream, too, but only a hiss came out. A numbing chill was seeping into her brain and bones, robbing her of all thought and feeling. At the wedding, Timothy had promised that his cloak would warm Gwynneth against "life's deadly chills," but not even the thickest cloak could ward off such cold. Gwynneth had just enough presence of mind to mouth, *Gaelathane, help us! Please don't let Mirrah and me die out here! Save us, Gaelathane!*

Just then, a shining cloud of dremlens swarmed down. Encircling the tree from top to bottom, they created a living curtain that separated Gwynneth and Mirrah from the borwogs. Cocooned in light, Gwynneth felt warmth slowly returning to her stiff body.

"Mirrah, can you hear me?" she hoarsely whispered.

She felt the sinews tighten against her body as Mirrah moved. From the tree's other side came the wobbly words, "Yes, I can."

"What are those dremlens doing, anyway? They won't try to harm us or turn us into toads or something horrible, will they?"

"I don't think so," Mirrah replied. "They've never done anything to hurt us before. Sometimes, they lead us to a lost sheep or warn us away from danger. I like to watch them. They help me forget my problems. Dask hates the dremlens. He throws stones at them whenever they settle on the trees around our campfires at night."

"Well, whatever they are, by shielding us from the borwogs, your dremlens have kept us from freezing to death," Gwynneth said. "Do you have any idea why they would come to our defense?"

"Don't talk!" Mirrah hissed. "You might scare them off."

However, the dremlens remained with Gwynneth and Mirrah all during that long, dreadful night. Comforted by the light, Gwynneth dozed off, sagging against her bonds. She awoke at dawn just in time to see the dremlens disappear. Yawning, she tried to stretch, but the sinews held her fast. If only she had tucked a knife into her tunic before leaving the tower to greet her wedding guests!

In the morning stillness, she heard soft footfalls approaching. Someone was coming to rescue them! "Help!" she cried. "We're over here, tied to this ash tree!" Then Dask's face popped into view.

"Eh!" he gasped. "Still alive—the both of you?" Frowning, he circled the ash three times before stopping in front of Gwynneth. "How did you do it?" he demanded, his face inches from hers.

"Do what?" she returned innocently.

"You know very well what!" he growled. "How did you and this useless servant of mine escape the borwogs? They should have sucked the life right out of your miserable bodies. Now talk!"

Dask pulled a wicked-looking knife from his belt and waved it in Gwynneth's face. "Tell me, or I'll have your nose and ears!"

Gwynneth swallowed. "It was the dremlens."

Dask's eyes gleamed with rage and blood lust. "Why did they help you?" he rasped. "What did you promise them—gold, jewels, silver? How did they protect you from the 'wogs? Did they—?"

A sudden commotion cut him off. Green-cloaked figures were running through the trees toward them, shouting as they came.

As Dask raised his knife defensively, Gwynneth's heart nearly burst out of her chest. She knew those baying voices. Lucambra's finest bloodhounds had tracked her down! Magnificent and terrible to behold, Timothy, Elwyn, Rolin, Scanlon, Marlis and Bembor were rushing down the dale, hair streaming and hoods flapping.

CHAPTER 10

DELIVERANCE AND DISASTER

Having awakened the outringers, Owen alerted them to the noises outside. "It's *her*!" they cried and tore out of the cave. Wondering at their excitement, Owen hurried after them. He didn't want to be left behind in the cave!

When he caught up with his friends, they were approaching a knife-wielding man clad in sheepskins. It was the swordsman who had attacked Owen for trying to liberate the rustled sheep!

Timothy and the stranger began arguing over a young woman tied to a nearby ash tree. Her delicate features and blond hair recalled Marlis's. A dark-haired girl was tied to the tree's other side. Both were struggling in vain to free themselves from their bonds.

Owen's heart sank. Neither of the women resembled Melina.

"We're saved, Mirrah! My family is here!" cried the blond.

"Gwynneth!" Marlis shrieked, and she threw herself on her daughter. "We've found you at last! Thanks be to Gaelathane!"

"Who are you and why have you tied my wife to this tree?" Timothy was saying to the rough-hewn man. "I demand that you untie her at once! If you have harmed her in any way, I'll—"

The man tensed. His narrow gaze measured the newcomers. Seeing that Timothy was unarmed, he lowered his knife hand.

"The name's Dask, but what's it to you? She's mine now, and there's nothin' you can do about it. Ain't that right, girls?"

Gwynneth and Mirrah kept silent, but their pleading eyes spoke volumes. *Please, please, rescue us from this horrible man!*

Dask grinned. "You see?" he said. "We was just having ourselves a little harmless fun. No need to get all riled up. Plenty of other pretty girls wander into the Deadwood every day. You can have your pick of them. Now, why don't you folks move along?"

"We're not going anywhere without Gwynneth!" Timothy retorted. He stepped toward Dask, his face as hard as solid slate.

As Dask backed away from Timothy, his eyes abruptly went flat and dead. Owen was reminded of a snake coiling before it pounced on its prey. With a deft flip of his wrist, Dask reversed the knife. Now he was holding it by the tip of the glinting blade.

"Timothy!" Gwynneth gasped. "Look out! He's going to—"

Her warning came too late. Dask had already flicked the knife underhanded at Timothy, who barely managed to deflect the spinning blade with his staff. Snarling, Dask whipped out a long-sword and was springing upon his defenseless foe when he froze mid-lunge with a pained expression. His back had sprouted an arrow shaft tipped with a bouquet of black feathers. Gracefully, he crumpled to earth and pitched forward onto his face. Blood stained his coat.

Snatching up Dask's knife, Timothy cut away the cords that bound Gwynneth and Mirrah. Gwynneth fell weeping into his arms, while Mirrah slumped into Rolin's. After hasty introductions all around and more tearful embraces, everyone looked to see who had shot Dask. Only Marlis and Scanlon were armed with bows and arrows, but neither of them had done the bloody deed.

Rolin removed the arrow jutting from Dask's back. "This is crudely made, but very effective," he remarked. "I thought perhaps Emmer or another scout had caught up to us and was trying to even the odds. However, this arrow isn't one of ours. Lucambrians always use griffin feathers, but as you can see, these are raven feathers."

Fanning out, the Greencloaks scanned the forest for signs of intruders. An early-morning breeze ruffled the tops of the trees clothing the valley's slopes, but otherwise, nothing stirred. Then a tall, grizzled man wearing a sheepskin coat stepped out from behind a beech. Deliberately, he unstrung his longbow and approached.

"Hail, stranger!" Rolin greeted him. "This poor wretch seems to have stopped a stray arrow. Have you lost one, perchance?"

"I have," the bowman replied. "I am called Wolf. That is my arrow—and my man, good riddance to him!" He spat on the body, adding, "Dask was his name. He was a fine hunter but also a cruel and wicked scoundrel. We all lived in fear of him; not a few of us lost hands, noses or ears to his sword. Now it belongs to me."

Wolf wrenched the weapon from Dask's dead grasp. "I cut him once or twice with my knife, but this sword always gave him the upper hand, and he knew it. I could never get close enough to sorely wound or kill him." Wolf shook his bow. "That's why I made this—and the arrows to go with it. If Dask had known what I was really up to, he would have watched his back more carefully."

Gwynneth told Rolin, "Wolf is a good man, Father. While I was staying with him and his men, he protected me from Dask."

"That reminds me," said Wolf. He whistled, and more figures emerged from the forest. One was dragging a slender, mop-haired young man after him. The youth was raising a terrible fuss over his poor breakfast and the shabby clothing he was wearing.

As Wolf's companions trooped up, he said, "My men and I only wish to live and let live in this wood. You are welcome to join us. Otherwise, put some distance between us. This is our territory." He glanced at Gwynneth. "These are friends of yours?"

"My husband and family," she replied, her eyes fastened on Timothy. She introduced him and the rest of her relatives but stopped short when she came to Owen. Seeing her predicament, Marlis supplied Owen's name. Wolf's men stared at him curiously.

"Where are you from, boy?" Wolf asked him.

"Swyndon," Owen replied, lowering his head respectfully.

Wolf nodded. "I thought as much. You dress like a shepherd. You know, we could use some extra help, now that Dask is dead."

Owen nervously jogged from one foot to the other. "If it's all the same to you, sir, I'd rather stick with my friends here. We've been through a lot together, if you understand my meaning."

With a shrug, Wolf said, "Suit yourself." He turned a gloomy gaze on Gwynneth. "I reckon you'll want to go with your husband and relations. I'm glad they found you. No hard feelings here."

"Thank you for all you've done," said Gwynneth awkwardly. "I will . . . miss you and your men. You've been most kind to me."

"But now I'm taking her home," Timothy hurriedly put in.

Wolf's followers guffawed and slapped their knees. "Home?" they howled. "Ain't anybody told you about the Deadwood yet?"

Gwynneth blushed. "They still don't know."

"Know what?" Scanlon asked.

"There is no way out of this wood," she said softly. "We are trapped here. You can't get out the same way you came in."

"'Green the Ghostwood! Dark the Deadwood! Never shall you leave the Dreadwood!'" the men mockingly recited. "In a few days, you'll come crawling back to us—what's left of you, that is."

"We'll take our chances," Rolin calmly replied.

"So be it," said Wolf. "What about Mirrah, then? She belongs to us. Without Gwynneth and Dask, we're shorthanded as it is."

"No!" Mirrah screamed. Weeping furiously, she scrambled up the ash tree and crouched on a limb. Gwynneth climbed up after her and tried unsuccessfully to talk her into coming down again.

While the outringers hid amused expressions, Wolf scratched his beard and scowled. Then a rueful grin tugged at the corners of his mouth and he said, "Can't say as how I blame her for not wanting to come with us. Dask kept her on a short tether—and shorter rations. The other fellows and I took turns slipping food to her when Dask warn't looking. I done us all a favor by putting that arrow in him. He would have slaughtered your men and taken your womenfolk for himself. I've seen him do it before."

"We are quite capable of defending ourselves," said Scanlon.

"In a fair fight, maybe," Wolf replied. "But Dask never did fight fair. He'd as soon cut your throat in your sleep as wink at you. Since I saved your lives just now, I'm asking you to return the favor. If you want Mirrah, you've got to take *princey*, too." Wolf jerked a thumb toward the young man, who assumed what might pass for a princely pose. His companions sniggered behind his back.

"Who is he?" asked Rolin. "Another of your captives?"

"He's the Deadwood's captive, not mine. Calls himself 'Prince Percy,'" said Wolf with a disgusted look. He waved an arm at the forest. "We're scavengers, not kidnappers. What the tide brings in, we keep. Can you blame us for that? Ask Gwynneth. She'll tell you we're only trying to survive in this place. You'll learn that lesson, too—if you're lucky enough to live. Now may your fires never go out!" Nodding curtly, he shouldered his bow and led his men back the way they had come. Percy was left standing awkwardly by himself. He looked more forlorn and pathetic than princely.

"It seems you're joining up with us, like it or not," said Scanlon with a sigh. "Why didn't Wolf want you in his band, anyway?"

"Blackguards!" Percy blustered. "Good riddance to that lot!"

After climbing down from the ash tree, Gwynneth introduced her family and Owen to the prince. Then she described how he had fallen in with Wolf and the other mutton-men. Beginning with her wedding, Gwynneth next retold her own misadventures.

"Touch-torsils!" Bembor declared. "That's convenient. Lately, these old bones haven't taken too kindly to tree-climbing."

"Convenient? Hardly!" countered Gwynneth. "I told you what Thinbark said. You still have to climb the trees as you would ordinary torsils if you want to make proper passage. Otherwise, you'll go only halfway. That's how the trees here work, anyhow."

"Halfway-torsils," Elwyn mused aloud. "This I must see!"

"That still does not explain how we landed in this place," Marlis pointed out. "None of us in the search party touched any trees."

"Maybe we got into a patch of torsil-grass," Elwyn snickered.

"It's the fog," said Owen. "Nobody escapes it—not even me."

Gwynneth raised an eyebrow. "The fog did roll in just before I found myself in this forest. But why would fog cause me to make passage? I'm certain I didn't step into another faery ring, either."

"Then we are right back where we started," Rolin said glumly. "We can't climb these torsils you've described, because they're too tall, too high limbed and too smooth barked, even if we could find one that led to Lucambra. Where exactly does that leave us?"

"In the Deadwood—to stay!" Mirrah called from the tree.

She shinnied down the ash in a shower of leaves and lichens. Steering clear of Dask's body, she returned to Gwynneth's side.

"We had better not be stuck here," Marlis declared. "Meghan is waiting for us at home, the poor dear. The next time we set off on one of these harebrained escapades, we're bringing her with us."

"And I'm bringing my wife along, too!" Scanlon muttered.

"It's a shame she had to leave after the wedding," said Rolin.

"Yes, it is," Scanlon agreed. "As queen of the worldwalkers, she never likes to stray far from her beloved Golden Wood. If she were here, I'm sure she could have helped us search for Gwynneth."

"How did you find me in the first place?" Gwynneth asked.

"You can thank Owen for that," said Rolin, wrapping an arm around Owen's shoulders. "Without him, we might all be dead."

Rolin recounted the outringers' search and how they had met Owen in the forest the day before. "He and his firefly friend—"

"A dremlen," Mirrah interrupted.

Rolin frowned. "Very well, he and his *dremlen* friend led us to a cave where we took refuge from those creatures of the night—"

"Borwogs," Gwynneth corrected him.

Rolin heaved a deep sigh. "Borwogs, then. Early this morning, Owen heard your outcries and awakened us. I'd say we arrived just in the nick of time to rescue you from Dask and his knife."

"May Gaelathane have mercy upon that villain's soul," said Bembor fervently. "Speaking of Gaelathane, are we not remiss?"

"Indeed we are," said Rolin, and he sank to his knees. The other outringers joined him in thanking the King of the Trees for His guidance and deliverance. Mirrah and Percy stood off to one side, listening. Feeling out of place, Owen chewed on his nails.

Afterwards, Marlis asked him, "What kind of bird is that sitting up there in the tree? It sings very prettily, like a song sparrow."

Peering into the ash, Owen spotted a familiar brown ball perched on a limb. He laughed for joy as the bird alit on his shoulder.

"Welcome back, Sparrow," he cried. "I've missed you! Where have you been all this time, anyway? You helped me find dear old Tabitha; can you lead my friends and me out of this forest, too?" He held out his hand, and the sparrow demurely fluttered onto it.

Owen's companions stared at him quizzically. He had forgotten again that his words and actions no longer fell upon deaf ears and blind eyes. Living in his own private world, he had been free to do and say as he pleased without the risk of appearing foolish.

"Is this the bird you've been telling us about?" Marlis asked.

"Yes, it is," Owen replied, his face burning.

Gwynneth and Mirrah exchanged a flurry of hand motions. Mirrah ended the conversation with a scornful headshake.

Timothy gaped. "What were you two doing just now?"

Gwynneth flushed. "The mut-, I mean, the *Deadwood* people converse in sign language when the borwogs are about. I learned a few of the signs from Mirrah. I was just asking her whether all the feathered creatures in this forest are so tame as Owen's sparrow."

"And no, they're not," Mirrah declared.

Stroking his beard, Bembor asked, "Does this sparrow of yours talk to you the way you talk to her, Owen son of Tadwyn?"

Owen recoiled at the question. Was the outringer making cruel sport of him? "Of course she doesn't. Oh, she chirps at me, but I don't understand any of that. I doubt she understands me, either. If she wants me to follow, she—well, you can see for yourself."

Warbling plaintively, the sparrow fluttered off a few yards. Then she flew back to Owen and hovered in front of his face. Back and forth she went, until even Prince Percy took notice.

"Whatever is the matter with that bird?" he grumbled. "Can't you stop it from making such a dreadful racket? It's giving me a headache. Whenever I have a headache at home, Mother prepares me a special herbal ointment that makes the pain go away. I don't suppose you *peasants* brought along such a thing with you."

Rolling his eyes, Scanlon said, "Talk about a headache! Now I know why Wolf was so anxious to get this fellow off his hands."

Still the sparrow flew to and fro, twittering insistently. Marlis observed, "I do believe that bird really wants us to follow it."

"Then what are we waiting for?" Rolin said. "Let's go!"

While the outringers collected their belongings from the cave, Owen, Mirrah and Percy foraged for food outside. Owen found a strawberry patch, but Percy argued he had found the patch first.

Anxious to avoid a squabble, Owen moved off to find something else to eat. Near the cave, he spied a pair of oversized insect wings lying on the ground. Picking them up, he was astonished to discover they were attached to the figure of a tiny, green-garbed woman. Having a perfectly formed head and limbs, she lay like a sliver of ice in his palm. Gently, he warmed her frozen body with his breath until her eyelids fluttered open. Seeing Owen, she shuddered with shock. Using his thumb for support, she sat up and then stood.

"You!" she cried. "Truly, you are the shepherd's son. Wait until Gisella hears about *this*. Fare thee well!" Her wings beat tentatively like a newly hatched butterfly's. Then with a *whir*, she was gone.

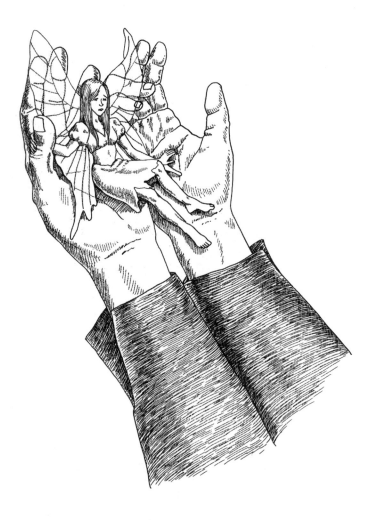

Athyrea. Dumbfounded, Owen stared at his empty palm. Had he imagined the dainty winged woman with the voice of his firefly rescuer? And who were "the shepherd's son" and "Gisella?"

He was still reeling from this encounter when the outringers emerged from the cave. At Rolin's request, Owen took the lead, tracking his sparrow by hips and hops through the valley and west toward the foothills. The wise bird would fly nearly out of Owen's sight before waiting for her two-legged followers to catch up.

Beyond the dale, the ten companions came across a few borwog holes, but the black pits dwindled in size and number as the ground rose to meet the mountains. At noon, the party halted for rest and a meager lunch. Having eaten little since leaving home the day before, Owen was grateful for the sweet chestnut-flour bread the outringers shared with him. He tossed a few crumbs to the sparrow, and she gobbled them up. Percy sniffed at his portion before delicately nibbling on it. Still famished after their kidnapping, Gwynneth and Mirrah devoured their bread down to the last morsel.

Meanwhile, Scanlon had shot a deer with his bow. Timothy and Elwyn helped him cut up the carcass, while Owen built a fire. Before long, everyone was enjoying strips of fresh roasted venison.

After the travelers had eaten their fill, they set out again. As he hiked, Owen idly listened to the discussions that drifted up from behind him. Bembor and Marlis's particularly caught his ear.

"I don't understand it," Bembor was telling Marlis. "I've never met a bird like this one. Ordinarily, sparrow-speech is among the easiest of bird languages to follow, and the little creatures are friendly, too. Yet, I can't make out a word this bird is saying."

"I can't either," Marlis replied. "It's all 'cheeps' and 'chirps' to me. You would think she was just making up sounds, like a baby still learning to talk. Yet, this sparrow looks full grown."

Owen glanced over his shoulder at the two speakers. If he had heard them aright, Bembor and Marlis—and no doubt their companions as well—could comprehend bird-speech. The notion that wild creatures possessed their own languages came as no particular surprise to Owen. He himself had often suspected as much. Making sense of those languages was quite another matter. No wonder

Bembor had questioned him so closely about the sparrow. He had wanted to know whether Owen understood bird-speech, too!

Raindrops were spattering on their heads when the exiles gained the summit of a rocky hill. Taller hills marched ahead, crowding up to yet loftier, snow-clad peaks. In Clynnod, Owen had heard of mountains whose tops were snow bound year 'round. Swyndon Hill was often blanketed with snow, but it melted away by spring.

"Where is that dratted bird taking us?" grumbled Percy. "I suppose we will have to climb all those mountains before our journey ends. I for one would rather make camp on this hill and rest."

"It's too wet and windy up here to build a fire," Mirrah pointed out. "You know very well we can't spend the night in these woods without a fire. Do you want the borwogs to come calling again?"

Climbing down the hill's west side proved both difficult and dangerous going. So many boulders lay precariously balanced in loose scree that every footfall threatened to bring down the whole slope. To keep from slipping or falling, the hikers held hands.

They had almost reached the bottom when a stone rolled under Owen's foot. He slid the rest of the way, dragging Elwyn and Timothy with him into a torsil. Instantly, the three were caught up in a raging thunderstorm. Lightning crashed around them in splashes of garish light. Bellowing screeches blasted the night sky as an enormous black bulk swayed by, crushing the trees and bushes in its path. At once, three hands slapped the torsil's smooth trunk.

"That was close!" Elwyn exclaimed as he staggered away from the tree. "With these touch-torsils, it's 'easy in and easy out.' That creature might have flattened us all like a batch of oatcakes."

Owen couldn't help laughing at his shaken friend. "No, it wouldn't. We weren't really 'there,' remember? Look at yourself. It was raining buckets, but none of us got any wetter than we already were. I'll admit I was frightened, too, but if we had remained in that other world, that big beast would have passed right through our bodies. Not even the lightning bolts could have harmed us."

Timothy and Elwyn chuckled ruefully at themselves. Then the three rejoined their companions at the hill's base. Rolin had decided to set up camp in a dense stand of touch-torsils. Beside the grove, water coursing down the hillside had gouged a deep, narrow ravine littered with jumbled logs, boulders and piles of pebbly silt.

"It's about time we stopped," Percy said. "I'm starving, and I couldn't walk another step. My feet will never be the same again." He grandly lowered himself onto a log as if it were a gilded throne.

Owen, Elwyn and Timothy set about gathering firewood, while Rolin and Scanlon heaped up some moss-tinder in a dry spot beneath the dripping trees. Once enough kindling was arranged over the tinder, Scanlon began striking a piece of iron against his flint.

Sparks flew, but none burned hot or long enough to set the tinder afire. Owen nervously peered among the forest's gray pillars. Already he fancied the borwogs' chill shadows were creeping through those darkling trunks. As dusk drowned the landscape, a familiar sweet odor wafted down from the treetops.

Scanlon was blowing on a promising spark when a dull thud sounded on the hill above. A shower of small rocks clattered into the torsil grove. Then a chorus of thumps, rumbles and crashes blended into a roaring crescendo, as if a great ocean wave were bearing down on the firewatch. Dust flew up from the hillside.

"Avalanche!" shouted Rolin. Awestruck, Owen gazed up at the boiling mass grinding toward him. Never had he seen such a monstrous force spawned of mere dirt and stone. Then Scanlon grabbed his arm and screamed in his ear, "Run! Run for your life!"

Trailing after his friends, Owen sprinted across the avalanche's path, coming up short on the brink of the erosion gully. "In we go!" cried Scanlon, and he hopped over the edge. With a gulp, Owen followed. Rolling and sliding, he tumbled to the bottom with his bruised and battered companions. Already mountainous boulders were bounding down the ravine behind them.

"Keep going!" Bembor bellowed above the deafening din. Deeper into the gully they dashed, food, fire and knapsacks all forgotten. Rocks boomed and burst, sending stony shards whizzing through the air. Owen felt a stinging pain in the back of his head and another in his leg. Then he stumbled into a cool, dark cavern.

After the groaning and growling of tortured stone had died away, Rolin brought out a lightstaff. The company had taken refuge in a tunnel blocked at the back with avalanche debris. Water meandered underfoot through a slippery slurry of mud and slime.

"Where are we?" asked Elwyn. His voice echoed eerily in the confined space. Rocks shifted nearby, and Owen's heart found his mouth. Where was his sparrow? Had she managed to escape the avalanche, or was she buried now under tons of rock and dirt?

"Flash floods must have delved this hole," said Bembor. With a sucking sound, a clot of gooey mud dropped out of the ceiling, leaving an oozing scar. As the old man carefully examined the tunnel by staff light, the furrows in his face gathered shadows.

"This soil is overburdened with water," he observed. "I fear the avalanche may cause these already weakened walls and roof to cave in. We must leave this place immediately!"

The outringers wore grim looks as they picked at the rockfall. "It could take weeks to dig our way through this landslide," Rolin remarked. "There's no telling how far back the blockage extends. It might be only a few feet thick, or many yards. Disturbing the pile might bring more boulders down, and maybe the roof as well."

"We wouldn't have to tunnel all the way through the slide in order to open a passage to the surface," Scanlon argued.

"That's true," Rolin admitted. "Even so, we still don't know how far away the surface lies. Besides, any passage we dug through this loose rock could easily collapse around our heads."

"What are you suggesting, then?" Bembor asked him.

Rolin climbed down off the rock pile. "If we cannot go back, we must go forward," he said. "I'll admit it sounds risky, but what other choice do we have? We didn't bring enough provisions to last us long, and the air may go bad before we run out of food."

Rocks rattled faintly somewhere high above, and every head turned upward. "Hello down there, if you are still alive!" a muffled voice called. "A loose boulder can work some powerful damage, cain't it? I hope you'll enjoy your nice, new tomb!" An unpleasant laugh echoed through the stones, fading into a deathly silence.

"Dask!" Mirrah wheezed, and she fainted.

106

CHAPTER 11

THE DAM BURSTS

I t was Dask, all right," said Gwynneth as she helped her
mother revive Mirrah. "I'll never forget that voice. We all
lived in constant fear of it, day and night. Dask delighted in
tormenting us, knowing we were weaker than he and unable to
defend ourselves. I am not surprised he pursued us all this way."

"How could he have survived being pierced with Wolf's arrow?"
puzzled Rolin. "I myself drew that arrow from his body. You all saw
it. And we have traveled many miles from the spot where he fell.
No one so badly wounded could possibly have followed us."

"Yet apparently he did," said Bembor heavily. "Revenge oft
drives wicked men beyond the limits of mortal endurance. Surely
Dask's hatred of us must be exceedingly great, though he has only
himself to blame for his downfall. We must forgive him his cruelty,
for bitterness will otherwise cloud our minds at a time when clear
thinking and level heads are most needed." The other outringers
quietly bowed their heads in agreement.

"I should have known we were being followed," Scanlon said.
"Earlier today, I heard a noise behind us in the forest, but I put it
down to foxes or raccoons. I wasn't thinking, because of course the
borwogs have made such animals scarce in these parts. When I was

stalking that deer, again I thought I heard someone or something creeping up through the woods. It must have been Dask. No doubt he set off this avalanche, intending to kill us all."

Marlis put an arm around his shoulders. "Don't blame yourself," she said. "Who would have thought Dask could have recovered from such a serious injury? Anyway, there's no use crying over torn cloaks. We must find a way to escape this underground prison."

"Marlis is right," said Rolin. "Dear friends, let us pray. Without the King's help, this tunnel may well become our tomb."

While the outringers spoke by turns to their invisible Friend, Owen fretted. Water was seeping through the bulging walls and roof, pooling on the ground. At any moment, he expected a cave-in to bury everyone under a mountain of mud. Mirrah and Prince Percy must have shared his fears, for they kept glancing from wall to wall, wall to ceiling, and ceiling to the circle of outringers.

After prayers were finished, another dollop of cold, wet clay landed smack on the back of Owen's neck. "Ugh!" he grunted. "We've got to get out of here while we still have the chance!"

As he and his friends plodded away from the rock slide, more gobs and glops of sticky sludge rained down on them. With a horrible slurping sound, a section of the ceiling gave way, narrowly missing Mirrah. An ominous rumbling noise filled the tunnel.

"Hurry!" cried Rolin. Owen forced his mud-caked legs to slog more swiftly through the mire. Then the tunnel came to an end. The flash floods had wedged a welter of rocks and uprooted trees into a chokepoint, almost completely blocking the passage. Stripped bare of their bark during their jostling journey, the splintered logs resembled giant white toothpicks in the staff light.

Owen followed his companions in ascending the log pile. At the top, he saw that the flash-flood tunnel met another, much wider passage just a few yards away. A dark river ran swiftly through it. The rest of the party stood beside the river in a pool of staff light, waving at him and shouting. The rumbling was growing louder.

"I can't go any faster," Owen grumbled to himself. Then he realized the others weren't only waving at him. Partway down the pile, Marlis was pulling on her leg, her face twisted with pain.

When Owen climbed down to her, he found Marlis's foot was caught in the space between two timbers. Straddling one of the logs, he worked the foot back and forth until it finally came free.

"Thank you!" Marlis said. Owen was helping her navigate the heap of tangled logs when a thunderclap rolled down the flash-flood tunnel. Then a shrieking hurricane plucked the two climbers from the log jam like a couple of bugs from a branch and hurled them into the river's frigid waters. Grabbing Marlis's hand, Owen clawed his way to the surface and swam to shore.

He was coughing up water when with a mighty roar, the flash-flood passage disgorged a stream of mud, logs and rock, damming the river. The water below the dam drained away into the darkness, leaving a muddy bed alive with flopping fish and slithering eels. Owen shakily found his feet and helped Marlis find hers.

Halos of staff light bobbed toward them. Then Rolin was crushing Marlis in a fierce embrace. "Are you all right?" he asked as the other outringers gathered around with Percy and Mirrah.

"Thanks to Owen, I am," Marlis said, wringing out her hair.

"Bless you, son of Tadwyn, for saving my wife!" Rolin said.

Dazedly, Owen sputtered, "What just happened?"

Pointing his staff upriver, Scanlon explained, "The side tunnel's collapse forced out all the air in a gust. Then the debris shoved that log jam ahead of it into this passage, blocking it."

"Truly there is no going back now," said Bembor grimly. "Fortunately, Gaelathane has made another way of escape for us. Still, we must make all haste down this riverbed before the dam bursts."

Everyone's eyes fastened on the debris flow, which plugged the passage from wall to wall and floor to ceiling. Already muddy water was seeping and trickling through cracks in the dam's base.

Handing Owen his lightstaff, Rolin said, "Since the avalanche has cut us off from your sparrow, we can follow her no longer. Yet, you have made a fine guide so far. May your heart and feet still lead us in safe paths and true until our journey's end. Perhaps this staff will help you find your way in this dismal river passage."

"Thank you!" said Owen, taking the staff. Unbidden, a thrill of joy surged through his despairing soul. Clearer than the purest diamond or crystal, the staff weighed heavily in his hand. Though its light dazzled his eyes, the rod was as cool as mountain granite.

After taking his place at the head of the procession, Owen set off downriver. To avoid becoming bogged down in riverbed silt, he hugged the tunnel wall. His feet unerringly picked out the best path, as if the lightstaff had lent them eyes that pierced the darkness.

Leading people, he discovered, was little different than herding sheep. Every so often, he had to stop for stubbed toes or bruised shins. With her sprained ankle, Marlis in particular found the going difficult, and she leaned heavily upon Rolin's steady shoulder. To complete the pastoral picture, Prince Percy bleated in complaint from time to time, though even he realized the need to maintain a steady pace. Great danger lay behind, and in his mind's eye, Owen saw himself driving his sheep before a following fog.

Although Rolin's lightstaff was a comfort in the dank, dripping darkness, Owen missed Sparrow's companionship. Her cheery songs, sure wings and sharp eyes had oft guided him along perilous paths. Unable to speak in the tongues of men, Sparrow had instead warmed his flagging spirit with the silent language of devotion.

A shadow slid up beside him. "How are you faring?" Gwynneth asked. "That was quite a spill you and Mother took in the river."

Owen shrugged. "I'm just a little wet," he said. How could he explain his loneliness to one who was surrounded by family?

"Wolf told me an exploration party once set off for the western mountains but never returned," Gwynneth went on. "Why do you think your sparrow was taking us in that direction, anyway?"

"She didn't tell me," Owen wryly replied. "You should have asked her yourself, since you seem to understand bird-speech."

Gwynneth's eyes betrayed her shock and alarm, but before she could answer, a deep, agonizing groan rolled down the tunnel. To Owen, it sounded as if some great blind beast of the watery darkness were moaning in mortal distress. Growing louder by the minute, the groaning noises were punctuated with sharp creaks and cracks.

Under the pressure of the water mounting behind it, the debris dam was failing. Owen felt the pent-up river's rising flood poised at his back. If the dam should burst, he and his friends would die.

Rolin called a halt to the march. Then he and the other out-ringers bade one another farewell. Kissing Marlis tenderly, Rolin murmured, "Take courage, my sweet bride. Our lives will soon be over, but Gaelathane and Gaelessa await us on the other side."

Trembling, Marlis buried her face in the hollow of Rolin's shoulder. "Hold me!" she murmured. "I cannot bear to look. And think of poor Meghan! How will she survive without her parents or brother or sister? I suppose my father will have to raise her."

Timothy was embracing Gwynneth. "At least we were married," he told her, weeping. "I only wish I could hold back those flood-waters until you and your family were out of harm's way."

"I'm glad you found me!" Gwynneth tearfully replied.

Owen was marveling at the composure with which the outring-ers were facing the prospect of death when a current of sweet air coiled under his nostrils. He breathed in deeply. Yes, there it was again—the refreshing scent of sun-drenched growing things.

"I smell fresh air coming from downriver!" he announced.

BOOM! Rocks shook with the throbbing thunder of a breached dam. Needing no prompting, Owen and his friends raced down the riverbed. Everyone except Percy, that is. Wresting the lightstaff from Owen's grip, the prince pranced off with it—upriver.

"You blind fools!" he shouted down the tunnel. "You're going the wrong direction! Can't you feel it? The fresh air is coming from behind us! You missed a side passage. We must go back!"

Charging after Percy, Scanlon snatched the lightstaff from him and slung the protesting prince over his shoulder. The two had just caught up to their companions when the tunnel ended. "We're out!" Owen was about to shout, but the words died on his lips.

The passage had expanded into an immense underground grotto. At the far end, a weir partially dammed the river, forming a shallow pool. A thousand feet above, tapering stalactites hung from the high-domed ceiling like glittering, polished lances. Their stalagmite mates grew from the floor, a serried army of stolid stone men. On each stalagmite soldier's knobbly "head" sat a tiny "hel-met"—a nut encased in a milky mineral film. Owen could only conclude that he and his friends had found a squirrel's larder!

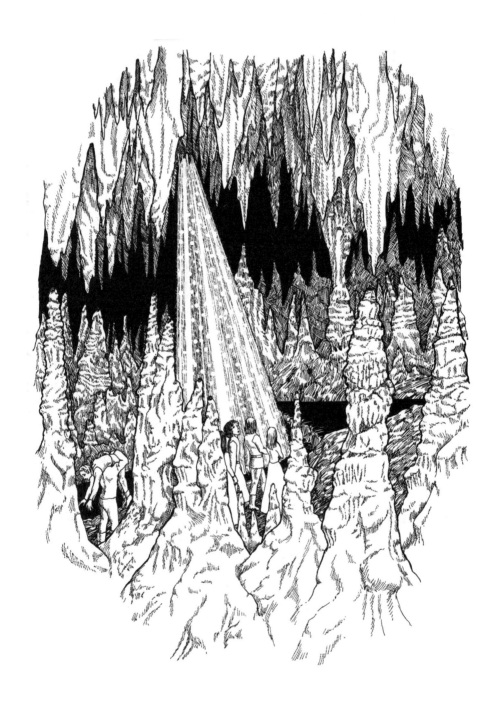

No one spoke for a dumbstruck minute. Finally, Marlis breathed, "We must be the first to find this awesome place!"

"The first?" said Bembor. "Nay, we are not the first. Look above us, and you will see that *others* arrived here before we did."

Slanting through a small hole in the roof, a ray of wan sunlight illuminated the spacious cavern. Suspended in the sunbeam like floating dust motes, hundreds of stars rose and fell, fell and rose in a looping dance between ceiling hole and water. Owen was reminded of the waterfall-lights that had held off the borwogs. Bright, joyous voices raised in song echoed through the cavern, while ripples danced upon the placid pool where the lights alit.

Such voices Owen had heard in waking dreams while wandering over the misty Downs. They whispered to him when the fog was engulfing the sleepy afternoon hills, or as it fled under the morning sun like the etched frost melting on his windowpane.

Suddenly, the wind picked up, rising to a gale that howled through the grotto. The stalactites shivered, and several plummeted into the pool below, raising frothy plumes of water. As if alarmed, the dancing lights swarmed into the ceiling outlet and vanished.

Scanlon unceremoniously dropped Percy into the muck. "That's not fresh air blowing toward us," he informed the prince. "It's a water-wind, and we are in the water's path! Unless you wish to die by drowning, I suggest you look for a way out of this cavern."

Owen understood. Bursting through the breached earthen barrier, water by the ton was roaring down the tunnel, scouring the very air out of its path. His ears popped as the air pressure rose. Several more stalactites broke loose, but instead of falling, they were blown upward through the roof hole. Now the stalagmites were shaking, too, some toppling like dominoes. Doom was hurtling down upon the ten travelers. They took refuge behind a teetering boulder.

Rolin glanced frantically about. "My kingdom for a sorc!" he cried. Owen didn't bother asking what a "sorc" was. He was too busy searching for a way of escape. Borrowing Scanlon's lightstaff, he played its rays upon the rock walls. More stalactites came crashing down, this time right among his companions. Mirrah started screaming, while Percy desperately clung to a stalagmite.

There! Owen spotted a series of steps recessed into the cavern's opposite wall. "Over here! This way!" he yelled. His friends followed him across the miry riverbed, fighting the freshening wind all the while. Upon reaching the slanting stairs, Owen moved aside to let Mirrah, Marlis and Gwynneth climb first into the dark stairwell. Then Percy shoved his way up the steps, followed by Rolin and Scanlon with Bembor. At Owen's insistence, Timothy and Elwyn went next. Just as they disappeared, the wind rose to a screech, and a dark, churning debris bubble bulged at the tunnel's mouth.

Owen's ears popped again and his chest ached under the compressing air. Dodging a deadly hail of rattling stalactites, he raced up the stairway. Legs pumping, he took the steps two at a time. A cushiony wall of air propelled him ever higher. Rising to a banshee wail, the water-wind blew him out of the stairwell. A gush of water followed. Arms flailing, Owen landed on grassy earth.

Picking himself up, he was dusting off his tunic when Rolin screamed, "Get down!" Owen dropped as the earth shuddered and exploded upward with a terrific roar, hurling stalactites and giant stone slabs high into the lightening sky. Following a blast of air, a column of water and mud geysered from the ground, soaking Owen and company with chilly spray. Its force spent, the fountain sank beneath the earth, its rushing waters reduced to a sullen gurgle.

After dodging falling rocks, Owen crawled closer to the geyser-hole. Measuring over fifty yards across, the toothless mouth swallowed all light falling upon it. Water trickled back into the dark, churning pool that nearly filled the now-roofless grotto.

"What happened?" Gwynneth spoke into the gray twilight.

Timothy answered, "All that air trapped in the flooding tunnel was seeking the nearest way out, so it blew off the cavern roof. The water that followed just finished the job by widening the hole."

"Did everybody else get out safely?" Rolin called. One by one, Bembor, Scanlon, Marlis, Elwyn, Mirrah and Percy spoke up.

Shivering, Owen had just answered the roll call when Marlis cried, "Oh! Look up there! What are those lights in the sky?"

The company had emerged in a lush, bowl-shaped valley surrounded by snowy peaks. High above, a sheet of pure silver was fanning across a blushing patch of mountain-framed sky. On clear summer nights, Owen had often gazed up at the stars wheeling in their milky majesty above Swyndon, whose feeble lights could never dim the splendor of those heavenly ones.

However, this fire in the firmament banished the stars, the dawn and the sheltered basin's shadows. The glorious display spread from horizon to horizon, thinning and dispersing like a glowing nebula drifting through space, until only a luminous haze remained. Then five greater lights appeared beside the grotto hole as if fallen from their appointed places in the heavens.

"What are those?" Elwyn whispered to Owen.

Owen did not know. Circling the hole, the bobbing lights approached him. They were shining men unlike any he had ever seen. Taller than Swyndon's torches they stood, and fury chiseled their stern faces. Fair, goldspun hair fell freely across their backs and shoulders. Their dazzling garments were woven of the very starlight, and long spears they held to stab the sky. The tallest of their number lowered his spear point directly at Owen's chest.

"You are fortunate the Spirewalker was occupied elsewhere this morning, *dustling*," he said. "If she had perished in that cataclysm, we would have slain you and your companions on the spot. Who are you, and whence have you journeyed to our valley?"

"I am Owen son of Tadwyn," he answered. "My friends and I have come from afar. Now we are lost and weary and hungry, for we have fled great peril over and under the earth, and we do not know which way to turn. Who are you, and can you help us?"

"My name is Trellisant," said the shining man. "I am captain of the Caerillion Guard." He pointed his lance at the hole. "How came this breach in the ground where there was none before?"

Rolin stepped forward and bowed before the bright strangers. "As Owen has told you, we arrived at this place by no fault or intent of our own. Avalanche and flood drove us underground; the flood forced us out here and also tore open the earth. All this is Gaelathane's doing, for it is He Who has protected us thus far."

A quiver ran through Trellisant's frame, and he said, "We reverence the King's name as well. Nonetheless, death is the penalty for damaging but one of the singing spires, and you have destroyed the entire Glynnspire Cave. Now you must come with us—or die."

Rolin bowed again. "We are your guests. Lead us onward!"

The outringers had no need of their staffs to light the way, since their escorts' bright robes lit up the ground for yards around. Singing as they worked, other shining figures were tending the sweet-scented shrubs, herbs and flowers that carpeted the valley floor. Owen breathed in the rich fragrances of lavender, thyme and wild rose; phlox and valerian; mint and myrtle; lilies and sweet peas; honeysuckle and heliotrope. Here and there, more of Trellisant's grim guards stood at attention among the bushes. On second glance, Owen recognized the "guards" as pale, lifelike garden statuary frozen in stiff poses. The blending of scent and song lulled him into a wakeful sleep even as his feet carried him numbly along.

Percy paused to poke his nose into a white trumpet lily, provoking a resounding sneeze. "Mudder always warred me nod do spell eddy flowers because dey stubb ub by dose," he snuffled, and he stuck his "dose" into another lily bloom for a second sniff.

Following Trellisant, Owen heard the outringers talking in hushed tones behind him. The word "angels" threaded through their whispers, raising the hair on the back of his neck.

"Where are these fellows taking us?" he asked Elwyn.

Beneath his dripping cloak, Elwyn's thin shoulders rose and fell in a shrug. "I don't know," he said. "I just hope we'll find some food and a place to sleep at the end of this march. We must have walked miles and miles since that meal of roast venison."

A demure sun was peering around the highest peaks when the company climbed out of the broad basin and its fragrant gardens. Now the travelers wound among aromatic groves of sweet bay, magnolia, incense cedar and white pine. Just when Owen felt he could go no farther, the forest poured into a secluded alpine valley, where two rows of tall torsils stood like twin bulwarks against the shorter trees on either side. The torsils' leafy crowns lifted skyward in billowing majesty, sweeping the fading stars from the sky. Far down the colonnades gleamed an archway of gold set in a massive, snow-streaked mountain. Shadows lurked beneath the arch.

Trellisant held up his hand, and the ragged procession halted. A distant humming disturbed the still air. The humming became a thrumming, the thrumming, a throbbing. Muted lightning flashed against the mountainsides as a shining cloud descended upon the onlookers. Radiant figures beyond count blurred by on whirring wings, flying out of the craggy dawn like a huge swarm of bees.

Funneling between the rows of touch-torsils, the torrent of liquid light poured into the archway like a mighty colony of bats returning to their roosts. On and on came the cloud, until Owen imagined all the stars in the heavens had come down to lodge in the mountain. A fragrant breeze whirled by in the cyclone's wake. Then all fell as breathless and expectant as the first day of creation.

"What in the name of Elgathel was that?" Scanlon exclaimed.

"Dremlens—but they wouldn't hurt us," said Mirrah.

"How do you know that?" asked Percy doubtfully.

"Because they saved Gwynneth and me from the borwogs."

"What *are* dremlens?" Timothy asked.

The answer never came, for stabbing between two peaks, the sun's first full rays flooded the torsil colonnades. Lifting their spears, Trellisant and his fellow guards turned east toward the morning. Rapture lit their faces as they sang in clear, resounding voices,

Hail, Star of the Dawn, the Dancer of Days!
The Bearer of Warmth and Revealer of Ways!
To thee we sing, in the name of the King,
Who maketh all things for His purpose and praise!

Grower of green that ripens the fruit,
Drives off the dew and hardens the shoot;
Rise o'er the earth to bring a rebirth
To seed and to egg, to blossom and root.

Now lend we our hands to the labors of light,
For in blessing His bounty is all our delight;
To bring forth a flower in the space of an hour;
To save the new bud from the blackening blight.

Friends, fly swiftly and true to the place of your birth,
To toil until dusk with the creatures of earth;
May your wings speed your ways; may the Ancient of Days
Grant you strength in your singing, your playing and work.

"Come," said Trellisant. He and the other sentries started down the grassy aisle between the soldierly lines of touch-torsils. Owen and his friends followed. Because of the trees' great height and girth, the colonnades turned out to be much longer than they had appeared at first glance. The sun had been warming the earth for the better part of an hour before the exiles reached the gleaming archway, which framed the yawning mouth of a tunnel. In keeping with the deceptively foreshortened rows of trees, the hole in the mountain had seemed much smaller from a distance.

Rolin craned his neck back to look up. "This entrance must measure one hundred and fifty feet high, if it's a foot!" he declared. "Not even Lucambra's stoneworms can delve tunnels so large."

"In you go," Trellisant ordered, pointing at the opening.

Percy groaned. "Not another tunnel! We've already spent days knocking about nasty hollows and holes. I absolutely refuse to go one step farther until I know what is waiting inside that entry."

"We spent a few hours underground," Mirrah corrected him. "It just *felt* like days. Now stop whining and start moving! If you want to be a king, you'll have to put up with some hardship. You had better wipe that pout off your face, too, or I'll do it for you."

Percy's face and ears burned a flaming red. "No one has ever spoken to me so cheekily before, not even my nurse!" he retorted. "If I were at home, I would have you thrown into my father's dungeon for such insolence. Do not forget I am still a prince!"

Planting her hands on her hips, Mirrah eyed him narrowly. "You're no better than the rest of us, *princey*. Look at yourself. You may be royalty, but you sure don't look the part. Now get going!"

Chuckling, Owen reflected that Maid Mirrah had a knack for cutting the prince down to size. In spite of himself, Percy was warming to her. A volatile romance seemed to be brewing between the two. Owen couldn't imagine a more unlikely couple.

Percy rubbed the dark, stubbly growth on his pinched face and picked at his borrowed rags. His mouth turned up in a wry grin. "I suppose you are right," he allowed. "Lead on, *cheeky!*"

Following their shining escorts, the travelers tramped into the tunnel. To Owen's relief, the walls and ceiling were bare of bats. When the daylight dimmed, Trellisant stopped. Raising his spear like a battle standard, he called out words in a melodious tongue. A shimmering haze appeared down the passage. Owen's heart leapt into his throat. Had the Gray Death followed him even here?

Yet, the misty Downs lay many miles and a world away. As the cloud floated toward him, Owen saw it was only more dremlens. The tiny beings settled on the ceiling and walls, illumining the tunnel like a million candles. The company moved on again.

Presently, an even brighter glow shone in the distance, as if the mountain had caught fire. Out of the light resounded countless voices singing in the same language Trellisant had spoken.

The tunnel swung in a gentle curve—and ended in another world. Owen gasped. The entire mountain was hollow inside, forming a chamber spacious enough at its forested base to encompass all of the Downs, with plenty of room left over for fifteen or twenty Landon Lakes. Echoing with a musical murmuring, the hollow extended a mile or more into the peak's heights, where hawks and eagles lazily soared. Myriads of shining dremlens clustered thickly along the cavern walls and flitted through the clear air, creating curtains of light as warm and soothing as the sun's.

"Oh, look!" Gwynneth said. "They're everywhere—in the air, on the rocks, in the trees—everywhere! What a grand sight!"

"Who would have dreamed that such a magnificent kingdom of light and space could thrive within a mountain's heart?" Rolin marveled. "Surely this hall rivals the beauties of Gaelessa!"

"Caerillion is but a pale shadow of that fair land," Trellisant told him. "Still, it is our home. Welcome to the City of Light!"

CHAPTER 12

THE LAST SPIREWALKER

After dismissing his fellow guards, Trellisant led the way down a flight of stone steps to the cavern floor. Sheltered from summer's heat and winter's frosts, flowers, shrubs and trees grew luxuriantly here. Neat paths fringed with daffodils, snowy sweet alyssum and ice-blue forget-me-nots wound among thickets of azaleas with their fragrant, trumpet-shaped blooms.

Timothy picked a golden daffodil and wove its stem into Gwynneth's hair. Giggling, she kissed him on the cheek, and together, they strolled along the path hand-in-hand. Reminded of Melina, Owen turned away with a pang of raw grief and loneliness.

The azaleas ended in a smooth green sward sprinkled with daisies and violets. In the midst of the lawn sat a green pavilion. Running up to the dome-shaped tent, Owen saw it was actually a circle of slender living poplars whose springy tops and branches had been bent over and woven together in the center. As they grew, the trees' crowns and limbs had created a cool, leafy roof.

Just then, cold, wet needles stung Owen's face. Raindrops! How could it rain inside a mountain? Seeing no other shelter from the indoor downpour, he was about to take refuge under the leafy pavilion when Trellisant strode up and firmly gripped his arm.

"Not so hasty, young one," he said. "Allow me to enter first and prepare the Spirewalker. I shall return for you and your friends when she is ready to receive guests. Do try to be courteous!"

As Trellisant disappeared inside the poplar pavilion, Gwynneth, Rolin and the other outringers joined Owen. Mirrah and Percy straggled up at the rear, holding their hands over their heads to ward off the rain. Mirrah seemed both amazed and perplexed.

"Well, I never! It's raining inside!" she exclaimed. "How did the dremlens manage that? And what a funny-looking tent this is."

"It's a very ingenious one, too," Rolin remarked. "I don't know why none of us ever thought of making a living tent of trees."

Trellisant reappeared from behind some low-hanging foliage to summon the travelers inside. The pavilion's overarching canopy of restlessly fluttering leaves cast a dappled green light upon the soft grass. In the lawn's center stood a leafy, wicker-like throne that evidently had been formed in much the same way as the tent itself, by planting, plaiting and pruning poplar switches.

On the living throne sat the loveliest woman Owen had ever seen. Her silver hair cascaded loosely over her shoulders and shimmering gossamer gown, while her ageless, pale-blue eyes bespoke a profound wisdom and humor. A wavering poplar-light played over her comely, expressive face. Darting dremlens swarmed about her head like drones attending a queen bee.

Bowing to her, Trellisant announced, "The visitors, milady." With a nod to his guests, he added, "Forgive me; I must now return to my post." Then he backed out of the poplar pavilion.

After Trellisant had departed, the willowy woman arose and held out her hands. "Greetings, strangers, who name the name of Gaelathane," she said. "I am Gisella, the Spirewalker of Feirian."

Gisella. While Rolin introduced himself and his traveling companions, Athyrea's words rang in Owen's head: *Truly, you are the shepherd's son. Wait until Gisella hears about this. Fare thee well!*

Like Trellisant and his guards, Gisella possessed long, lithe limbs and fingers; a sharp chin; a pert, upturned mouth; a long, pointed nose, and widely spaced eyes set beneath a high, smooth brow. She was the twin of the sleeping woman in the golden cave.

Gwynneth said, "When I visited the Isle of Luralin, Gaelathane mentioned a place called 'Feirian.' Does that mean 'Faeryland'?"

"Hush, girl!" Marlis scolded her. "It's impolite to interrupt."

"After six hundred years and twenty, I welcome the occasional interruption," said Gisella. "However, the name 'Feirian' does not refer to faeries. It means 'the Beautiful Land,' for so this world once was before the darkness, and so we strive still to make it."

"My friends and I are honored to make your acquaintance," said Rolin. He was recounting their harrowing underground adventures when Gisella raised a delicate hand to stop him.

"I care not how or why you have come to the Valley of Glynnhaven," she said, folding her arms. "By the Code of Caerillion, your presence here merits the death penalty. Barring that, People of the Dust who stumble upon our hidden refuge are escorted back to their own lands by ways devious and dark, and only after swearing a solemn oath never to return upon pain of execution."

Owen's companions blanched and exchanged dismayed looks. "We would be glad enough of the lesser penalty, good lady," said Bembor hoarsely. "Our only wish is to go home again."

Gisella's face softened. "Please do not misunderstand me. We have never put any innocent to death, for it is not in our nature to harm, only to heal. Still, if you were to leave this place and return with others of your kind, you would be imperiling our race and all the worlds we serve. Indeed, we already stand at the doorway to our doom, and we have lost all hope of deliverance."

Rolin asked, "Who are these 'People of the Dust'? Are you referring to the dust of our travels that clings to our clothing?"

Smiling, the Spirewalker said, "I should be a poor hostess indeed to find fault with my guests' appearance. Nay, I was speaking of the short-lived race of men. From the dust you all are made, and to the dust you return, for brief is the glory of man."

Scanlon countered, "Though we may resemble ordinary men, Gaelathane fashioned us *long-lived* Lucambrians from the very leaves of the Tree of trees, or so our ancient legends tell us."

"Be that as it may," Gisella said, "of all Gaelathane's created races, ours lives the longest. Even the Wood Folk—nymphs and dryads—cannot outlive us. Theirs is the lifetime of a tree, but we outlast the very mountains and hills."

"But who—or what—*are* you?" Bembor asked.

"Although we have gone by many names in many places and ages, we call ourselves 'the People of the Glen,' or 'glynnies.'"

Gwynneth clapped her hands. "That's what Thinbark called you! I thought the temperamental tree was talking nonsense."

Gisella's eyebrows rose. "If you can understand forest speech, then you must have breathed the sweet odor of *orella* trees."

"Indeed we have, though we call them *amenthils*," Rolin said. His eyes met Owen's, and he added, "Some of us have, that is."

"Then your people aren't angels?" Marlis wistfully asked.

"We are not," said Gisella. "Hear our Rhyme of the Races:

Men walk the waking worlds, creating with their minds;
In thought and purpose, like they are to Gaelathane;
They name the creatures, all of His created kinds;
To men is granted over earthly realms to reign.

The angels fly betwixt the heavens and the earth;
Unseen by mortal eyes, they work His perfect will;
Their task to help the children of the second birth;
Their highest joy to see His ways in men fulfilled.

To glynnies all the innocence of earth belongs,
To cherish and to tend as only glynnies know;
At morning and at dusk we sing our gladsome songs,
Wherever sweetest daffodils and daisies grow.

Gisella brushed a stray hair away from her forehead. "Angels and glynnies serve the same Creator but within different spheres, although Gaelathane may otherwise direct us. Angels assist the children of men who have believed upon the King and His Tree. We glynnies minister to most other living things—trees, flowers, ferns, mosses and mushrooms; insects, birds and land animals; fish, frogs, turtles and other creatures of pond, lake, river and sea."

Gwynneth made a face. "But what *are* glynnies?"

"Most People of the Dust know us as 'faeries,'" Gisella said.

Tears streaked Bembor's bearded cheeks. "Behold a living myth! We have found the kingdom of the tylwyth teg." Turning to Elwyn, he said, "What did I tell you? Now you owe me a new blowpipe and darts, and be sure to bind fresh griffin feathers on the darts. I don't want cattail down. It makes the darts fly crookedly."

"I still don't believe in faeries," said Elwyn stoutly. "Where are their wings? You always taught me the tylwyth teg had wings."

"We do, but not throughout our lives," Gisella broke in. Raising her head, she sang out words as shrill and lilting as rippling birdsong. Instantly, the pavilion filled with faeries, lighting up the leafy tent more brightly than the moon on a cloudless night.

Gisella spoke another command, and the faeries dimmed, revealing their true forms. Owen gaped. Dressed in loose, flowing frocks of tans, reds and greens, the women might have been Athyrea's cousins. The men wore neatly tailored tunics and trousers.

Some of the glynnies were dark of hair and eye, their skin burnt to a walnut brown, while others were fairer than a shepherdess shut away from the summer sun. All had wings as sheer as a bug-eyed dragonfly's yet as full and shapely as a silk moth's.

"What changed them from those firefly lights into winged creatures of such comeliness and grace?" Marlis asked Gisella.

"They merely hid their *talisynds* under their garments."

"What are talisynds?" asked Scanlon.

With a mischievous glint in her eye, Gisella replied, "I am surprised you do not recognize Tree-staffs when you see them! You must not presume the King has bestowed the gift of His light only upon those of your own race. See, here is my old talisynd."

Reaching into a pocket, Gisella drew out a tiny rod and held it between thumb and forefinger. "Every glynnie bears one of these, shaped from a twig of the risen Tree. With our talisynds, we help seeds to sprout; buds to leaf out and bloom; fruits to form and ripen with their seeds in them; baby birds to hatch, grow their feathers and stretch their wings. We guide the butterfly, the hummingbird and the bee to their nectar and the eagle to his eyrie; we help the fox to find his mate and the bear her den. Without our care and nurturing, all the living things Gaelathane has created to populate His worlds would soon weaken and die out."

"I knew the dremlens were Good People!" Mirrah said.

"Why don't *you* have wings like these others?" Owen asked.

Gisella held out her hand, and a glynnie alit on it. "All faeries begin their lives as *wispwings* like Tilia here," she said. "With each passing year, we grow a little larger. Nowadays, when we reach about a yard in height, our wings shrivel and drop off. Thereafter, we are called *slipwings*, and we walk about on the earth as you do."

"What causes your wings to wither?" asked Bembor.

The Spirewalker sighed. "After Felgor's rebellion, we glynnies have declined along with the rest of creation. In the beginning, faeries of all ages could fly. The King made our lightweight bodies and wings to last us a lifetime of lifetimes. Then the eldest among us began losing their wings. With each generation, *wingshed* has occurred earlier, until our wispwing years have grown briefer than a winter's day. How I miss those light-winged, fleeting hours when I danced with the stars and rode bats and birds bareback!"

Bembor suggested, "Have you ever tried eating starflower berries? They cure a wasting disease peculiar to griffins. Drinking gold dust may help, too, although gold is difficult to come by."

"We have already tested those remedies and many more besides," Gisella replied. "Starlyss, the first Spirewalker, discovered the cure for our condition, but she took her secret to the grave."

"Is there a cure, then?" asked Rolin eagerly. "Whether it be a nut or a seed, a fruit or a flower, or a drought of Glymmerin water, please tell us! If it still exists in any world, we will find it for you."

Gisella shook her head. "Neither food nor drink will restore our fallen wings," she said sadly. "We must be . . . *bitten*."

Horrified looks passed across the faces of Gisella's listeners. "Bitten?" Bembor echoed. "By what, in the name of Elgathel?"

"By an insect. Starlyss spent years delving into the secret ways of Feirian's wild creatures. At last, she ferreted out the fabled roosting-place of a rare dragonfly whose bite not only preserved our wings but also regrew them, even in the most aged slipwing."

Owen shuddered. The bloodthirsty, swarming insects that preyed upon his flocks often bit him as well. However, dragonflies were supposed to be harmless. He had never heard of any that bit people. "Doesn't the dragonfly cure work anymore?" he asked.

"Only Starlyss knew how to 'call' the creatures," Gisella said. "We have tried all sorts of ingenious lures, but without success. No one has even seen such a dragonfly in hundreds of years."

"Then how did Starlyss attract them?" asked Rolin.

"With sounds," said Gisella. "While exploring Mt. Morwynion here, our people came across some veins of a metal that Starlyss called 'glynniant,' for it shone like glynnie wings in the sun. From glynniant and wood, she fashioned a harp whose notes drew the insects to her in great, buzzing swarms. Unfortunately, the harp was broken in a rockfall. Before Starlyss could make another, she fell ill and wandered off, never to be seen again in this world."

"Couldn't you make another harp yourselves?" Owen said.

"Nay, *dustling*. Our cleverest craftsmen have tried to recreate Starlyss's instrument, but their every attempt so far has failed."

"But what can slipwings *do*, being wingless?" Marlis asked.

"Once we lose our wings, we rarely venture outside the bounds of our own world, lest the locals hunt us down. Our task is looking after Feirian's leafy, feathered and furry creatures. You must have seen slipwings tending the Glynnhaven Valley's gardens. Yet every year, our burden grows greater as our numbers dwindle."

"Since wispwings and slipwings all obey your commands," said Bembor, "I must conclude you are the Queen of the Glynnies."

"Not at all," said Gisella, dipping her head. "No glynnie may wear Feirian's crown until the Royal Prophecy has been fulfilled. Every 'walker has longed to see that day. Alas, our hope will die with me, for I am the last of my line. My husband Blethryn and I had an only child, a daughter who was to succeed me in this honored office. Soon after her wingshed, she and Blethryn fell into darkness. I was bereaved of both in a single day. Now I am also bereaved of my beloved Glynnspire Cave, and I shall perish!"

Just then, Trellisant entered the pavilion carrying a bulky gray object over his shoulder. "Here is one of the spires we recovered largely intact," he announced. With a grunt, he drove the cone-shaped stone pillar blunt-end first into the earth. Standing upright in place, it resembled the tooth of some gigantic fanged creature.

Trellisant dusted off his hands. "There!" he said. "Forgive my gouging your grass, milady, but I thought this rock might bring you some cheer. It may no longer respond to you, but it will suit for other purposes, should the Caerillion Council invoke the Code.

"I do hope that we shall find a few more whole spires. Most of the others, I am sorry to say, have been smashed beyond repair or washed away. May your wings bear you to the home of the Myndyn-Maker." Thus excusing himself, Trellisant took his leave.

"Feirian's spires have fallen, as I feared," said Gisella. She bowed her head, and bitter words poured from her bloodless lips.

> To walk among the spires again, to touch each spine,
> My hands and heart I'd freely give, to make them mine;
> For lost they are beyond the sea, and shattered sore;
> Their shards alone still whisper tones upon the shore.
>
> My kindred, too, have perished from the pining earth—
> The mate I loved and her to whom I once gave birth—
> How many days and years shall pass my aching eyes,
> Until I join them in that land beyond the skies?
>
> When time and age shall still the 'walker's winsome voice,
> How shall her roving people make the proper choice?
> What visions of a wasting world shall lead them on?
> What wisdom strengthen and direct when I am gone?
>
> Alas, the freezing net fast gathers 'round our feet,
> Though glynnie hearts be bold and beating wings be fleet;
> In time, our joyful songs of worship shall descend
> Into the pit of blackest breath, where love will end.

Scanlon's brow furrowed. "Trellisant said something about using this spike for 'other purposes.' What did he mean by that?"

"By order of the Caerillion Council," Gisella replied, "anybody that steals, damages or destroys one of our stone spires may be put to death by impalement upon the same or another such spire."

CHAPTER 13

FAERY HOSPITALITY

The outringers traded stricken looks. Prince Percy's face turned ashen. "Do you not think impalement a harsh penalty for marring a mere pillar of stone?" he asked.

"Not if you knew what those spires meant to us!" Gisella shot back. A shadow passed behind her eyes. "The Glynnspire Cave was not only our water source and our refuge from enemies. It was also the Spirewalker's window into the King's creation. We called it *Myndyn Hall*—our sole repository of myndyn worlds."

"What are 'myndyns'?" Marlis asked.

"Those are the trees of travel that fill our land," Gisella said. "The name means 'sweet-trees,' for their highly fragrant blooms open at dawn and at dusk. Gaelathane placed the first myndyn here. Over the years, we have planted more trees from its nuts."

"Torsils," said Scanlon. "She means the touch-torsils."

"I never want to see another of those trees again!" Gwynneth declared. "Why would Gaelathane create a world forested by just one kind of tree? How utterly boring! Back home, our torsils grow mostly in scattered groves, not in pure stands like these trees."

Timothy said, "We've seen pines and firs here, too, as well as maples and ashes, hemlocks and beeches, oaks and cedars."

"But not in great numbers," Rolin reminded him.

"You may find our myndyns tiresome, but we do not," Gisella said. "We visit other lands through them; we hide in them; we even live in them. Without the myndyns, we People of the Glen would have no purpose for our existence, and other worlds would eventually wither, leaving only our dying race to inhabit Feirian."

From behind her throne, Gisella brought out a shining staff similar to those the outringers carried. Standing before Trellisant's spire, she tapped it with the staff. The stone column gonged like a great brass bell, and the Spirewalker disappeared.

"Where did she go?" everyone gabbled at once. A minute later, the spire rang again, and Gisella reappeared, staff still in hand.

"What happened to you?" Rolin asked her, looking shaken.

"I just viewed the land of Drowdon, which is now a desert, since the Drowdonians cut down their myndyns years ago. Glynnies no longer go there, for this spire remains the only way in or out."

Owen ran his fingers over the stone's smooth surface. Though dry, it felt soapy or greasy. "How could you visit another world just by striking this spike?" he asked. "Did you use faery magic?"

"We shun all magic!" Gisella replied. "Gaelathane instructed Starlyss to place a nut from a different myndyn tree upon each floor spire in Myndyn Hall. Dripping stone has entombed those nuts, preserving them for all time—until you and your friends brought the flood. Spirewalkers once struck the stones with wooden rods, but in these latter days, Gaelathane has given us staffs from the Tree of trees to use instead. Even so, convincing these rocks to ring requires much practice and patience, for too sharp a blow will shatter the spire, and too dull a one will produce no tone at all."

"I believe I understand now," said Bembor, pushing his way to the front of the gathering. "In and of itself, a torsil—or rather, a *myndyn*—nut cannot take anyone anywhere. However, tapping one of these stalagmites sets up a strong vibration that somehow coaxes the nut inside to grant passage." He shook his head. "Wouldn't it be far simpler just to touch a myndyn tree instead?"

"Simpler, perhaps, but certainly far more perilous," Gisella replied. "Our common foe—and Gaelathane's—seeks to destroy the Spirewalker's line. He knows if he succeeds, our race will fade away for lack of guidance, and all worlds will fall into ruin. He has nearly achieved his aim, for the Spirewalker's heir has perished, and the Glynnspire Cave is gone. Without my spires, I am deaf and blind, unless I touch every myndyn tree in the wood."

Bembor nodded. "Our enemy is hoping you will do just that, for you would be exposed and unprotected above ground."

"In days of old," Gisella sighed, "we had nothing to fear from the forest. Then the encroaching darkness forced the dwindling remnant of our race higher into the hills. Finally, we retreated into the Valley of Glynnhaven, our last outpost. Here we lived in trees and shallow caves until Gaelathane Himself came to our assistance.

"'For this very day and hour I have prepared you a secret refuge,' He told us. 'No longer shall you all dwell in danger beneath the pitiless sky, enduring winter's chill and summer's relentless heat.'

"Then He led us to a pile of boulders at the foot of this mountain. Behind them lay an echoing tunnel. When Mt. Morwynion erupted years earlier, much of the molten rock escaped through a side passage of its own making, the very tunnel through which you entered. By the time the fiery rivers had ceased to flow, they had emptied Morwynion, leaving it with a hollow, habitable interior."

"Amazing!" murmured Rolin. "A world within a world, secure from all outside enemies that might attempt to assail it."

Bowing her head, Gisella said, "Though we may be secure without, we are withering within, for the darkness has steadily weakened our will to go on." She raised her arms toward the poplar canopy, her hands brushing its fragrant leaves. "What good is the Spirewalker without her spires?" she cried. "How many generations of us have walked among them and rung them? No more shall I tend the Glynnspire Cave's torch-fires. Now all worlds are lost to me! Camaron and Cornobonne, Blethys and Borweggion, Plennestyr and Portmorgoron—all have been washed down the River Blynnys into the Sea of Thionne. Thence they shall not return until the Last Day, when Gaelathane will renew all things."

She turned fierce eyes upon her shocked audience. "Had I the power to weep as you do, I would weep for my injury."

"I apologize for the collapse of your cave," Rolin told her. "If we could restore that hallowed hall, we would gladly do so."

Gisella lowered her arms. "Please forgive me. Spiteful words mend no losses and serve only to poison the speaker. Alas, I have neglected to offer you the hospitality due even condemned guests."

At the Spirewalker's crisp command, her wispwing servants shot out of the pavilion like a school of frightened fish. Returning promptly, the glynnies each bore a nut meat, an orange fairybell fruit, a boiled bird's egg, a bit of wintercress or wild lettuce, or a baked groundnut. Owen also recognized some jellylike, white-spined mushrooms that he knew as "gray hedgehogs." They grew on decaying logs and branches in cool, wet weather. He often ate the rubbery hedgehogs raw on the Downs when his water bag had gone dry. Though tasteless, the fungi made a moist, chewy snack.

The faeries deposited these dainty morsels in piles upon a white linen cloth they had laid out on the grass. Altogether, it hardly seemed enough food to satisfy ten starving travelers.

"I believe you will enjoy this repast, since our tastes are similar," said the Spirewalker. "Do not be put off by the small portions, for you may eat as much as you please." Sure enough, after Rolin had given thanks for Gaelathane's provision, everyone had plenty to eat. As quickly as the food piles shrank, the wispwings replenished them. Feeling comfortably full after nibbling his way through this faery feast, Owen reflected he would not be wanting his supper that evening. Then he helped himself to another bird's egg.

Afterwards, Gisella clapped her hands, and the wispwings strung long bundles of golden, brown and black fabric between the poplar trunks. Pulling apart one of the stretchy skeins, Owen found it was a lightweight sleeping-sling made of a smooth, supple material. He felt the sudden urge to lie down and sleep on it.

"These hammocks were woven from the hairs of our own heads," Gisella said. "Faery hair is finer and lighter than silk. Our wee wispwings weave the hair into a cloth that slipwings later make into hammocks and garments, blankets, quilts and tents."

A perplexed look creased Rolin's forehead, and he said, "I have seen hammocks much like these somewhere before."

"So have I," said Marlis. Her face lit up. "I know! It was in the Beechtown market. Every year, someone sets up a stall full of these. I always thought the vendor looked, well, a little *different*."

"Beechtown?" said Gisella. "I know the place. Few myndyns still grow in that world. Your vendor, Madrielle, was born there."

"Born there!" Scanlon exclaimed. "Why aren't your children born here in this world, where you can best care for them?"

"Because Gaelathane has ordained otherwise," Gisella replied. "No glynnie is born in Feirian. Only in the Outer Worlds do we bear our young, so that the wispwings will better come to know the trees and flowers, birds and other wild creatures of those lands. Once trained, wispwings will resettle in Caerillion, but they usually return to their birth worlds to serve, though not to live."

Seeing that the wispwings had not touched any of the leftover food, Owen asked, "But what do faeries, er, *glynnies* eat?"

"As wispwings," said Gisella, "we can survive quite nicely on flower nectar and pollen, with a little honey thrown in for good measure. As slipwings, however, we need more substantial fare."

Rolin said, "Come to think of it, my father once saw a faery sitting on one of his beehives in the moonlight, eating some honey. He told only me about it, for fear he was losing his mind."

Winking at him, Gisella said, "Perhaps you shall find our hospitality ample repayment for that stolen honey, even if our council may have other ideas. Now, dear guests, it is time for sleep, though the morning has but lately dawned. When you are suitably rested and refreshed, I will show you more of Caerillion. In the meantime, may your dream-wings bear you to Gaelessa, Land of Joy."

Never having slept in a hammock before, Owen wasn't sure how to approach one. The fabric trough seemed entirely too flimsy to support his weight. Finally, he turned around and seated himself on it. Then he swung his legs up. The hammock swiftly tipped over, dumping him onto the ground with a jarring 'thud.'

More surprised and embarrassed than hurt, he picked himself up to a chorus of tinkling wispwing laughter. With dazed expressions, Percy, Mirrah and Marlis also lay on the grass beneath their still-swinging hammocks. Owen couldn't help grinning. At least he wasn't the only one to fall out! After two more attempts, he tamed the hammock, balancing himself with his knees and arms.

Still, he couldn't find a comfortable position. No matter which way he shifted, he ended up facing the Drowdon spire. In the lazy, shifting shadows, the stalagmite darkened, as if stained with blood. Owen could hardly believe Gisella would condemn him and his companions to impalement upon such a spire, but the gruesome prospect still haunted him. Hordes of wispwings would seize and lift him above the pillar before dropping him onto its pointed top. As this vivid vision replayed in his mind, he began to sweat.

Lulled by the hammock's swaying, he was finally drifting off to sleep when a faint breeze tickled his face. Opening one eye, he found a wispwing hovering above him, her fluttering faery wings fanning his skin. Clad in green, she wore a circlet of fern leaflets on her flowing, dark hair. As she alit on his chest, intense interest animated her lively hazel eyes and pale, sprightly face.

It was Athyrea.

CHAPTER 14

DAY AND NIGHT FAERIES

T hank you for saving my life," she said in a wispy voice like the faint chirping of high-soaring swallows. "After I led you and your friends to Sheltering Cave, I lost my only talisynd. Without it, I could not stave off the cold that burns like fire. I was very near death when you found me. I am forever in your service." Raising her dainty arms, she executed a graceful curtsy.

"As I am in yours," Owen said. "Without you, I would have died of thirst and starvation in Swyndon. I owe my life to you!"

A tiny red spot appeared on Athyrea's wan cheeks as she blushed. "Any glynnie worth her wings would have done the same," she said. "I was looking after some sword ferns when Celembrose sent me to help you. I am a fern-faery, you see. Ferns and mosses flourish under my care, here and elsewhere. Have you ever tasted the sweet dewdrops that dangle on the tips of a luxuriant lady fern? I have. Or have you seen the spore-dust drifting from beneath those lacy fronds? I have. And when the wood fern's fiddleheads appear in the spring, I am there, helping them to unfurl and spread out."

Owen blinked in surprise. He had never given much thought to the workings of nature. How or why ferns and other plants grew was a mystery to him. Now he was beginning to understand.

135

Propping himself up on one elbow, he told Athyrea, "Perhaps before I leave Caerillion you can show me your favorite ferns."

"I would love that!" she said. "In some worlds, ferns grow as big as trees, and the people there build their houses in them."

The tallest ferns Owen had ever seen were the bracken that grew chest-high in moist places on the Downs. He loved the sweet smell of their fronds when he waded through a patch. When eaten in the curled fiddlehead stage of spring, the delicate plants made a tasty cooked vegetable somewhat like asparagus. In full leaf, however, they were poisonous both to people and to sheep.

"Are all faeries fern-faeries?" he asked sleepily.

Athyrea laughed with the soft, silvery sound of rain dripping from new leaves into a forest pool. "Goodness, no!" she said. "It all depends upon the clan you're born into. Some glynnies watch over trees or birds; others over mushrooms, mosses or ferns; still others over certain flowers. There are dandelion-glynnies, daffodil-glynnies, violet-glynnies, iris-glynnies and gooseberry-glynnies (a prickly sort, those are), just to name a few. Broadly speaking, we are either 'night-faeries,' *glynnion-naifalon*, or 'day-faeries,' *glynnion-daifalon*. By my looks, you can probably guess which kind I am."

"Since you are fair skinned, you must be a night-faery," said Owen. "But why would you want to work at night, when the forest sleeps? I should think you would find little to do then."

"Quite the contrary!" said Athyrea. "After dark, the forest comes to life. The trees whisper their deepest secrets then, and many small creatures go about their business. Night-blooming flowers release their richest scents into the cooling air, delighting moths, bats and especially us glynnies! We truly prefer the night, when we can fly about more freely under the cover of darkness."

It struck Owen that he and his companions had arrived in the Valley of Glynnhaven just in time to see the day-faeries departing for their labors and later, the night-faeries returning from theirs.

A flash and a whirr interrupted his thoughts as a mossy-haired wispwing flew into the pavilion to land beside Athyrea. The two exchanged words as quick and sharp as knitting needles. Then Mossy-hair handed something to Athyrea and flew off in a huff.

"That was my brother, Osmund," said Athyrea apologetically. "He is a fern-faery, too, but he prefers mosses more. We often work together, even though we don't always get along very well."

Owen decided he liked Athyrea's ferny circlet better than the abandoned bird's nest of moss sprigs and twigs tangled in her brother's unkempt hair. "Osmund seemed rather cross with you over something," he observed. "What was the matter, anyway?"

Athyrea sighed. "I love my brother, but sometimes he hovers over me as if I were still a wet-winged wispling. He was most upset I had lost my talisynd and brought me another one so I could leave tonight with my companions. We can work without our rods, of course, but they help light our way in the darkness, and the virtue of Gaelathane resides in them to bless every living thing they touch." She raised the tiny talisynd, transforming herself into a star.

"Follow me, and I will show you what glynnies can do with the King's help!" she said. Owen sat up in his hair-hammock, which overturned, tossing him out on the ground again. Grumbling, he got up and followed Athyrea out of the pavilion. The wispwing led him across the lush lawn into stately groves of beech trees, where more glynnies were already busily working. The trees' leaves dripped with water that left puddles on the soft earth.

"How can it rain inside a mountain?" Owen asked his guide.

"That's not rain," she replied. "Long ago, we diverted some of Morwynion's streams and waterfalls to flow into the mountain's heart. Entire glynnie clans are devoted to ensuring that Caerillion is evenly watered. Without the sun and wind to rob us of moisture, we require only a few light showers now and again to keep everything fresh, green and flourishing year 'round."

"But how can anything grow in here without the sun?"

"All living things thrive better under the Tree's light than in the sun's," Athyrea answered. Owen had to admit she was right. Everywhere he looked, tall trees rose above the cavern floor, their leaves lightly shading the flowering herbs and bushes beneath. Wispwings flitted here and there, touching this plant or that with their shining talisynds. Circling to a stop, Athyrea hovered above a clump of columbines struggling beside a massive bay tree.

"Here we are," she said. "I am sure whoever is looking after these flowers won't mind if I add my talisynd's touch to hers."

With that, Athyrea pointed her talisynd at the columbine clump. A needlelike light beam shot out of the rod and played across the languishing plant. The columbine's drooping leaves perked up. Then sprightly green shoots sprouted from the clump's center. Buds formed at the tips of the lengthening shoots. To Owen's astonishment, nodding ruby flowers burst forth from the buds.

"That should do for now," said Athyrea, and she flew up to land on Owen's arm. "Before we part, you should know that Gaelathane has granted me the gift of prophecy, and this I say to you in His name, son of dust: 'The borwogs shall be thy bane!'"

Athyrea's talisynd flashed, and she whirred off. Making his way back to the poplar pavilion, Owen collapsed into his hammock and fell asleep. In his dreams, borwogs lurked outside Caerillion's entrance, waiting to drag him down into their dark, freezing holes.

Later that day, Owen's world turned topsy-turvy. Elwyn had flipped his hammock upside-down. Owen flopped out and landed on the matted grass in a befuddled heap, groaning and yawning.

"Rise and shine, sleepyhead! You've almost missed supper!" Elwyn cheerily told him as he helped him to his feet.

"Why did you have to do that?" Owen mumbled.

"I didn't have to; I wanted to!" Elwyn shot back with a good-natured grin. Grumbling, Owen followed him to Gisella's linen cloth, which was neatly laid out with cheeses, breads, nuts and fruits. Though his friends were just finishing their simple meal, Owen was relieved to see that plenty of food remained for him.

Unexpectedly famished, he tucked into a loaf of bread, piling it with slabs of cheese. Between bites, he asked, "How did the wispwings carry all this here?" The cheeses alone must have weighed five pounds apiece, and the bread loaves weren't much lighter.

"They didn't!" Elwyn replied. "Our supper was served courtesy of Trellisant's guards. Say, where did you go earlier while the rest of us were sleeping? I noticed your hammock was empty."

Owen told his friends about Athyrea and Osmund, of giant ferns, faery habits and waterfall rain. He didn't mention Athyrea's prophecy, however. He didn't think anyone would believe him. He wasn't sure he believed the wispwing's prediction himself.

Scanlon said, "That's all very quaint, but must I remind everyone we are under a death sentence for coming here and bringing down the Glynnspire Cave's roof? I say we leave Caerillion before Gisella and her council decide to have us impaled on this spire."

"Even if we were allowed to leave," said Rolin softly, "where would we go? We still don't know how to escape this peculiar world, let alone find our way home through a Lucambra torsil."

"Uh, oh," said Elwyn. "Now we're in trouble!" He pointed at the Spirewalker, who had just entered the pavilion with Trellisant.

"Come with us," Gisella said, beckoning to her visitors.

Hastily stuffing his unfinished supper in his shepherd's purse, Owen caught up to his friends as they followed Gisella and the guard through the gardens and up the stairway. Meanwhile, Caerillion's light was fading. Wispwings by the thousands were dropping off the walls and funneling into the tunnel, filling it with talisynds and flittering wings. As Owen entered, the tiny creatures flowed around him like swimming schools of vivid, varicolored fishes.

Outside, the myndyn colonnades stood cloaked in evening shadow as the sun sank behind Mt. Morwynion. Thin clouds were curling across the sky like snippets of freshly shorn wool. Gisella gathered her guests beneath a tree until the wispwings had all swarmed out. Then she pointed up at the myndyns. Bright lights were flying out of the trees' cup-shaped, maroon blossoms. Waves of delicious perfume flooded the air. Gwynneth wrinkled her nose.

"That scent wafts out every evening," she said. "I remember first smelling it before I came to Feirian. The next thing I knew, a very large, hairy man was chasing me through a strange woodland."

The other outringers nodded, and Rolin said, "We all smelled that fragrance in the fog just as the Downs disappeared."

The honeysuckle odor reminded Owen of his first visit to Feirian with Sparrow. What could have happened to her? If she was searching for him, she would never find him in Caerillion.

Timothy stamped his staff. "Touch-torsils I can understand, but what sort of faery magic breeds scents that transport people?"

"This is Gaelathane's creation at work, not magic," said Gisella. "Breathing the aroma of myndyn blossoms will whisk you into Feirian as surely as touching one of the trees—if you are not there already. In other worlds, the opening flowers also release a mist or fog that helps conceal the wispwings flying out of them."

"Do wispwings hide in the myndyn flowers?" Owen asked.

Gisella replied, "Yes, and they live in them! Not all wispwings sleep in Caerillion, save in winter. Many of them make their homes inside myndyn blossoms, sipping their sweet nectar. At eventide, the blooms release the glynnies of the night while also receiving the weary glynnies of the day, who will sleep safely in the tops of the trees. At dawn, the flowers will open again to send forth those faeries, making room for the returning glynnies of the night."

"That still doesn't explain how we could walk into a faery ring in our world and walk out of it into Owen's world," Scanlon said.

"Our folk do not cause such circles to grow," Gisella answered. "However, we do enjoy dancing in them! Often, a ring will form around a stump or a dead tree and continue to expand long after the wood has rotted away. If the tree was a myndyn, then stepping in and out of the circle will take you to another land."

Bembor was grinning broadly. "So as the 'torsil-ring' grows, it takes on the virtues of the dead tree! How perfectly marvelous."

As Owen now understood it, Swyndon's welving rings marked the last remnants of the Greatwood's original trees—most of them myndyns. That meant Swyndon's missing sheep, shepherds and shepherdesses—Melina included—must have ended up in Feirian. Bright hope gleamed in Owen's heart like a polished talisynd.

Scanlon caught himself starting to lean against one of the myndyns. "What perilous trees these are," he muttered. "Touch or smell one, and you're exiled in Feirian or some other place."

The Spirewalker pointed her staff at the twin rows of torsil trees. "If you find our land harsh or inhospitable, please remember that Gaelathane never intended for men to live here. He made the myndyns to ease glynnie labors, not to snare the unwary. The flower-fragrance that brought you here has also called home many a glynnie stranded or lost without her tree in some strange land."

140

Even as Gisella spoke, a cloud of singing day-faeries descended upon the valley. Most flew through Caerillion's yawning entryway, but a number settled on the myndyn trees standing in front of the mountain. Their song went something like this, though I fear neither the tongues of men nor of angels can do it justice:

Back from the fields of fair flowers we fly,
Back from our errands where mountains meet sky,
Back to our blossoms to find blessed rest,
Back to our sweet-trees, back to our nests!

Lily and bluebell, laurel and peach,
Cherry, rosemary, lupine and beech;
All the King's creatures respond to our care,
For in love and in patience we heal and repair!

Dancing and spinning, laughing and playing;
Our burdens grow lighter with singing and praying!
For the love of the King we all gladly give,
Who surrendered His life that we glynnies might live!

In storm and in sunshine, in snow, sleet and hail,
We fly to our labors at dawn without fail!
Unseen and unsung, we swift make our rounds;
In serving the King, our joy knows no bounds.

Yet day after day, our deliverer delays;
While dronzils devour and blackness betrays;
Alone he shall hang 'twixt the living and dead;
For faeries and men he shall stand in our stead.

Back from the fields of fair flowers we fly,
Back from our errands where mountains meet sky,
Back to our blossoms to find blessed rest,
Back to our sweet-trees, back to our nests!

"You have already warned us against presumption," said Bembor dryly. "Still, I would guess your 'deliverer' must be Gaelathane Himself. Who else has hung betwixt the living and the dead?"

"This time, I sing not of the King's sacrifice," the Spirewalker replied. "Gaelathane never delays. He comes and goes as He pleases, and He has been pleased to visit us often in Feirian. Still, if He does not send us the promised deliverer ere long, the dronzils shall swallow up Feirian—sun, moon, mountains, stars and all."

Mirrah and Prince Percy looked perplexed until Gwynneth explained, "By 'dronzils' I think she means the borwogs."

Gisella raised her staff toward a snowy mountain. "See how the sickle moon hangs upon yonder peak? She rises early this evening. According to legend, when the waning moon hooks herself around Mt. Crygmor, the deliverer shall come to save us. Ever since the first myndyn was felled in the world of Wesselwynd, hundreds of such moons have crowned Crygmor, but ever have our hopes come to naught. The darkness grows and our people perish still."

"Then may your deliverance hasten on the wings of eagles, Spirewalker of Feirian," Bembor gravely told her.

As Gisella led her visitors back through the entryway, Owen tarried outside. The crescent moon still cradled Crygmor's summit in its butter-yellow embrace. More day-glynnies straggled into Mt. Morwynion from worlds unknown. When Owen turned to leave, he thought he heard a forlorn sparrow chirping sadly in the dusk.

CHAPTER 15

A VOICE IN THE NIGHT

Over the next few days, Owen visited more of the City of Light and its surroundings, often in the company of Mirrah and Percy. The three friends tested all the myndyns in the colonnades to discover where each tree led. They were not disappointed. Wondrous worlds dawned before them at a simple touch, worlds ripe for the exploring—and without the risk of being detected by any of the inhabitants. Nowhere, however, did Owen see any sign of his elusive sparrow or of Melina.

After dark, when his companions were snoring in their hammocks, he would slip out of Caerillion to find Athyrea waiting for him in the forest. Since few borwogs inhabited the highlands, Owen would spend hours exploring Feirian and lands beyond while Athyrea ministered to ferns, flowers and other denizens of meadow and wood. From her, Owen learned to love the night, with its cool, still air, whispering shadows and the furtive sounds of small, wakeful creatures scurrying through the underbrush.

One evening, Owen was so frazzled from his moonlit escapades that he decided to stay in the pavilion and enjoy a full night's rest. He had just convinced his tippety hammock to let him lie in it instead of on the ground when he heard a voice softly calling.

"Owen."

He jerked upright, and the hammock tipped him out again. Lying bruised on the grass, he tried to regain his bearings. Who had called his name? Perhaps it was Athyrea. She had been most distressed to learn that Owen would not be joining her again that evening. Faeries, he had observed, possessed a virtually inexhaustible store of energy and enthusiasm. He decided their secret must lie in their simple diet or the talisynds they bore.

Picking himself up, he listened for the voice. There it was again, calling his name. This was no faery-summons. All of Caerillion seemed to be whispering, "Owen!" He crept outside the pavilion, but still the voice urged him on. Only a glimmering twilight shone inside the mountain, for the glynnies cloaked their talisynds at night. Along slipwing paths, up the stone stairs and through the access tunnel he hurried, following the mysterious voice.

Down the broad aisle between the ranks of myndyn trees flowed a silken river of light. At first Owen thought the moon had risen, but it had already sunk below the horizon. Drawn onward by the light, he moved along the grassy corridor. On either side, the myndyns stood at attention like so many silent sentinels. Once, he heard old leaves crunching. He told himself it was just a wild animal, but his heart beat faster. No wispwings flew about.

Floating along the light-river, Owen finally reached its source. At the colonnade's head towered an enormous tree, its transparent trunk and limbs shining like a giant lightstaff. The outringers had described the Tree perfectly. Owen walked all the way around it, marveling at its great girth, perfect symmetry and straight trunk. But how could a tree of such size spring up in the space of only a few hours? Mystified, he touched the Tree's bark.

Light shone everywhere around him, for the darkness had fled into a serene, cloudless sky. From beneath the Tree gushed a spring that became a river flowing between ranks of rustling poplars. Continuing on, the river slid into an amethyst lake bounded by smooth lawns. Bright figures were dancing on the grass. *Slipwings!*

Owen was looking for a place to ford the river when he came up against a nearly invisible wall. Yielding but firm, it shimmered like the veils that separated Feirian from every other myndyn world. Looking down, he saw his feet had left no dints in the lush grass.

One of the dancing figures appeared on the bank opposite Owen. This was no faery! Though clad in shining robes similar to a slipwings's, the sword-wielding young man wore a pair of white-feathered wings quite unlike the glynnies' gauzy ones. The winged warrior was gazing at him with familiar eyes as clear and gray as the light of dawn on the Downs. However, Owen was sure his rescuer had been wingless when they had first met in Feirian.

"Greetings!" said Celembrose. "You may not pass beyond the River of the Tree. The barrier dividing Gaelathane's worlds one from another is thickest here, lest mortal beings break through into the eternal. Only we angels and Gaelathane's children may enter His kingdom. He will show you the way, for He is the way."

Then Owen was back in Feirian beside the Tree. Seized with an awful anguish, he slumped weeping to the ground. Since leaving Swyndon, he had wept for himself, for his parents, for his loneliness and for Melina. Now, however, he wept for a loss so great that he could not fathom its depths. Of all the worlds he had visited, he knew he had to find a way into this one. If only Athyrea had been there to open a porthyl big enough for him to slip through!

"Only I can create such a porthyl, for I *am* the Porthyl."

Rubbing his eyes, Owen looked up to see an old man standing over him. The stranger held a shining shepherd's crook and wore a radiant robe that shone with all the hues of the rainbow. Even his eyes blazed so brightly that Owen couldn't be certain whether they were reflecting the Tree's light or the other way around.

"Who are you?" he asked.

"I am Gaelathane," replied the Man. "Others have told you about Me, but now you must know Me for yourself." He helped Owen to his feet and wiped away his tears with a tender touch.

"Receive My comfort," said Gaelathane soothingly. "Before sun, there must come rain; before laughter, there must come tears; before life, there must come death. I know how lonely and distressed you are. Touch the Tree's trunk here, and be strengthened." Where the Man was pointing, Owen pressed his finger into the bark.

In the beat of a faery's wing, he was home. He and Gaelathane stood beside Tadwyn and Gyrta, who were seated at the kitchen table before two empty plates. Their faces looked as lined and hollow as worn-out waterskins. Gaelathane reached out, and light streaming from His luminous hands bathed the grieving parents.

Lifting his head, Tadwyn said, "I can't explain why, Gyrta, but I have a feeling our boy will be coming home soon. I know it makes no sense after he's been gone so long, but there it is."

Laying her hand on Tadwyn's, Gyrta said, "I believe so, too."

The scene faded, and Owen found himself back in Feirian, hope and pain mingled in his heart. Gaelathane pointed out more places on the Tree's trunk for him to touch. This time, he and the King relived different events in Owen's childhood and youth. Among the most heartrending was the afternoon he had first met Melina.

"As bony as a half-starved sheep, you are," he had teased her. Through older eyes he watched Melina hurry home, wailing as she went, and he wept. How could he have been so cruel? He wished he could see Melina again and properly apologize to her in person.

Yannick, Melina's father, had later berated Owen for his thoughtless words. Touching the Tree again, Owen saw himself taking revenge on Yannick by letting his sheep out of their pen one night. Many of those sheep had wandered onto the Downs and into some welving rings. Owen had never confessed to the cowardly deed.

Prodding the Tree in different places called up more scenes of sorrow and despair. Owen saw his wrenching loneliness as an only child, especially when Swyndon's other children jeered and rejected him for his clumsiness. Some of those mockers were later taken untimely on the Downs. Observing their sheepshuns for the second time, Owen regretted he had not forgiven his tormenters earlier.

He saw the glad times, too, such as the day his father had presented him with a shepherd's crook of ash wood. Owen had beamed with pride. When he first tried to snare a sheep with the staff's hooked end, he tripped over the straight end and fell on his face. Now he wondered whether he would ever herd sheep again.

Overwhelmed with shame and regret, Owen finally collapsed in a heap at Gaelathane's feet. "I'm sorry; please, please forgive me!"

he tearfully told the King. He had never intentionally wronged this Man, yet somehow he knew that every unkind word he had ever spoken, every selfish act he had ever committed had wounded not only his own conscience but also the heart of Gaelathane.

Again the King raised him to his feet and dried his tears. "Today," He said, "you have become one of My sheep. I will never leave you or forsake you, though you lose your way in the wilderness as Tabitha did. Now I must place My shepherd's mark upon you."

From His robes Gaelathane produced a long, gleaming knife. Owen shrank back. Was the King about to prove His ownership by notching Owen's ears after the manner of Swyndon's shepherds with their wayward sheep? Melina's parents were rumored to have done the same to her. Owen had seen his friend's scarred ears only once, since she always wore her hair long to hide them.

Wincing with pain, Gaelathane deliberately drew the knife blade across His own right forearm. The cut reddened with welling blood, which the King gently smeared upon Owen's forehead.

When Owen moved to wipe away the blood, Gaelathane stayed his hand. "Leave it be," He said. "In a few hours, the stain will fade of its own accord. However, My mark of love upon your heart will never fade away. You will always be mine, and I will always be yours. Reject Me, and I will still love you for all eternity."

Owen felt whole and at peace for the first time in his life. Joy surged within him as Gaelathane touched the Tree with His staff. The landscape changed again. This time, Owen stood with Gaelathane and the Tree atop a mountain overlooking a sparkling blue lake. From the Tree's roots bubbled up the stream Owen had seen earlier. Warm light flooded the mountain and the lake, though no sun hung in the limitless sky. Owen saw no shadows.

"The last time you visited My world," Gaelathane said, "you could not enter. Now you may, although you cannot stay. I am granting you this visitation to encourage and strengthen you in the trials and challenges that lie ahead, for the time is short."

The King waved His staff, and the glimmering veil appeared again before Owen. He put out his hand to touch it, and it dissolved like dew beneath a summer's sun. Such scents! Such sounds! Such sights burst upon his senses! In a flash, Celembrose and several other angels had surrounded him with their great wings and bodies, shielding him from the onslaught of overwhelming sensations.

"Hail, son of the King!" said one of the angels. "We rejoice that you have sworn allegiance to Gaelathane. Content yourself with this glimpse of Gaelessa's glories, which earthly eyes and ears can endure but briefly. The longer you tarry in the Blessed Land, the more difficult you shall find it to return to the worlds of men."

Owen's heart sank. Already the cords that bound him to his former life were loosening. How much better it would be to remain in Gaelessa and fellowship with Gaelathane and His angels!

"Be not downcast," Celembrose told him. "We shall meet again, beyond pain and sickness and death, beyond the bitter sorrow of mortal partings. Your place in Gaelessa is already reserved for you against that day when you will come to live with us forever."

"Why could I pass through the veil just now but not earlier?"

"The Holy of holies parts only for those who have been sealed with the Blood upon their foreheads and with the Shepherd's love in their hearts," the angel replied. "All others must remain in the Outer Darkness, for nothing unclean may enter this place."

Owen was then escorted back through the barrier, where a smiling Gaelathane embraced him. "Do not grieve this loss," He said. "As Celembrose told you, one day you will come to live with Me in Gaelessa forever, where the Waters of Life never cease to flow from the Tree of trees into the Lake of Love. Here we have no need of sun or moon, for My boundless glory fills this place."

Gaelathane handed Owen His shining, curve-topped rod. "No longer shall you bear a shepherd's crook of wood," He said. "Instead, the Shepherd of shepherds gives you His own Tree-staff."

As soon as Owen took the staff, Gaelathane, Gaelessa and the Tree vanished. In their place appeared Mt. Morwynion's twin rows of myndyn trees. Weary beyond endurance, Owen lay down at the foot of one of the trees and fell into a deep, dreamless sleep.

When he awoke, the morning sun was streaming between the myndyn colonnades. Surely the Tree, the angels, Gaelathane and Gaelessa had all been a dream! As Owen stretched and rolled over, a sharp pain pierced his side. Sitting up, he discovered he had been lying on the shining shepherd's crook Gaelathane had given him. Then he heard the sounds of whistling and shouting.

"Owen? Owen!" people were calling. "Where are you? How could one lad cause so much bother? Owen! Answer us!"

Staggering to his feet, he was about to shout a reply when a meaty hand clamped over his mouth, and another hand drove him to the ground. He struggled to break his assailant's grip until he felt a searing pain below his ear, and blood trickled down his neck.

"Don't make a sound, or I'll slit yer scrawny throat!" growled an all-too-familiar voice. "I ain't forgotten that lump on the noggin you gave me. Nobody strikes Dask and gets away with it. Nobody!"

Dask! Having failed to eliminate Owen and his companions with the avalanche, was he bent on finishing the job now? Owen squirmed again, but the mutton-man only tightened his grasp.

Footsteps approached. "I heard something over here," said Mirrah's voice. Then she and Percy stepped into the sunlight. Before Owen knew what was happening, Dask had released him and was choking Mirrah in the crook of one arm, pressing a razor-edged flint knife against her throat with his other hand. Mirrah's eyes bulged with terror as she clawed at her captor's arms.

"Enough!" Dask roared, and he squeezed Mirrah's neck until she turned purple. "Now that I've got you, I'm never letting you go again. You're coming with me, wench, or I'll cut yer throat!"

"Leave her alone!" cried Percy, and he struck Dask in the back with his fist. The mutton-man grimaced with pain before kicking the prince aside. Owen noted then that Dask had tied his coat around his chest instead of wearing it across his shoulders, undoubtedly to protect the arrow wound in his back.

Dask coughed and spat blood. "Thought I was finished back there, didn't you," he rasped. "It takes more than a stick in the back to stop Dask. Wolf's arrow had to get through my sheepskin before it hit me. After you and your filthy friends left, I patched myself up. Once I figured you were heading for the mountains and freedom, I decided to bury you all and go it alone. Some day, I'll make the lot of you wish you'd died like rats under that rock pile!"

The mutton-man was dragging Mirrah away when he gestured at Owen's staff. "I'll take that, too, runt!" he said hoarsely. "I'm going to break out of this blasted wood, just as the dremlens do."

Owen snatched up the staff. "No!" he shouted. "Gaelathane gave me this staff as a present, so now it belongs to me, not you."

"Hand it over, or so help me, I'll cut this wastrel to pieces!"

With a lazy flick of his wrist, Dask drew blood on Mirrah's throat. The girl stiffened with pain and fright. Her eyes pleaded with Owen. *Please don't let him kill me! Just give him the rod!*

Owen held up his lightstaff. "You can have it—in exchange for Mirrah," he said. "It's a fair trade. You get what you want, and we get what we want." Owen wasn't accustomed to bargaining, but it was the best he could do in the heat of the moment.

Dask's eyes narrowed, and he tightened his arm around Mirrah's neck like a hairy vice. She made gasping and choking sounds.

"Stop it! You're hurting her!" Percy cried. He leapt onto Dask's back, but the other man shrugged him off like an annoying flea.

"You ain't in any position to haggle," Dask told Owen, spitting more blood. "The staff or she dies. Which will it be?"

Reluctantly, Owen tossed the lightstaff at Dask's feet. "Take it, then," he grumbled. "You won't get far with Mirrah. Alone, you might have had a chance of escaping, but now my friends and I will track you down and take her back, dead or alive. Be warned!"

"I'll be long gone before then, and you'll never find me!" Dask sneered. Grabbing a fistful of Mirrah's hair, he jerked her backwards. She tried to push him away, but he pulled on her hair all the harder, dragging her screaming into the surrounding forest.

Owen was casting about for a sharp stick with which to attack Dask when a brown blur flashed past him and exploded in Dask's face. Shrilly screeching, a bird was assailing the mutton-man with wings, beak and claws. Owen wondered whether the tiny bundle of feathers was defending her nest. In trying to ward off his tormentor, Dask released his hold on Mirrah. She fled like a frightened deer toward Mt. Morwynion. Prince Percy followed close behind.

Harassed by the swooping bird, Dask lumbered off, waving his arms as he went. Hoping to recover his staff, Owen hurried after him. Still the bird dove on Dask with the ferocity of a hawk. Suddenly, he stopped and with a violent backhand, knocked his flying foe out of the air. Leering at Owen, he continued on his way.

The sparrow. Owen knew it was she before he reached the tiny form lying motionless on the ground. He picked up her bruised body, and she quivered, her eyes rolling back in her head. One wing hung at an awkward angle. Her heart fluttered in his hand.

Forgetting Dask and the lightstaff, Owen raced down the myndyn corridor with Sparrow's body. Rolin, Scanlon and Timothy met him with drawn swords at the mountain's gold-arched entry.

"Are you all right?" Rolin asked him with a worried look. "Mirrah and Percy just came in, and they told us what happened. You were very brave to face down Dask like that. Where is he now?"

"I don't know," said Owen. Tears streamed down his cheeks.

"Where did you get a lightstaff?" Scanlon added.

"Look! He's bleeding at the neck!" said Timothy.

"I'll explain later," Owen said, brushing past the three outringers. Into the dark tunnel he rushed, for no glynnies awaited to greet him with their cheery talisynds. Once, he stumbled and nearly dropped his precious burden. Then Caerillion's lights came into sight, and Owen quickened his pace. Down the stone stairs, through the azalea gardens and across the springy turf he bounded.

Bending beneath the overhanging canopy of leaves, he entered the poplar pavilion. Inside, he found Mirrah, Percy, Bembor, Elwyn, Marlis and Gwynneth gathered around Gisella.

"There you are!" Mirrah greeted him with a hug and a kiss. "Thank you for saving my life!" Then she saw the sparrow lying in his hands, and a cloud passed across her face. "I suppose I should thank this bird, too. But what has happened, and where is Dask now? Surely you have not managed to kill him, have you?"

"Never mind Dask," said Owen, and he knelt before Gisella. After pouring out the tale of Sparrow's selfless act, he raised his hands to the Spirewalker in supplication. Had she not sung of the glynnies' healing arts? If anyone could save the sparrow, the Spirewalker could. "Please," he said tearfully. "Please help my friend. She's terribly hurt. Don't let her die. You can heal her!"

Gently, Gisella took the sparrow in her own hands and stroked its wounded wing. Then a curious light dawned in her large, liquid eyes and she turned a questioning gaze upon Owen.

"Why do you care so deeply for this bird?" she asked him.

The heat rose in Owen's face. "Begging your pardon, ma'am, but the sparrow and I met on a hill near my village. She brought me here to Feirian to find a lost sheep, and she led my friends and me nearly all the way to Caerillion. I don't want to lose her."

"Some hurts only Gaelathane can mend," Gisella said.

"Gaelathane is not here!" Owen protested. A chill wind like a borwog's breath came over him. He could not bear the thought of life without Sparrow. If she died, he would hunt down Dask and strike him dead, even if it meant visiting every myndyn world.

"Oh, but He is!" said Gisella. "He is present wherever and whenever we invite Him. Let me ask Him now to heal this sparrow. Then we glynnies will do what we can with the gifts He has given us." The Spirewalker bowed her head over the bird, her lips moving soundlessly. Then she sang out a string of musical notes.

Suddenly, hundreds of wispwings appeared under the poplar pavilion. Three darted down to land on Gisella's palm. One of them Owen recognized as Athyrea, who played her talisynd's light upon the sparrow while her companions went about setting the bird's broken wing. Owen watched anxiously as his friend's breathing steadied and the pulse in her breast grew stronger. Then her sleek head drooped and her whole body relaxed in Gisella's hand.

Dread seized Owen's heart. "Is she . . . dead?" he asked.

"No," the Spirewalker replied. "She is merely sleeping. The light of Gaelathane brings peace and rest to any creature it touches. This bird shall sleep long and deeply now. We will know in a few days whether or not she is to recover from her injuries."

"Why not use a full-sized staff on her instead of a talisynd?" Gwynneth suggested. "I should think the more light, the better."

The Spirewalker shook her head. "Too much of the light can overwhelm smaller creatures such as this sparrow. In the hands of a skillful wispwing, a single talisynd can work greater good in these cases than would the more powerful light of larger staffs."

That day, the wispwings built the bird a nest of twigs and faery hair under one of Caerillion's maple trees. There she lay, moving only to sip the nectar the faeries fed her. Owen kept vigil at her side, hardly eating or sleeping, despite his friends' pleas. What if Sparrow should die while he was asleep or away from his post?

Then one evening, Rolin and Scanlon rushed up to Owen, their faces flushed with triumph. After spending many fruitless hours searching for Dask around Mt. Morwynion and elsewhere, they had nearly given up. Then Scanlon had spotted what appeared to be a fire at the bottom of a canyon. Upon investigating, the two found a "fire" of an unexpected sort: a curve-topped lightstaff.

Leaping to his feet, Owen took the shining crook from Rolin. "This is the very staff Dask stole from me!" he marveled.

"I've never seen the like of it," said Scanlon. "Is it yours, or did you borrow it from Trellisant or one of the other slipwings?"

"No, this one is mine," Owen said, admiring its smooth lines. If only shining it on Sparrow would heal her! Recalling Gisella's warning, however, he pointed the staff well away from the bird.

The other outringers were strolling up to the maple when Rolin asked Owen, "Then where did you get a staff of your own?"

Owen described his encounters with Gaelathane, the Tree, Gaelessa and the angels. When he had finished, his friends regarded him with a newfound respect and admiration.

"So Gaelathane gave you His very own staff, eh?" said Scanlon doubtfully. "We have never known Him as a shepherd before."

Marlis quickly put in, "The King must think very highly of you, to invite you to visit His country. Death is the usual doorway by which most people enter Gaelessa, and very few ever return."

Bembor combed gnarled fingers through his long, white beard. "If it weren't for this staff, I wouldn't have believed a word of your tale," he told Owen. "The Tree of trees is a *myndyn*? Who would have guessed it! I always assumed we had to climb the Tree to enter other worlds, just as we do our Lucambrian torsils."

"Maybe the Tree acts like a myndyn only in Feirian," Elwyn suggested. After some discussion, the others agreed. Owen thought Elwyn's idea made sense, too, though he was new to the Tree.

Afterwards, everyone embraced Owen and welcomed him to Gaelathane's family. He found the attention refreshing but bewildering, for even his parents had not lavished such affection upon him. Would he ever see Tadwyn and Gyrta again, and if so, would they believe the stories of all his marvelous adventures?

Putting aside his homesickness, he returned to his sparrow-vigil. Despair seized his soul. Despite the glynnies' ministrations, the bird was growing weaker by the hour. That night, Owen knelt and prayed beside the pitiful bundle of brown feathers.

"Dear Gaelathane," he said. "I've met You only once, but my friends tell me once is enough. I do know You've changed me on the inside. Please, change Sparrow on the inside, too. She is so badly hurt the glynnies cannot help her. I don't want her to die."

When he looked up, the bird was breathing more easily, and her heartbeat seemed stronger. Tears of gratitude welled in his eyes.

After the night-glynnies had departed, leaving Caerillion in twilight, Owen surrendered to sleep himself. As soon as his eyelids closed, he was walking the Downs again, Melina at his side. To his dismay, she looked as pallid as sun-bleached sheep bones.

A bright light awoke him. Gaelathane was bending over the sparrow. Picking up the battered bird, He cradled her in His hands. Owen saw a brief glow and heard a feeble chirp. The chirp became a trill, and the trill, a full-fledged warble. With a flash of wings, the sparrow flew into Caerillion's lofty heights. Her joyous song echoed through the airy cavern, and then she was gone.

Gaelathane turned and smiled at Owen, but before the shepherd boy could thank Him, the King had disappeared. Reassured that all was well, Owen lay back against the maple trunk and slept.

CHAPTER 16

THE PLENION OF GAELATHANE

O wen dozed most of the next day. When he awoke, the empty nest convinced him he hadn't been dreaming. Thanks to Gaelathane, his sparrow had mended. She had flown back into the world outside. Would she ever return to Caerillion?

The outringers had left him some bread and broiled fish beside the maple tree. He had just tucked away the last crumb when Gisella came floating toward him through the trees. Her feet hardly seemed to touch the ground. Owen straightened his slept-in clothes and ran his fingers through his mop of hair, but Gisella gave no sign she was displeased with his rumpled appearance.

"I rejoice with you over your feathered friend's recovery," she said, though her eyes were deep wells of pain. "As I have told you, some wounds Gaelathane alone can heal. His touch works more wonders than a hundred of our talisynds. Now I wish to speak more freely with you of matters that concern us both. Come with me to a special place where we may talk more privately."

The Spirewalker led Owen through acres of trees and flowers where other slipwings were at work picking, pruning and weeding. Near the cavern's center, Gisella stopped beside a high, curving stone wall. A clear stream ran from underneath it. Owen half expected to see Athyrea and Osmund flitting among the mosses and ferns covering the wall. Gisella circled the enclosure until she reached a door set in one side. Taking a key from her gown, she opened the door and ushered Owen through the arched entrance.

Inside, he found a quiet garden. Murmuring through it, the stream lingered in a placid pool ringed with birches. A pinkish-white film resembling spent cherry blossoms lay lightly upon the water. Around the pool stood more carven slipwing figures like those Owen had seen in the Valley of Glynnhaven. A skilled sculptor had etched the lines of ancient sorrows upon their noble faces.

"Welcome to the *Glynniard-alffornion*—the Losswing Gardens," Gisella said, guiding Owen to a stone bench beside the water. "You are the first of your kind ever to enter this place. All the streams that pour into Caerillion eventually gather in the Wingwater Pool here and flow hence by this brook to join the River Blynnys."

Owen had just seated himself on the bench when a slender wispwing girl about three feet tall fluttered awkwardly over the wall and landed heavily on the bank of the pond. Tensing her muscles, she tried to fly again. Her dull gray wings trembled like a dying butterfly's before lifelessly drooping down her back.

The Spirewalker put a finger to her lips as the wailing wispwing shook her body the way a dog shakes water from its fur. Like withered autumn leaves, her wings dropped off and floated to earth. Trembling, she picked them up and kissed them. Then she flung the faded gossamer wisps into the pool. Without looking back, the new slipwing fled the Losswing Gardens by way of the door.

Gisella sighed, her alabaster hands lying limply in her lap. She gazed wistfully at the discarded wings as they sailed down the stream and under the wall. "Wingshed is an important rite of passage in a glynnie's life," she said. "Most wispwings come here to shed their wings and cast them into the pool. The wings journey down to the Sea of Thionne, where it is said the angels gather them for glynnies yet unborn. 'Losswings' often tarry in this garden for weeks, grieving over their newly earthbound state. If one looks long and deeply enough into the pond, he will glimpse the faces of glynnies who have strewn their wings upon the water."

Owen sneaked a peek at the pool, but he saw no faces.

"After mourning their fallen wings," Gisella went on, "the loss-wings put on a slipwing's garb, which is woven from the bark of the risen Tree. You might say we thereby 'put on the Tree,' reminding us throughout life of the King's death on our behalf."

"Why did you bring me here alone?" Owen asked her.

Gisella gazed at him earnestly. "Outside this sanctuary of silence, wispwing tongues are apt to wag, and no whispered word escapes the dronzils, even in their deepest, darkest *slunge* pits."

"That's impossible. The beasts have no ears!"

"Hush!" said Gisella. "Not all hearing comes by the ear. Have you not noticed how voices die when dronzils appear? They draw all things into themselves—warmth, light, sound and life itself. Even in Caerillion our secrets are not safe, for the cavern magnifies noises and funnels them through our tunnel into the outer world.

"For that reason, we take counsel only by the Wingwater Pool. These thick walls and the ferns that festoon them tend to trap stray sounds, while the babbling of running water further masks our voices. Also, the 'fuzzy birches' we have planted around the pool help deaden sounds with their hairy leaves and soft bark."

Owen rubbed a birch leaf between his fingers. Its downy coating had the texture of fine felt. When he poked the tree's trunk, its spongy bark yielded to him like the flesh of a living creature.

Reaching beneath one of the birches, Gisella plucked a large, tan-capped fungus with a bulbous stem. "In my former wispwing days," she said, "I looked after *campions*, as we call mushrooms." She wafted the fungus under her nose. "This *Bolytarn*—'King Campion'—is my favorite, both for its pleasing odor and flavor.

"Whether you realize it or not, Owen," she continued, "Feirian's fate may depend upon you. The *Plenion*, Gaelathane's prophetic riddle, may speak of you. It goes like this in the tongue of men:

When trees are felled, and joy is quelled,
And glynnies 'neath the mountain dwell;
When all is lost in fire and frost,
As darkness oozes in the dell—

Then he shall come, the shepherd's son,
From healing hills, the willing one;
With feathered guide he will abide,
Till death has doomed and deed is done.

Of mortal mold, his hand shall hold
A glynnie dying of the cold;
Though others still the chill may kill,
This friend will free us as foretold.

But ruin he brings to all that rings
Within the grotto where she sings
Who lights the fires and strikes the spires
To bring the Light to living things.

To heal the sore, set right the score;
Through bleeding breach send back the boar
Who takes the place of all his race,
That brought the blight and bitter war.

No sheep will do, no ram or ewe,
But only one of faithful few
Who dares to plunge beneath the slunge
And give his life to pay their due.

Before the end, the slunge will send
Its loathsome legions for revenge;
Prepare the fire and flee the ire
They bring upon the faeries' friend!

If twice he dies before their eyes,
Then every world shall be their prize;
To fight the flood, bring back the blood
That strips away their dark disguise.

The Plenion's words left Owen in the grip of a sudden chill. "Why are you telling me this?" he asked. "'Darkness oozes in the dell' sounds like the dronzils, but does the 'feathered guide' mean the sparrow? *Who* is doomed to death? *What* deed is done?"

In answer, Gisella quoted, "'Of mortal mold, his hand shall hold a glynnie dying of the cold.' When Athyrea told me how you had saved her life, I suspected you were the long awaited 'shepherd's son,' one who would restore our world to what it was before the Wasting began. After you and your friends brought 'ruin' to the 'grotto,' I became even more convinced you were the one."

Owen found himself saying, "But why must this person be a shepherd? Why not a cobbler or a baker or a smith or a miller?"

The Spirewalker replied, "Perhaps our deliverer must be a shepherd because sheepherders have cleared so many myndyn forests to make way for pasturelands. Indeed, shepherds have felled more trees even than woodcutters, who at least have an eye for the health of their woodlands. Sheep themselves have destroyed many a thriving forest by grazing and trampling the tree seedlings. Since shepherds have caused our people such grief, should we not expect that a shepherd should also redress those wrongs?"

Owen was feeling more and more uneasy. "I have never cut down any trees—except maybe dead ones," he said firmly.

"Maybe you have not," said Gisella with a wry smile. "However, your own people have leveled vast forests in bygone years."

Recalling tales of the Greatwood's destruction, Owen winced. Although his sheepherding ancestors had laid waste to that forest more out of fear than from greed, they and their children had profited when grass sprang from the ashes of the Great Burning.

"I . . . I still don't see what any of this has to do with me," he said, avoiding Gisella's gaze. "What difference does it make if my people—or any people—want to cut down their own trees?"

"It makes a great deal of difference if some of those trees are myndyns," said Gisella. "All myndyn trees point to Feirian, and without them, you and your sheep are doomed! Grass and clover, flax and spelt—all would die without our help. Where you graze your sheep today, there once waved the largest myndyn forest in any world. Now the door to your homeland is all but closed to us, and our land languishes because death's debt remains unpaid."

"How can I help?" asked Owen, bewildered. "I cannot undo what has been done; I cannot replant all the myndyns that my folk have felled. Sheep, not trees, are what I know best. I only want to return home and help my parents see to their flocks and garden."

"Home has been within your grasp, if you had wished to go."

Owen stared at the Spirewalker. "What are you saying?"

"Athyrea told me how she opened a porthyl in the *gwanlen*—the veil between worlds—to help you survive in Swyndon. You could have done the same thing by using your friends' talisynds."

"Why didn't you tell me so before?" Owen cried. He clutched the staff Gaelathane had given him. With it, he could burn a hole in the pesky gwanlen-veil. Then he could walk up to his parents' front door to be *seen*, to hold and to be held, to touch and to be touched, to speak and to be spoken to. Life would be satisfying and good again, except for Melina. He would always miss Melina.

"I did not tell you earlier because you cannot leave Feirian until the Caerillion Council determines your fate. For the present, please do not reveal the gwanlen secret to your companions."

"Why—I mean *what*—is the gwanlen for?" he asked.

"Its main purpose is to separate worlds one from another, but thanks to the myndyns, we glynnies can move about behind the gwanlen without being seen. Only when we actually reach our destination—be it a clump of heather, a hawk's nest or a beaver's den—do we enter through a porthyl and go about our business."

"Begging your pardon, good lady," said Owen, "but when will your councilors make it *their* business to decide upon my fate?"

Gesturing toward the pool, Gisella said, "They already have."

Owen glanced about the garden, seeing no one but the statues. "It appears to me we are alone in this place," he said.

"We are—and we aren't," the Spirewalker lightly replied. She pointed at the slipwing statues. "Behold the Caerillion Council!"

Owen gulped. "Those sculptures aren't really alive, are they?"

"They aren't sculptures," said Gisella. "As glynnies age, we fall into a dreaming state between waking and sleeping. Gaelathane may call us home then, or He may leave us in Feirian to serve Him longer. All the Spirewalkers since Starlyss are still here in this garden, no doubt dreaming of their carefree wispwing years."

"Are you telling me they stand there motionless day and night?" Owen asked. "Do they sleep that way, too? What do they eat?"

"'Sleepwings,' as we call them, may remain sitting or standing in one spot for months or years. With difficulty, these sleepers can be awakened, but otherwise, they do not respond to the world around them. They neither eat nor drink, for they draw their strength and sustenance from the collective light of our talisynds."

"But what good is a sleeping council?"

"Do not underestimate my ancestors. Awake or asleep, their wisdom and knowledge are beyond measure. Patience is necessary if one is seeking answers from a sleepwing. Go ahead, touch one."

Approaching an elegant, ivory-skinned woman, Owen touched her warm but wrinkled hand. "When may I go home?" he asked.

If the sleepwing had heard his question, her face did not betray it. Though her eyes and mouth remained closed, Owen heard a whisper like the soft fanning of faery wings. "The shepherd's son cannot leave. He must make amends for the Myndyn Hall."

Owen was about to touch the next "statue" when Gisella struck a listening pose, and a look of alarm spread across her fair face. Owen heard nothing but the pleasant purling of the stream.

"We must leave immediately!" she cried. "Caerillion has been breached!" Rising from the bench, Gisella darted out the door.

"Leave?" Owen called after her. "We just got here, and I haven't talked with all the sleepwings yet." Grumbling, he followed the Spirewalker out of the Losswing Gardens. As soon as he opened the door and stepped outside, a buzzing sound assaulted his ears.

Some distance away, a swarm of chattering wispwings was noisily hovering over a grove of trees. Owen was reminded of the way angry bees will attack a hungry bear that has ripped open their nest. Setting off at a lope, he threaded his way through crowds of agitated slipwings before reaching the center of the faery swarm.

The wispwings were at war. Rival faeries must have broken into Caerillion and were waging a fierce battle with their foes. At least, that was how matters first appeared to Owen. Then he realized the wispwings were not actually fighting with one another. Rather, they were spinning about a stand of dying myndyn trees.

Pushing between more slipwings, Owen entered the glade. He found the Spirewalker sitting alone beside a myndyn, her head bowed. Owen felt a gnawing chill as he knelt next to her.

"What is the matter?" he asked. "Why is everyone so upset?"

Gisella began rocking back and forth. "It is too late," she moaned. "We cannot escape. I warned them. Oh, how I warned them not to plant these trees here. But they would not listen. Now comes the reckoning, and a harsh, harsh reckoning it shall be!"

Owen cast about for the cause of Gisella's grief. A patch of darkness was spreading like a pool of poison beneath the withered myndyns. An aching cold benumbed his face as he crawled closer to the pool and thrust a long stick into it. The end came away white with frost. The slunge had come to Caerillion to stay.

"There you are!" Rolin called out to Owen, shoving his way through the throngs of slipwings. "Where have you been, anyway? We've been searching Caerillion high and low for you."

As Owen described his visit to the Losswing Gardens, his other companions popped into the grove. The outringers trained their staffs on the hole, sending bright light-beams lancing into it.

"You are wasting your time," said the Spirewalker dully.

"I suspect you are correct," said Rolin. "However, you must not surrender to despair. Your people still need you. We all need you. Please tell us why this black pit has appeared in this place."

Only the Spirewalker's mouth moved. "What is there to tell? Because someone has cut down one of these myndyns, we are all doomed. In a matter of months, the dronzil-slunge will consume Mt. Morwynion from the inside out, even if no other trees are felled. The People of the Glen must now seek another home, but where shall we go? Slunge pits have polluted nearly all of Feirian."

"I don't understand," said Marlis. "If somebody cut down a myndyn tree on the other side, where is the fallen log? Where is the stump? Whatever happens to a torsil in one world happens in the other as well. Everybody knows that. It's basic torsil lore."

"Not all passage-trees are alike," Gisella reminded her. "To ensure us an open door to all of Gaelathane's worlds, He created each myndyn as two identical trees, not one. Regardless of what happens to its twin 'on the other side,' as you put it, the myndyn living in Feirian ordinarily remains alive and unscathed."

"Ordinarily?" said Owen.

Gisella looked up at him. "Yes. Nobody realized until it was too late that killing one tree of a myndyn pair creates a rift or crack in the curtain between worlds, letting in the slunge. In time, that creeping darkness will devour the live tree remaining in Feirian."

Rolin and Marlis glanced at one another, and Rolin said, "We were just discussing that mystery last night. It seems to us that these dark pits are places where Limbo has broken through."

"Limbo? What is that?" Gisella asked.

Marlis explained, "Limbo is our name for the void that lies between worlds. Rolin and I once fell into that void, and were it not for our lightstaffs, we might be trapped there still. Limbo is never satisfied; no matter how much it swallows, it still has room for more light, more worlds, more of the King's created works."

"Indeed," Gisella gloomily remarked.

"Whatever you want to call it," Scanlon put in, "we still don't know how to get rid of it. These black pools erupt like weeping sores across the land, only they weep darkness and death."

Although he couldn't be sure, Owen thought Gisella looked sharply at Scanlon. "To heal the sore," the Plenion had said. What kind of sore had Gaelathane meant when He spoke those words?

"That still doesn't explain the borwogs, or dronzils," Mirrah pointed out. "What are they, and why do they live in those pits?"

She never received a reply, for with a *WHOOSH*, all the wisp-wings in Mt. Morwynion fled, leaving their slipwing elders to mill around in twilight. As Owen raised his shepherd's lightstaff to drive back the darkness, the smell of smoke trickled into his nostrils. Fire was threatening Caerillion, and he was trapped inside.

CHAPTER 17

THE UNWILLING ONE

F ire!" cried Gisella, her face blanching beyond its usual pallor. "Must we face two foes on the selfsame day?"

Trellisant trotted in. "The fire is afar off, milady," he said. "We are safe enough for the present. The flames cannot reach us in here. Wispwings are fanning the smoke away from the entrance to prevent our air from fouling. I have posted lookouts around the mountain to warn us when the blaze approaches our valley."

"When?" Gisella echoed. "Can we not turn aside this fire?"

The guard hesitated. "According to the lookouts, the flames stretch in an unbroken wall across the Glynnion Wood from north to south. High winds are driving them toward us faster than a wispwing can fly. We may need to block the entrance."

"This is Wolf's doing!" said Gwynneth. "He has been threatening to burn the Deadwood, as he calls it, to wipe out the myndyn trees. He and his men must have set those fires this morning."

"The fools!" Gisella groaned. "I might have known men were behind this mischief. They destroy what they do not understand."

Owen understood all too well. The mutton-men were burning the only trees that could take him back to the Downs, to Swyndon and to his parents. Home was slipping through his fingers.

"Fire always burns most swiftly uphill," said Scanlon. "Those flames may well reach us ere dawn. We can take refuge inside this mountain, but what about the glynnies caught outside?"

"What indeed?" Gisella said with a bitter laugh. "If the myndyn trees burn, most of the wispwings serving in the Outer Worlds will be forever trapped there. They will become exiles." The Spirewalker's eyes dulled with resignation as she murmured, "The end comes upon us in fire and frost, just as the Plenion predicted."

"The Plenion?" asked Bembor. "What is that?"

Nervously pacing, Gisella recited the Plenion of Gaelathane. When she had finished, the outringers looked at her expectantly.

"If you are asking us what this prophecy means," Rolin said, "I am afraid we won't be of much help. I suspect you would know better than any of us how to interpret Gaelathane's words."

"You are correct," said the Spirewalker. "Yet, until your arrival here with Owen's 'feathered guide,' the Plenion's verses were murkier than a myndyn-mist. By bringing 'ruin' to the Glynnspire Cave, you have already partially fulfilled the Plenion. To complete it, 'the shepherd's son' must accomplish all that is written of him."

"And who is the shepherd's son?" Marlis asked.

The Spirewalker pointed a long finger at Owen. "It is he."

Owen's friends turned doubting eyes upon him. Scanlon said, "How can you be so sure Owen is the one? After all, many a shepherd's son must have found his way into Feirian over the years."

Gisella came to Owen's rescue. "But none of them has fulfilled the Plenion as completely as Owen son of Tadwyn has done."

"What is this 'shepherd's son' supposed to *do*?" asked Rolin.

Gisella's brow knitted. "The second half of the Plenion remains unclear to me. Someone is to 'send back' a 'boar' though a 'bleeding breach.' If you are right about the slunge, it is a 'breach' in Limbo. Yet, wild pigs have never roamed Feirian's forests."

"Not unless you count *princely* pigs," Mirrah muttered.

"I beg your pardon!" huffed Percy. "My manners are impeccable! Besides, I refuse to set foot anywhere near those nasty freezing holes. Taking such foolish risks is the proper task of servants."

Mirrah glared at him and snapped, "Who made that rule?"

Raising an arrogant eyebrow, Percy said, "I did."

Owen cleared his throat. "I am the Boar." Then he told his listeners the tale of his desperate battle with the tusked beast.

The Spirewalker paled. "If Owen son of Tadwyn is both the shepherd's son and the boar, the Plenion decrees he must throw himself into a slunge pit to heal Feirian and all other worlds."

"That is absurd!" Marlis exclaimed.

"No, Mother, it makes perfect sense," said Gwynneth. "Once a month, Wolf and his men sacrifice a sheep to the slunge pit they call 'Black Lake.' Feeding Day is supposed to help keep the borwogs in check, but they still attack and kill people. Now I think Gaelathane is saying the sacrifice must be a man, not an animal."

As the Plenion's scattered pieces fell into place, Owen began to shake. He thought of the many sheepshuns he had witnessed. Was he about to play the part of the helpless ram or ewe, slaughtered to appease an enemy whose very presence froze the blood?

Marlis gave Owen a sickly smile and patted his hand. "The Plenion does say the shepherd's son must be *willing*. No one can force you to go through with such a terrible sacrifice. No one."

"Do not forget that the Code of Caerillion demands a reckoning for the Glynnspire Cave's destruction," said Gisella heavily. She lowered her head. "Knowing your love of Gaelathane, I have so far shielded you from the Caerillion Council. I can do so no longer. The council is now demanding the ultimate penalty."

She regarded Owen with mingled pity and severity. "First, I must ask the shepherd's son his decision. Are you willing to die?"

Terror turned Owen's heart into a wild thing threatening to burst out of his chest. His tongue swelled in his parched mouth, and all his limbs went limp. Unable to speak, he shook his head.

Disappointment and understanding flowed from Gisella's eyes. Then she drew herself up. "In that case, I must now pronounce sentence upon you and your friends. For your offenses, one of you must die by impalement tomorrow at dawn. Who shall it be?"

The outringers leapt to their feet. "None of us shall die for your arbitrary code!" Rolin roared. "What right have you to sentence Gaelathane's servants to death? I contest your verdict!"

Gisella held up her hands. "Although our code may seem arbitrary to you, it is nonetheless the law of this land, and you have transgressed it. You may not appeal. If I could change your fate, I would. Now, who will step forward to take the Drowdon-spike?"

"I will," Rolin growled. "As Lucambra's king, it is my duty."

"No, my husband, you must not!" cried Marlis. "Let me!"

Scanlon stuck out his chin. "What keeps us from walking out of Caerillion today and returning home as free men and women?"

The Spirewalker's hands dropped loosely to her sides, and she said, "You would not be allowed to leave. Our slipwings are well armed and would strike you down if you attempted to escape."

"Must one of us truly die?" wailed Marlis.

Gisella's mournful gaze strayed back to Owen. "The council has granted me one concession," she said. "If the shepherd's son will embrace his prophetic destiny, his death shall also satisfy the Code of Caerillion's demands, and the rest of you may go free."

"Noooo!" yelled Owen, and off he ran. Dashing up the stairs, he darted through the great tunnel. Outside, haze from the burning forest tinged the evening light a sickly yellow. The acrid smoke seared his laboring lungs. Bending over, he gasped for breath.

Was it his fault the Glynnspire Cave's ceiling had collapsed? If the glynnies wanted someone to blame, Dask was their man. Let *him* be impaled upon the Drowdon-spire and appease the council with his blood. Then Owen and his friends could go home.

Cupping his hands around his mouth, Owen shouted, "Dask! Dask? Where are you? You can come out now! All is forgiven. Dask! I know you're still hiding somewhere in these woods. If you show yourself, you may even have my staff back. Daaassssk!"

Batting at the smoke and coughing, Owen continued searching the forest and calling Dask's name. The mutton-man did not appear. Dejected, Owen sat on a log and wept. What was he to do? He could not return to Caerillion, where he was certain the outringers would have him impaled or thrown into a slunge pit to save their own skins. He had to flee to another world. Now that he owned a lightstaff, he could easily break through the gwanlen and escape.

"Where would you go without your friends?"

Owen practically jumped out of his tunic. Gaelathane was sitting on the log beside him. Owen scooted away from the King.

"With or without my friends, I am returning home to Swyndon," he declared. "Why should I sacrifice my life for Gisella's silly old code? What happened to the Glynnspire Cave was not my fault."

"Whoever tries to save his life will lose it," said Gaelathane gently. "And whoever loses his life for My sake will find it."

"What does that mean?"

"Look at Me."

Owen forced himself to stare into Gaelathane's ageless eyes. He found no condemnation there, only love and acceptance.

"Do you remember the day you saved Melina from the boar?"

Owen numbly nodded. How could he forget? The wild beast's savage attack had marred his legs with deep, disfiguring scars.

Gaelathane said, "I, too, was cruelly wounded at the hands of an enemy. Behold the Scars that shall never fade for all eternity!"

For the first time, Owen noticed angry stripes crisscrossing Gaelathane's hands and arms. Even His face bore the telltale marks of terrible wounds inflicted by the likes of whips or knives.

"As you once risked your life for Melina and your sheep," Gaelathane said, "I am the Good Shepherd Who laid down His life for His sheep. They were straying far from Me, but now I am bringing them together into one flock that they may cease their wandering ways. If you would face death for the sake of a shepherdess and a few sheep, will you not do so to save an entire world and its people? If Feirian falls, all creation falls with it."

"You can always make more worlds," Owen sullenly replied.

"I cannot make another Feirian like this one, or another Rolin or a Marlis or a Gwynneth or a Timothy—or an Owen. Neither shall I force My will upon you. Yet I beseech you by My scars to consider this: I died for all, the holy for the unholy, that all might live in the spirit. Will you not obey that all may live in the body?"

"I don't want to die!" Owen cried, and a dam burst in his soul. Sobs racked his body as tears poured down his cheeks. "Why me? Why can't Dask or Bembor or Rolin or Percy or . . . or somebody else suffer the spike? I don't deserve to die; I'm too young to die!"

"No one is too young to die," said the King. "The fear of death enslaves, but I shall make you free. You dread facing the unknown, yet My presence will comfort you. I died alone so that you would not need to, and I delivered you from Gundul's fires."

"Then deliver me again this one last time," Owen pleaded.

"So I shall, yet not here and not today. This day you must be lifted up that many lives may be preserved. Now I bid you farewell. If you choose love, great shall be your reward."

"Wait!" Owen cried, but the King had already disappeared.

"I shall send you another comforter," His voice whispered. Then the smoke-filled forest fell silent again, as if all of creation were awaiting Owen's decision. Would he be the willing one?

Owen bowed his head. He knew what he must do, but his body refused to budge. The birds twittered in the myndyn trees as dawn's first faint light kissed the land. Owen had spent the entire night with Gaelathane, yet it had seemed but an hour or two.

The bushes parted, and Trellisant appeared carrying a spear. He did not point it in Owen's direction. "Hail, shepherd's son," he said. "The Lady Gisella, your companions and Feirian itself await your presence in Caerillion. May it please you to come with me."

On wooden legs, Owen rose and stiffly followed the guard back through the woods. The smoke was so thick now that he could scarcely see, but Trellisant moved along swiftly and surely. Reaching the corridor between the twin rows of myndyns, they turned toward Mt. Morwynion, now wreathed in a heavy haze.

Other guards met them at the entrance, falling in behind Owen as he followed Trellisant into the tunnel. *Tramp, tramp, tramp,* their feet echoed along the passage, sending chills of fear up Owen's spine. He was a condemned prisoner going to his death.

Inside, Caerillion was brightly lit, but the usual hum and buzz of faery wings and faery voices was absent. Countless wispwings flocked the tree branches overhanging two facing lines of silent slipwings. Still flanked by guards, Owen descended to the city's main level and trudged between the ranks of watchful slipwings.

Would the glynnies grieve for the shepherd's son when he was gone? Would the outringers tell his parents what had befallen their boy? Owen reminded himself he was already dead to everyone who had known him in Swyndon. Today would merely make his death official and his sheepshun final. He regretted that his parents and Melina would never hear his loving words of farewell.

Too soon, the slipwing gauntlet ended at the dying myndyn grove. Owen was shocked at how rapidly the slunge had spread beneath the wilting trees. Even from a distance, he could feel the oily darkness draining the warmth and strength from his body.

A few yards ahead of him, the dreaded Drowdon-spike stood half-buried in the earth. High above it, Rolin hung splayed out, suspended with ropes tied to his arms and legs. Owen's knees buckled at the sight, but Trellisant and another guard supported him. The outringers were doing the same for Marlis, who stared back at Owen with pleading eyes full of anguish and despair.

Trellisant led Owen to a myndyn where Gisella stood with several slipwing attendants. The Spirewalker was pressing a knife against a taut rope tied to the tree. Owen could not bring himself to imagine the consequences if she were to cut through that cord.

Bowing to his mistress, Trellisant said, "I bring you the shepherd's son of his own free will, as you have instructed me."

As Gisella looked up at him, Owen felt an uncanny calm come over him, and he shook off Trellisant's arm. Knowing what he knew, seeing what he had seen, he was sure of what he must do.

"Hello, Owen," said Gisella with uncharacteristic familiarity.

Owen bowed to her. As his head moved, he felt a weight drop onto it. Had one of the ropes broken? Touching his hair, he found a warm ball of feathers. His faithful sparrow had returned.

"Why have you come back to Caerillion?" Gisella asked him.

"As Gaelathane's son, I must fulfill His will," he firmly replied. "As the shepherd's son, I must accept the sentence laid upon me by the Plenion of Gaelathane and by the Caerillion Council." At these words, the murmuring of many voices ran through the assembled glynnies, echoing like a waterfall through the vast cavern. With a whimpering sigh, Marlis fainted into her brother's arms.

The knife trembled in Gisella's outstretched hand. "Do you understand what is being required of you?" she asked Owen.

His heart thudded loudly, painfully. "I do."

"Are you still willing to accept your doom?"

Owen swallowed a hard knot of fear. "I am."

The Spirewalker lowered her hand, her face a marble mask. "Then on behalf of the Caerillion Council, I, Gisella, Spirewalker of Feirian, pronounce this judgment upon you. Owen son of Tadwyn, the shepherd's son, of your own accord you have consented to stand in the place of all your race. You shall commit your living body unto the death of the pit, whence there is no returning to the lands of the living. In exchange, your companions shall be free to sojourn in Feirian or to journey wherever they wish without fear of penalty. Let this sentence be carried out forthwith."

Owen suddenly felt lightheaded, but once again, Trellisant steadied him. At Gisella's command, other guards carefully lowered Rolin to earth and released him from his bonds. Then the ropes were repositioned to hang directly over the slunge pit.

Owen wordlessly pointed to the spectators, and Trellisant nodded. Going to his friends, Owen embraced and wept with each in turn. Last of all, he came to Marlis and Rolin. Sobbing, Marlis clung to him and wet his neck with her tears. "Thank you, dear boy," she whispered in his ear. "Though Rolin and I have known you only a short while, you have become like a second son to us. May Gaelathane have mercy on you for your sacrifice this day!"

When Owen embraced Rolin, the outringer could not speak.

Recalling how Rolin and Marlis had escaped Limbo using their lightstaffs, Owen turned to Gisella and raised his own staff. "May I take this with me?" he asked. A slim hope was better than none.

The Spirewalker shrugged. "You may. But what of the bird?"

Owen had forgotten about his friend. Gently, he plucked her from his head and held her in his hands. "Good-bye, Sparrow," he said. "I am going away now. I won't be coming back this time. You must stay here and lead my friends safely to their homes."

He opened his hands, and the bird flew out. Alighting in a tree, she watched Owen with the glittering eyes of fear.

Following Gisella's instructions, Owen lay face down on the ground. Trellisant and three other guards then tied ropes to his wrists and ankles. Those ropes in turn were attached to the main anchor rope. Pulling on it, Gisella's attendants raised Owen above the earth, and he swung toward the waiting slunge pit. The ropes bit into his flesh as he swayed slowly back and forth over the pit. *This day you must be lifted up that many lives may be preserved.*

Dizzy and sick to his stomach, Owen at last came to rest some fifteen feet above the slunge. His body stiffened with cold, and the crowd's wailing cries faded as Limbo siphoned all sound into itself. Borwog eyes burned redly beneath the slunge's surface.

Come to us! the beasts taunted him. *Come to us, and we will devour you, body, soul and spirit! When we have sucked the life out of you, we will gnaw on your frozen flesh for eternity. Despair and die!*

Owen was ten again, crawling back across a frozen Landon Lake. Then as now he was suspended above a frigid grave. He had tried to spread his weight evenly across the ice, but fractures spiderwebbed beneath his trembling body. Water welled through the widening cracks, and with an awful shriek, the ice gave way.

Into the freezing lake he fell. Icy water closed over his head, stinging his skin with liquid fire. His heavy boots and wool coat dragged him down. He was sinking, dying for the sake of a swan.

While collecting firewood that fateful morning, he had come upon a swan trapped in the frozen lake. After inching across the creaking ice, he used his shepherd's staff to break the bird free. Before he knew it, cracks were snaking from the hole toward him.

Rescued from the lake, he was standing shivering on the shore when his Guardian's voice had told him, "You must return home." Now as he dangled above the slunge-pool, he knew no angelic arms awaited to save him this time. He was returning to a home where suffering, death and darkness had been banished forever.

Then he heard a softer voice in his ear as a wisp of a wing settled on his shoulder. "Take courage, dear friend," said Athyrea, shuddering in Limbo's icy grip. "With Gaelathane, hope and love never die. Farewell in this life! May we meet again in the next."

Athyrea flew away, her prophetic words ringing in Owen's mind like a death knell: *The borwogs shall be thy bane!* He groaned as the ropes went slack and the slunge pit rushed up to engulf him.

The shock of plunging into Landon Lake could not compare with falling into the black pool. Owen dropped his staff and screamed as the slunge burned him with icy fire, smothering his agonized shrieks. Sinking into the frosty, featherbed blackness, he sensed another hapless creature struggling above him, soundlessly thrashing as its life ebbed away. Borwogs rose to meet him, draining the remaining warmth and breath from his helpless body.

He thought, *What if I was not the shepherd's son? Is my death in vain?* Then his limbs froze solid and his heart ceased to beat.

Far above Owen's lifeless form, the witnesses to his sacrifice stood weeping in amazement. "I did not think he could do it," Rolin murmured. "He was a brave lad to take my place like that."

"What of the sparrow?" Marlis said. "She flew right in after him! Why would she throw away her life for a two-legs, anyway?"

Gwynneth remarked, "That bird rarely ever left Owen's side. I think she truly loved him, and she loved him to the end."

"Now we have lost both our guides," Scanlon sadly observed.

All at once, the slunge pool began to bubble and boil. Great tarlike globs formed in the oily blackness. Heaving themselves out of the pool, the lumpy shapes sprouted stumpy legs and arms with clubbed feet and hands. Neckless, earless heads lacking noses or mouths budded from stocky torsos. Silently, the black beasts waddled away from the Limbo pit that had spawned them.

"Dronzils!" Trellisant cried. "Make way for the dronzils!"

Like walking holes, the stolid creatures bored their way through the natural world of light and color. Ignoring the screaming, warm-blooded spectators scattering from them, the dronzils trooped up the stairs, through the entrance tunnel and disappeared outside.

Watching them leave, Gisella gasped, "Never have I seen the dronzils come out after daybreak! Where are they all going?"

Bembor pointed at the tarry pit. The pool had shrunk to a puddle. Then it vanished altogether. "Like rats deserting a flooding cavern," he said, "our freezing foes are fleeing Limbo."

CHAPTER 18

THE LAST SHEEPSHUN

Warmth. Blessed warmth. He was floating in darkness, no longer falling, no longer in pain. He felt only peace, blessed peace. A Star appeared in the blackness, flying toward him at a terrific speed. Its glory engulfed him, and Limbo fled away, for it could not endure the Light. He was caught up in the Light. Its rays shot through him, filling him with the sweetest freedom and gladness he had ever known.

Owen lay in grass so green it hurt his eyes. He stared at and *into* a single blade, seeing every intricate detail of its marvelous inner workings. He was still studying it when a voice commanded his attention, and he looked into the radiant face of Gaelathane.

"Welcome back to Gaelessa!" said the King, and Owen came to stand on his feet. He was dressed in a simple white robe that shone like Gisella's. A fierce joy welled up within him, and words in song sprang to his lips, although he had rarely sung before:

When the darkness had dragged me down into the deep,
And the slunge's slow singing had lulled me to sleep,
Then the King of all kings did reach down with His hand
To deliver my life from the dread Limbo-land!

Now give praise to the One Who in death dealt us life;
By His scars we are healed from the soul's inner strife;
For His love made a way for the lowly to rise,
To a dream after death where the soul never dies!

Praise to Him Whose great heart faced His enemies' hate;
As a sheep before shearers He suffered His fate;
So He left an example for all who would see,
That a life worth the living means dying to *me*.

As Owen sang, other voices joined his. Winged angels beyond count were soaring and circling above him, their faces aglow.

"Let us go," said Gaelathane, smiling. "The Lake awaits us."

Before Owen could blink, the scenery changed. Now he was standing with the King beside the same boundless blue lake he had seen on his earlier visits to Gaelessa. Despite the water's beauty, he shuddered at the memory of his near-drowning in Landon Lake.

Stepping onto the water, Gaelathane walked a few feet across the lake. He turned and beckoned to Owen. "Come," He said.

Owen hesitated. He couldn't swim, much less walk on water.

"You have nothing to fear on the Lake of Love," said Gaelathane warmly. "Join me, and you shall find the desire of your heart."

Curiosity overcoming his dread, Owen planted one foot on the lake, then the other. The water felt cool and firm beneath his feet. Following Gaelathane, he trod the lake's glassy surface, his fear melting into wonder. Everything in Gaelessa was so *different*!

The King's voice rang in his mind. *Yes, My love has perfected Gaelessa, making it unique among worlds. Here, you and I can converse in the language of the spirit, unfettered by flawed mortal speech.*

Communing without words, the two were approaching the lake's center when Owen spied another person on the water. Clothed in light, she was facing away from him, her faery-fine hair streaming down her back like a golden waterfall. In that instant, he *knew*, and in the knowing, his heart raced. His feet followed, carrying him swiftly and effortlessly across the Lake of Love.

Hardly daring to hope, he said, "Melina? Is that you?"

She spun into his embrace, repeating his name. "Owen, Owen, Owen! You're alive! We're alive and together again as one! For so many days I have longed to hold you in my arms but could not."

"Melina, my precious Melina, I have found you at last!" Owen sobbed. *Surely we shall stay here in paradise forever*, he thought. Seeing the look on Gaelathane's face, he knew they could not.

The King said, "Now you both must return to Swyndon and offer a sheepshun of thanks with the lamb whose ears are uncut."

In the snap of a faery's wing, Gaelessa had shrunk to a bright spot. Still holding Melina, Owen hurtled backward through starry space. Then his feet sank into soft earth. He and Melina stood awash in green waves that lapped against familiar low hills. A moaning wind cut through Owen's old homespun tunic. Still spangled with slunge-frost, his shepherd's purse dangled stiffly on his hip.

Wearing her woolen shepherdess's blouse and trousers, Melina looked up at him with tender eyes. "Where are we?" she asked.

"If I'm not mistaken, we're back on the Downs," he replied. Weeping, he drew the shepherdess against him. "Dear Melina! How I have missed you! Where have you been all this time? Please forgive me for calling you 'as bony as a half-starved sheep!'"

Melina's eyes twinkled as she held him at arm's length. "I was thinner than a stick in those days, all right. Do not trouble yourself over spent words. All is forgiven. As to my whereabouts, son of Tadwyn, I have stayed right beside you nearly every day, though you did not recognize me at the time. I was your song sparrow!"

Owen could not believe what he was hearing. *The sparrow.* "But . . . how could you become a bird and change back again?"

Melina laughed. "Come with me, boar-boy, and I shall tell you all while we walk. Since you have lost your staff, we will have to make for Swyndon before the fog rolls in and catches us."

The fog. After years of yearning, she had finally given in to it. One afternoon, she had tarried with her sheep on the Downs. Having taken his flock elsewhere that day, the Boy was not around to prod her back to the upland pastures. Her own sheep sensed when it was time to leave and had ambled homeward. Sitting cross-legged in the tall grass, Melina had waited for the Gray Death.

She wasn't unhappy. Her parents loved her well enough, though few others did. She simply didn't belong in Swyndon. Since she had come from the mist, to the mist she would return.

Breathing in the sweet myndyn-blossom scent, she had found herself in Feirian's forests. When the borwogs came out after dark, she was forced to spend a chilly night perched in the top of a tall tree. In the morning, she was climbing down the tree when her body began to shrink. Her legs shortened and her toes shriveled into curved claws. Feathers sprouted all over her. The longest ones grew from her arms and fingers, forming wings. Her lips froze in a sharp pout, becoming a beak. She had turned into a song sparrow.

"Wait," said Owen. He had been sucking on a grass stem, trying to take in Melina's tale. "How could climbing a tree turn you into a bird? I've never heard of such a thing, not even in Feirian."

Melina shrugged. "I don't know. Being a sparrow wasn't all that pleasant. Even though flying came easily to me, I couldn't get the knack of sparrow-speech, so the other birds ignored me or chased me away." Her lower lip trembled, but no tears filled her eyes.

"As a sparrow, I recalled much about my former life that I have already forgotten now. Still, it was terribly lonely in that 'bird world.' I spent weeks there hopping from myndyn to myndyn, trying to find the tree I had originally climbed. Instead, I happened upon a myndyn that sent me back to Clynnod. After escaping Feirian, I returned straightaway to Lone Oak Hill and waited for you."

Melina and the sparrow had been one and the same! "I enjoyed your companionship on the hill," Owen confessed. "After listening to me read from my journal, you must know of my love for you."

Melina cupped Owen's cheek in her hand. "More than anything and anyone else, I missed my Boy! While we were herding our flocks together, I fell in love with you. I didn't realize it until I had become a bird. Knowing you loved me made my feathered form all the more frustrating, because I wanted to say I loved you, too."

A warm glow spread throughout Owen's body. "When Dask struck you," he said, "I was so afraid of losing you! How daring you were to distract him when he was trying to kidnap Mirrah. But how did you end up in Gaelessa with me? Did the borwogs—?"

Melina smiled. "Didn't you know? I joined you in the slunge pit. I couldn't bear to be separated from you in life or in death."

A lump grew in Owen's throat. "Such love I could never deserve or repay, though I should live a thousand years." Through his tears, Melina-the-shepherdess looked as fetching as ever in the afternoon sun. He did a double take. Melina's striking features and ageless, widely spaced eyes reminded him of a young slipwing's.

"Why didn't you tell me before?" he said quietly.

"That I loved you? I was a sparrow then, remember?"

"No, that you were a glynnie."

Melina snorted. "Me, a glynnie? You must be joking!"

"I'm serious. You look and talk like a glynnie," Owen said.

"Well, I'm not one!" Melina's cheeks and eyes reddened. "All my life I have tried to fit in by looking and acting like everyone else. Now you're telling me I still don't belong. I hate you!" Wailing bitterly, Melina ran ahead, her cries floating back on the wind.

Catching up to her, Owen said, "I am sorry. Please forgive me; I won't bring it up again." Melina twisted away from him, her shoulders as hard and brittle as a ram's horns in his hands. When she finally turned back to face him, her wounded eyes were dry.

"You cannot cry," he said, brushing the hair from her face.

Melina clamped her quivering lips together. "I never could, not even when Papa clipped my ears. He always thought me such a brave girl, but I *couldn't cry*." Her chest heaved and she made sobbing, hiccupping sounds, yet not a tear moistened her lashes.

"Hush, my sweet little sparrow," crooned Owen. "We will speak no more of these matters, at least not here on the Downs and not now. Let no ill words dampen this gladsome day. Look! Here is Swyndon Hill, where I expect a joyous homecoming awaits us."

However, Swyndon did not open its arms in welcome to the pair. Passing the ring of torches, Owen and Melina came across a young girl drawing water from the well. Seeing them, she opened her mouth, dropped her bucket and ran back into the village.

"Wait!" Owen cried, but the girl had disappeared.

"At least we know she saw us, though she must have thought we were the ghosts of the departed," Melina wryly remarked.

"For a while, I thought we were, too!" said Owen.

The couple found Swyndon deserted, its houses shut up against them. They knocked on a few doors, but none opened.

At Melina's home, she pounded on the door. No one answered. Then she shouted through it, "Mama! Papa! It is I, Melina! Owen is with me. Please let us in! We are both anxious to see you again!"

The door opened a crack and Yannick's thin nose poked out. Seeing his long-lost daughter and Tadwyn's missing son, his eyes grew as round as harvest moons. *Bang!* He flung wide the door.

"Come on out, Mahilka!" he bellowed. "It's really them!"

As Yannick's wife threw herself weeping on Melina, he explained, "We didn't open the door because we thought you were spirits. After all, no Taken One has ever returned to Swyndon."

As the neighbors crept out of their huts to greet Owen and Melina, the questions began to fly. Slipping away, Owen trotted down the path to his former home. He found his father in the sheep pen, patiently wrapping Callie's leg. She was kicking and bleating, but Tadwyn held the leg fast. He looked old and worn, as if he had lived two lifetimes since Owen had last seen him.

Owen stood silently watching his father tend the sheep's injury. "Do you need a hand with Callie?" he finally asked.

"No, thanks," Tadwyn began. Then he looked up. His face went white, and he released the sheep's leg. Callie limped off, trailing her bandage. Father and son stared at one another for a frozen heartbeat. Then Owen leapt over the gate to embrace Tadwyn. The old man's chest spasmed with racking sobs to match Owen's own.

"Owen, my dear son Owen, I never hoped to see you again!" he grunted, rubbing away his tears. "Where have you been all this time? Your mother and I thought you were dead. Your mother—"

Tadwyn kicked open the gate and hurried into the house. Owen heard a squeal. Then his mother rushed out, drying her hands on a rag. Taking one look at Owen, she dissolved into tears.

Owen met his mother at the corral gate and threw his arms around her. At last his parents could see him and feel him and hear him! "I missed you, Mother!" he cried. "How I have missed you both! I have come back, and I'll never be *teithlin* again."

Then all of Swyndon poured into the front yard to rejoice with Owen and his parents. Pushing through the throng, Melina clung to him. "I love you, Owen!" she shouted over the happy din.

"I love you, too!" he shouted back. Nothing could spoil his joy on this festive occasion. He was home again with his sparrow.

Owen allowed himself one fervent kiss before he broke away from Melina and climbed the old rowan tree onto his home's thatched roof. Laughter and applause greeted him from the villagers below. "Speech! Speech!" they roared gleefully up at him.

Raising his hand for silence, he began, "Friends and neighbors, Melina and I have returned to you through flood, fog and frost. We have walked perilous paths and tasted the bitterness of death. Now let us celebrate a sheepshun of joy, not of sorrow!" Then prophetic words not of his own composing poured from his lips:

A sheepshun prepare, but bring not a sheep!
Of darkness beware; neither slumber nor sleep!
You must take a stray, with ears whole and pure;
The lamb shall you slay, and its blood be your cure.

That afternoon, Owen, Melina and their parents joined the *menestr* as he led a procession of rejoicing villagers down the hill. In one of the welving rings stood a snowy-white lamb. As the throng approached, the lamb ambled across the ring's dark green border.

The good people of Swyndon gasped, for the lamb did not disappear. Instead, it stood calmly nibbling on a clump of grass.

The menestr examined the lamb's ears. "Truly, this is a stray," he pronounced. "It belongs to no one, since its ears are uncut."

Elder Crowlyn stepped up and raised his staff. "This day we are gathered in gratitude for the return of Owen son of Tadwyn and Melina daughter of Mahilka. Where do they walk this hour?"

"They walk among us!" the villagers shouted.

"Shall they lead their flocks into pastures of green again?"

"Yes, they shall, for they have returned!"

"Shall they drink at the stream that flows from the hill?"

"Yes, they shall, for they have returned!"

Now Crowlyn faltered, but Owen improvised for him. "We have returned to Swyndon, thanks to Gaelathane, the King of kings!"

Opening the menestr's box, Owen removed the knife and chalice. Keeping the knife, he handed Crowlyn the cup. Following an inner urging, he placed his hands upon the lamb's head and prayed, "I ask You, my Lord, to let the punishment of my people's wrongdoing fall upon this guiltless lamb. Please lift the darkness that has bound our longsuffering land." Then as Tadwyn had done, he pulled back the head of the unresisting lamb and cut its throat.

Even as the lamb silently collapsed, Crowlyn quickly thrust the chalice under its neck to catch the streaming blood. Feeling sick, Owen looked away. Killing the lamb seemed such a waste, making a somber end to a day of jubilation, but Gaelathane had commanded it. Owen had obeyed, though he did not understand.

When the chalice was full, Owen took it from Crowlyn, much to the menestr's surprise. Moved by another inner impulse, Owen held up the bloody knife and announced to the onlookers, "We shall need this no more, for today, you have all witnessed your last sheepshun!" Cocking his arm, he flung the knife spinning toward Lone Oak Hill. All of Swyndon gasped, and Tadwyn frowned.

The menestr stared pointedly at the lamb, which still lay outside the welving ring. "Shall I bring out the ropes?" he asked Owen.

"We won't be wanting them this time," Owen replied, although he could not explain why. "Leave the lamb where it has fallen."

Taking the chalice with him, Owen left the gory scene. He and Melina were hiking up Swyndon Hill when the words of the Plenion's fifth stave stopped him reeling in his tracks. *Before the end, the slunge will send its loathsome legions for revenge; prepare the fire and flee the ire they bring upon the faeries' friend!*

Melina seized his arm. "Owen! What is the matter?"

"By escaping Limbo," he told her, "we cheated the borwogs of their prey. The Plenion predicts they will return to take us back!"

That evening, Owen and Melina helped their neighbors and friends prepare fresh torches and heap up brush to make bonfires. At dusk, Owen gave the order, and a ring of fire sprang up around the village, lighting the Downs for miles in all directions.

As the shadows slunk up the hillsides, doubts multiplied in Owen's heart. Had he interpreted the Plenion correctly? If the borwogs were thirsting for revenge upon the shepherd's son and his sparrow, he could be endangering everyone in Swyndon. Had he sacrificed himself in Caerillion only to see his own world overrun?

Worst of all, he was defenseless, having lost his lightstaff in Limbo. Alone, he was no match for Limbo's "loathsome legions."

Then he remembered Rolin's gift. With Tadwyn at his heels, he hurried back home to find his mother shuttering the windows. Brushing past her, he went to the fireplace, where the Tree-cone still lay where Gyrta had placed it on that sheepshun morning.

"How did you know that was there?" she exclaimed.

"I saw where you put it," he shot back with a sly grin. After pocketing the cone, he returned to Melina and the flaring torches, leaving his parents standing in open-mouthed astonishment.

As night fell, a deeper darkness invaded the valleys and besieged the hills. The torches dimmed, and a chill wind stirred among the restless villagers. Slinking away, they retreated to their warm houses, leaving only Melina still standing at Owen's side.

"Go home," he told her. "Go home and wait for me. If I do not return, then you will know I have perished and all is lost." Still Melina clung to him as the black tide surrounded Swyndon Hill.

"Leave me," Owen urged her. "You have lost your wings, my sparrow. Without them, you cannot fly away from your foes." If he failed, he could not bear the thought of watching her die.

"I will not let you face death alone!" she fiercely replied. Then she screamed as a host of red orbs drank in the torchlight. More borwog eyes than Owen had ever seen were encircling the hill.

"Go away!" he shouted. "Return to your black pits and trouble us no more! I command you in the name of Gaelathane. Go!"

The eyes winked out. Then a more profound darkness rose up and stalked forward, formless and menacing. The torches sputtered and died, while the bonfires sank down to sullen red coals. The breath left Owen's body as he threw his arms around Melina.

I am Oncollon, King of the Pit! hissed a voice. *You escaped us once, but we shall have you this time! Come back to us; come back!*

You cannot resist the Cold, the voice continued. *Feel it creeping into your heart and bones! Flesh and blood are no match for the People of the Pit. You belong to us, for we have left our mark upon you. Embrace us! Embrace the Cold, and become one of us!"*

"No—" Owen croaked. The word died in his throat. Looking down, he saw his hands and arms were mottled with black splotches. He was turning into a borwog himself. He felt so weary, so very weary. His eyelids grew heavy, and he wanted to lie down. Melina soundlessly collapsed to the ground beside him. The bonfires' last feeble flames flickered and went out. Even the stars in the moonless heavens shrank and lost their luster.

The fires in Owen's muddled mind were dying as surely as the ones surrounding Swyndon when he heard another Voice:

Let the Tree-cone burn bright, for the darkness draws near;
In the chill of the night comes an army of fear.
Take your stand with the cup, and the enemy rout;
With the King shall you sup; give a victory shout!

Owen plunged numb fingers into his pocket and drew out the cone. Its light blazed like a lightning bolt in that borwog-blackness. The darkness receded, allowing the bonfires and torches to spring back to life, and with them, the words of the Plenion's last stave:

If twice he dies before their eyes,
Then every world shall be their prize;
To fight the flood, bring back the blood
That strips away their dark disguise.

Revenge, it seemed, was not the borwogs' only motive for seeking to snuff out his life again. By some higher code than Caerillion's, if the creatures could kill the shepherd's son twice, they would gain mastery over all Gaelathane's created worlds.

Stiffly stooping, Owen retrieved the chalice from a hollow beside one of the torches, taking great care not to spill its contents. The lamb's blood shone black, as if the borwogs had infected it.

Holding out the chalice in one hand and the cone in the other, Owen cried, "As you have drunk the blood of innocents, so now drink the wrath of Gaelathane and the blood of the lamb!"

Then he hurled the chalice like a spear into the darkness.

Wailing howls raked his ears. Gradually, the suffocating darkness lifted. Bonfires and torch flames leapt high into the night, while the sprinkled stars revived and breathed forth their light again. After chafing the warmth and life back into his frozen limbs, Owen helped Melina to her feet. She groggily stared about.

"What happened?" she asked. "Where are all the borwogs?"

"They're gone," Owen said. Seeing that the skin on his arms and hands was restored to a healthy pink, he repeated, "They're really gone!" Contented at last, he enfolded Melina in his embrace.

As a warm spring wind frolicked over the hilltop, the villagers threw open their windows and doors. Pulling up one of the flaming torches, Owen waved it over his head. "Rejoice, O people of Swyndon!" he cried. "The lamb's blood and the Tree's light have defeated our enemies! No more shall we cower in our locked houses at night. No more shall we surround ourselves with burning torches like this one to drive away the deadly darkness. We are free!"

The bravest of his listeners ventured out of their homes to marvel at the frosty ground where the borwog army had gathered. Soon, most of Swyndon was peering cautiously over the hillside.

Elder Crowlyn took the torch from Owen and announced, "The son of Tadwyn has spoken the truth! Long years we have feared the darkness, but now it shall haunt us no longer. Down with the darkness and up with Owen son of Tadwyn!"

"Down with the darkness and up with Owen son of Tadwyn!" echoed his beaming parents. The other villagers took up Crowlyn's cheer, parading about the hill with Owen on their shoulders.

After the festivities had wound down and the last Swyndonian had staggered off to bed, Owen took Melina's hand and led her beyond the torches. Breathing in the fresh scents of growing grass and flowing water, the Boy and his Sparrow sat quietly together, watching the stars wheel in silent splendor over the hill.

CHAPTER 19

RESURRECTIONS

"Where do you suppose all the borwogs went?" said Owen. "And what happened to the lamb?" Melina added. At daybreak, the two had left Swyndon Hill for the dew-heavy grasses of the Downs. No sign of the borwogs remained, despite the hosts that had crowded the hillside the night before.

Equally puzzling, the dead lamb had also disappeared, leaving a patch of blood-soaked, matted grass near the welving ring.

"May I join you?" Tadwyn asked, striding up to the pair with a wicker hamper. His bald head gleamed in the morning sun, while the lines in his face had softened since Owen's homecoming.

"Gyrta and I were worried when you didn't come back last night. I brought you both some breakfast. I hope it's still hot!"

From the hamper, Tadwyn produced two bowls of steaming mutton stew, a loaf of bread and a lump of chilled butter. Melina and Owen devoured the lot without bothering to breathe between bites. Owen thought he had never tasted finer fare in all his life.

"I see you dragged the lamb across the ring after all," Tadwyn said. He pointed to the flattened grass where the lamb had lain.

Owen shook his head. "I haven't touched that lamb since yesterday's sheepshun. Maybe wolves or borwogs took the body."

Melina's lip curled in disgust. "Borwogs wouldn't bother a dead animal, if I know them. They feed only on the warmth of the living. I think I'll have a look around. That lamb couldn't have gone far."

"Borwogs?" Tadwyn asked his son after Melina had left.

"That's what we call those creatures of the night," Owen said.

Tadwyn chewed on his lip. "Now here's a puzzle," he said. "Wild beasts would have left a swath of crushed grass if they had made off with the carcass. On the other hand, they couldn't have eaten it here without leaving some bones behind. If I didn't know better, I'd say our lamb got up and walked away during the night."

Owen did know better. He had felt the lamb's lifeblood gush between his fingers as the ceremonial knife cleaved the animal's throat. He had felt its pulse falter and stop. That lamb had died.

"Oh!" Melina screamed. "Come quickly! See what I found!"

Owen and his father came running to find Melina pointing at something lying in the grass. At first Owen thought it was the lamb, but then he saw it had the limbs of a man. A dead man.

"Who is he?" Melina asked.

Tadwyn rubbed his shiny head. "I've never seen him before."

Neither had Owen. Searching farther, the three found scores of bodies sprawled about as if sleeping. Some were slipwings, but most were men, women and children of Owen's race. All were as pale as sheep's milk, and their skin was colder than frost. No blood or other marks of violence marred their lifeless forms.

"The meadows are full of them!" Owen said. "They weren't here yesterday. How could so many people die during the night?"

"The Downs take me if I know," Tadwyn grunted. "Say, isn't that old Borliman over there? He was *teithlin* years ago." Owen's father gestured at a corpse draped across a grassy hillock.

"I believe it is!" said Owen. He recalled the dreadful day when the well-loved shepherd had disappeared. More than once, Borliman had rescued Owen's sheep from welving rings. Owen recognized others whose names Swyndon no longer spoke. All had met the same mysterious fate. In vain the sun warmed their waxen faces.

Melina's own face turned pallid at the ghastly scene. "Soon these people will start to stink," she said. "Let's go back to the village."

"They need a proper burial," said Owen uncertainly as he took in the vast numbers of the dead. Working day and night, all of Swyndon could not bury such a multitude in a year's time.

Then he saw one who was still living, an upright figure weaving deliberately across the Downs amongst the dead. Dressed in shabby sheepskins, an old man was approaching, his shepherd's crook in hand. It was he whom Swyndon knew as the Gadabout.

"What is *he* doing out here?" said Tadwyn, scowling.

How the old shepherd had survived when so many others had perished was quite beyond Owen. Then the Gadabout was standing before him, leaning on his staff with a twinkle in his eye.

"I see your sparrow has recovered from her wounds and has returned home to roost," he said, pointing his staff at Melina.

Owen gasped. "How could you possibly know she was—?"

"I am the Sparrow-Watcher," replied the Gadabout.

Melina's face lit up as recognition dawned upon her. "It's You!" she breathed. "All this time, I never knew it was really You."

"It was *who*?" said Owen irritably.

"The Gadabout is the King, and the King is the Gadabout, silly goose!" she retorted. "Don't you see Gaelessa in His eyes? He has touched my life these three times now, but I never knew Him."

Owen looked again, and Gaelathane's features leapt out at him. As the rising sun crowned the King's hoary head with gold, its yellow rays fell upon an angry red scar encircling His throat.

"No!" cried Owen, and he sank to his knees. "You were the lamb?!" Wrenching sobs tore from his soul's core. With his own hand he had killed the King of the Trees and had not known it.

"You asked Me to take your place, and I have," said the King gently. "In this world you know as 'Clynnod,' I took not only your place but also the place and punishment of every erring sheep. You sang of this day in Gaelessa. Don't you remember, My son?

Praise to Him Whose great heart faced His enemies' hate;
As a sheep before shearers He suffered His fate;
So He left an example for all who would see,
That a life worth the living means dying to *me*.

188

"What is this mad fellow saying?" Tadwyn demanded. "Why do you even bother talking with him? He speaks only nonsense."

"I am the Lamb that was slain before the foundations of this world were laid," Gaelathane declared, and blinding light burst from His body and His staff. Reverently, Melina and Owen bowed low before Him, while Tadwyn fell on his face trembling in terror.

"What do You want with the likes of us, Sir?" he quavered.

"I desire your devotion and your service, Tadwyn son of Tarklin," Gaelathane replied, and He raised Tadwyn to his feet with a touch of His hand. "I must dine tonight in your home with you and your good wife, Gyrta. Invite your friends, neighbors and relatives, for I wish to meet them all, especially the children."

Owen had never seen his father so excited. "I would be honored to entertain You in our home!" Tadwyn said. "That is, if You don't mind mutton, leeks and potatoes. We haven't much, but we will gladly share what we do have with You and our other guests."

Gaelathane embraced him. "I have always loved your generous nature!" He said. "Your readiness to give is your greatest virtue."

"How do You know me, when I have always avoided You?"

The King laughed merrily. "I knew you while you were yet in your mother's womb, and I have seen all your days."

The color drained from Tadwyn's face. "You know the day of my birth and death? Tell me when—no, I don't want to know."

"I have come to abolish death and the dread of it," said Gaelathane. "In return, I give you life now and forevermore."

Owen asked, "Then why could You not have saved all these dead that lie upon the Downs? What brought them to this place?"

"And how did they die?" Melina put in.

Gaelathane replied, "They fell into darkness and have walked in death, cut off from My light. Though you shunned them, they came to you seeking the light, yet hating it. The warmth of love and companionship they sought also, but in their need, they stole the warmth of life. Only My blood could restore their bodies."

"Borwogs!" Owen exclaimed. "All these fell into the slunge and became borwogs! 'To fight the flood, bring back the blood that strips away their dark disguise.' But why do they appear so lifeless?"

189

"Though My blood has restored their bodies, their spirits still sleep," Gaelathane told him. "Thanks to the staff you left in Limbo, these dead shall now awaken." He pointed toward the green southern hills, where a rising full moon outshone the morning sun. Yet, no moon had ever risen south of Swyndon, nor had any moon shone so fiercely. Higher the glowing giant grew until it stood taller than the hills and the sun itself. Shading their eyes from that light, Tadwyn and Melina stared at the spectacle in fear and wonder.

"The Downs are burning!" cried Melina. "The flatlanders must have set the grass afire! Alas, alas, what will our sheep eat now?"

"That is no fire," Owen corrected her. "It's the Tree!"

"Do you mean a big tree has caught fire?" Tadwyn asked.

Gaelathane smiled. "Nay, the Light of Gaelessa burns neither flesh nor wood, though it can purge the deepest darkness from a living soul. Now you shall see the power of My risen Tree!"

As the Tree's light flooded the landscape, the former borwogs began stirring. Aroused from their long and dreadful sleep, they stood upon their feet and faced the Tree. With a collective sigh, they extended their arms towards that shining pillar, drinking in its warmth and light like blind men sunning themselves in spring.

Then a tumult arose among them. Some in the throng were fleeing from the Tree's presence, their faces twisted with rage and panic. Staggering toward Swyndon, one of them bellowed, "I'll have none of that trickster tree! I've escaped the Deadwood for good this time. No more dremlens and borwogs for me! I'm free!"

It was Dask. Seeing Owen and his companions, the mutton-man let out a howl of fury. Even as he rushed upon them, however, his form was changing. Darkness squirted out of every pore. His limbs shriveled and his skin split. Then his body collapsed upon itself like a rotten, hollow log. In a matter of moments, nothing remained of Dask the mutton-man but a shivering black shadow. Hanging over Owen, the threatening Dask-phantom wavered, broke apart and blew away like stinking smoke upon a chill wind.

"What happened to him?" Melina asked, looking horrified.

Sorrowfully, Gaelathane answered, "He loved the darkness rather than the light. From the darkness I delivered him, and to the

190

darkness he has returned. All who reject Me and the light of My Tree shall likewise perish. If only they would come to Me, I would grant them life everlasting in My blessed kingdom!"

All around, other shadowy figures were also wasting away as they fled the light. A stiff breeze carried the wailing wraiths away, leaving only the Tree's pure and undiluted radiance to dawn over the hushed Downs. Then the vast crowd of restored borwogs bowed as one to the King of the Trees. Their faces beamed with joy.

Gaelathane held out His hands in a gesture of warmth and acceptance. "Welcome to My kingdom!" he told the worshipers. "You who once walked in darkness must learn to walk in the light. Love one another as I have loved you. Return now to your homes and kindred, and I will be with you always." The King then pointed His shining shepherd's staff at the Tree. With a roar of jubilation, His people rushed toward the immense crystal pillar and began climbing it. Tadwyn stared slack-jawed after them.

"Where are they all going?" he asked Gaelathane.

"They are climbing back into their own worlds," the King replied. "Each branch of My Tree leads to a different land. As I create new worlds, the Tree continues to grow taller. In time, it will fill all worlds with its light, though the sun and moon cease to shine. Now be off with you. Your wife will want time to prepare."

"Yes, yes, of course!" Tadwyn stammered as he backed away from Gaelathane. "Do You know the way to our home?"

"Indeed I do. I have oft visited you, though you saw Me not."

Reminded of his own stint as his parents' invisible guest, Owen offered Tadwyn the Tree-cone. "Thank you for letting me borrow this last night, Father. It helped save my life and Melina's, too."

Tadwyn held up his hands in refusal. "Please keep it," he said. "Mainly, I used the thing as a lantern at night. I have a feeling you will find more important uses for it. Tell me, though, how did you know Gyrta kept it hidden in that chink in the fireplace?"

"As I told you before, I saw her put it there—the day of my sheepshun," Owen replied. Sitting on a rock, he recounted his adventures from the day the sparrow had first led him south in search of Tabitha until he and Melina had returned to the Downs.

Tadwyn scratched his chin. "The land of the faeries!" he said. "I've often seen bright lights flitting about of a summer's night, but I always thought they were fireflies. And I wondered why that bird kept hanging around our house. Now I'd best be going before Gyrta starts to fret about me." With a wave, he strode off homeward.

"What happened to Gaelathane?" said Melina. The King had quietly disappeared, leaving Owen and Melina alone amidst a sea of grasses hissing in the wind. Owen suddenly felt out of place.

"We don't belong here now," he told Melina. "We're not even invited to supper with my parents! I'm feeling invisible again."

"What are those?" Melina interrupted, pointing at the sky.

Owen looked up. A cluster of nine dark specks was rapidly approaching. Evidently, a flock of foul carrion birds had come to feast upon the corpses of the former borwogs. "You're too late!" Owen shouted. As the specks grew larger, he realized they were not birds at all, but some sort of winged, otherworldly creatures.

"What are they?" Melina uneasily repeated. Gripping Owen's hand, she drew him down inside a patch of tall, thick grass.

Still the flying beasts descended, landing heavily near Melina and Owen's makeshift hiding place. Fearsome in beak and claw, the creatures were a curious, furred-and-feathered blend of lion and eagle. Each one bore a two-legged figure on its broad back.

"You can come out of the grass now!" called one of the riders. It was Rolin. The rest of the outringers sat astride the other beasts with Mirrah and Prince Percy. All but Percy wore welcoming smiles.

"Our mounts spotted you from the air," Marlis explained as the pair sheepishly emerged from hiding. "They are hunters by nature. Being both eagle and lion, griffins have very sharp eyes."

Griffins. Owen rolled the word around in his mind. He had never heard of such strange beasts before, but after all his experiences in Feirian, very little could surprise him. He and Melina jumped when Scanlon's mount uttered a shrill, shrike-like call.

Scanlon said, "Ironwing was wondering whether you have any conies around here. He's feeling rather hungry at the moment."

Owen didn't care for the way the tail-twitching griffins were staring at him. Were the beasts cross, bored or simply curious?

"Conies?" Melina said. "If you mean rabbits, we have lots, and you're welcome to them. Their burrows are a real nuisance."

"How did you know we were here?" Owen asked.

"Gaelathane told us where to find you," Rolin said. "After you were dropped into that slunge pit, we never dreamed we would see you alive again. With the King, of course, nothing is impossible. Perhaps you can tell us later how you managed to survive."

I didn't, Owen thought, shuddering at the memory. "What about the forest fire?" he asked. "How did *you* all survive that?"

"When we prayed together," said Rolin, "Gaelathane sent a drenching downpour over the whole forest, dousing the fire."

"Who is your friend, Owen?" Bembor asked with a sly wink.

Owen replied, "Allow me to introduce the sparrow to you."

Melina's recounting of her own remarkable tale left her listeners speechless with doubt and amazement. Then Bembor observed, "We have only begun to discover some of the many types of torsils that serve as gateways between Gaelathane's worlds. In Feirian, we have already met the touch-torsils. Now we are learning of trees that can transform a climber into another creature entirely, in this instance, a bird. In the future, we all must be more careful about climbing unfamiliar torsils in strange lands!"

"Speaking of torsil travel," said Marlis, "we had better be leaving soon. Gaelathane made us promise to bring these two back to Mt. Morwynion, even if we have to carry them ourselves."

Groaning, Prince Percy stiffly clambered off his mount's back. "Well!" he said. "You may go where you wish, but I am staying right here where I belong. You ought to have warned me these horrid creatures could fly so high. I cannot abide heights, yet we flew so far above the earth that my head would not stop spinning. I am still dreadfully dizzy. It was most inconsiderate of you all, I must say. How anybody can practice this rustic, undignified and plainly hazardous form of transportation is quite beyond me."

Mirrah rolled her eyes. "Stop complaining. Do you want to walk all the way to Caerillion? Now get back on your griffin."

Percy stamped his foot. "I shall not! Nobody can tell me what to do in my own realm!" Up went his nose as he folded his arms.

"Very well," said Rolin. "Owen and Melina, since Percy wishes to keep his feet on the ground, you two may ride Sharpears instead. Remember to hold on with your knees—and don't choke him!"

Gingerly, Owen climbed onto the griffin and gripped its flanks with his knees as one might a barebacked horse. Melina jumped on behind him and clutched the beast's fur. Catching Percy's eye, she dryly remarked, "You're an awfully long way from home."

A befuddled Percy blinked and looked about. Then he nervously cleared his throat. "Yes, so it would appear. A long way indeed."

"The walk will do you good," Elwyn said with a hint of spite.

Percy was working himself into another foot-stomping frenzy when he paused with one leg still raised in the air. Cloaked again in His Gadabout guise, Gaelathane was approaching the prince.

Gwynneth pointed at the King. "I know that Man!" she told Timothy. "He came to our wedding. I wonder why a lone shepherd would want to show up uninvited at a Lucambrian wedding."

Then Gaelathane shed His sheepskin disguise, appearing in all His radiance. Percy's jaw dropped, and he collapsed in a quivering heap. When he managed to prop himself up on his wobbly knees, his face was as white as the griffins' neck feathers.

"Wh-who are You?" he squeaked.

"You are a prince only by My leave," said Gaelathane sternly. "It is time you behaved like one! Lay aside your childish ways, or I shall raise up another more worthy than you to become king."

"Yes, Sir," said Percy, his eyes downcast.

Gaelathane's tone softened. "You have grown much through your many trials, but you are not yet ready to return home to your servants and other privileges. If you were to wear Clynnod's crown tonight, your subjects would dethrone you. Instead, you shall live in the village of Swyndon and work as a shepherd. Perhaps you shall learn true humility through the dignity of honest labor. Besides, no king may reign wisely and justly over a people whom he does not know. Obey Me in this with all your heart, and I will honor you in time. Rebel against Me, and you will never sit upon Clynnod's throne, though you attempt to seize it with a mighty army."

Percy trembled as he asked, "What about Mirrah?"

"What of her? She is free to go wherever she pleases, and you should be grateful if she pleases to go with you. Mirrah was once an able shepherdess in her own right, although not in Clynnod. If you treat her with the proper respect, she might help you learn your new trade. In any event, a shepherd's life will afford you plenty of opportunity to reflect upon your calling and character."

Percy's fists balled, but he gave no other sign of hearing.

"Now take My hand as a man and a monarch," said Gaelathane. Reluctantly, Percy rose and gripped the King's hand. In turn, Gaelathane embraced him. "Go now and become Swyndon's finest shepherd," He said. "I will be with you and help you in all your endeavors, for I am the Shepherd of shepherds."

Then Gaelathane disappeared. As a sleeper awakens from a dream, Percy dazedly asked the outringers, "Does He always come and go like that at the drop of a pin? Where did He get to?"

Rolin laughed. "He's still here. We simply can't see Him, that's all. You ought to be thankful that He has taken an interest in your welfare. Despite what you may think, He really does love you."

"I suppose I had it coming," Percy grunted. "I called Wolf and his men, 'filthy, smelly shepherds,' and now I am about to become one myself. If word gets out that Prince Percy has stooped to herding sheep, I'll be a laughingstock." After asking Owen and Melina directions to Swyndon, he set off with slow and heavy steps.

"Don't leave yet!" cried Mirrah, and she slipped off her mount, whose name was Longbeak. Hugging Gwynneth, she wept on her shoulder. "Good-bye, dear friend!" she said. "You stood up for me when nobody else would. Do not forget me, wherever you fare!"

"Of course I won't forget you," Gwynneth replied. "But you don't have to go with Percy. You're certainly welcome to join us."

Mirrah pointed back at the prince. "Someone has to look after him. I know he isn't perfect, but he seems rather fond of me."

"He has a strange way of showing it," Scanlon muttered.

"As you wish," Rolin said. "You and Percy may want to fly to Swyndon instead of walking, in case Dask has followed us here."

"Dask is dead," Owen said. He retold the fate of the revived borwogs who had embraced the Tree—and of those who had not.

195

"I see now why we found your lightstaff in the woods, Owen," said Rolin. "In Dask's unbelieving hands, it must have refused to shine, and he fell prey to the borwogs. What a horrible end!"

"Dask deserved much worse, believe me," Mirrah declared. "Now he is doubly dead, and good riddance to him, I say. Still, I reckon I ought to forgive him. That's what your Gaelathane told me last night, anyway. Forgiving is easier than forgetting, I think."

Waving farewell, Mirrah ran after Percy. "Hold on, princey! Where do you think you're going without me? What's the rush?"

Percy turned to face her. "Why would you want to tag along with me? I thought you'd be glad to see the last of Prince Percy."

Wagging her finger at him, Mirrah said, "You can't shake me off so easily as that! Now do you want me to help you or not?"

A hopeful grin spread across the prince's face. "If you don't mind knocking about with a smelly shepherd, you are welcome to come along. You do have more experience than I herding sheep."

Mirrah dragged Percy back to Longbeak and patted the griffin's back. "Climb on, princey. We'll fly to Swyndon together."

"Done!" said Prince Percy gleefully. He and Mirrah leapt onto Longbeak's back, and the beast launched into the heavens.

"They'll need the Gift to get along with that griffin," Elwyn wryly remarked as Longbeak flew north toward Swyndon Hill.

Just then, the ground began shaking and rumbling. All eyes swiveled southward, where a mighty green wave was sweeping across the Downs toward the griffins and their riders. A rising wind flattened the grass and tore at the outringers' green cloaks.

"Fly!" Rolin cried, and the griffins lifted off the earth with frantic wingbeats. Melina gripped Owen's waist with both arms.

From a comfortably safe height, the pair of riders looked down upon an unfolding panorama. In the Tree's light, a new myndyn forest was erupting from the welving rings, leapfrogging toward Swyndon along a broad front. The Greatwood was being reborn.

CHAPTER 20

THE SINGING STRINGS

T here they are!" Gwynneth exclaimed. Riding a griffin named Crookedtail, she was pointing toward a spot in the faery forest's ruffled carpet lying far below. As the Greatwood had resprouted, the scent of its newly opening myndyn blossoms had transported the griffin riders back to Feirian.

Looking down from his perch on Sharpears, Owen spotted a telltale wisp of gray smoke curling ghostlike through the treetops.

From behind him, Melina said, "I don't see anyone on the ground. It's probably a tree still smoldering after the forest fire."

Then an arrow whizzed up from the woods, passing between Crookedtail and Sharpears. "Look out!" Owen shouted. Glancing back at Melina, he added, "Trees can't shoot arrows! I'd say somebody down there doesn't like us very much, wouldn't you?"

"He is a pretty fair marksman, too!" Melina replied.

When more arrows arced toward them, the griffins veered away, dove into the forest and landed on the outskirts of a burned-over clearing. On a stump beside a crackling campfire sat a sheepskin-clad man clutching a bow and arrows. As Owen and his companions approached, the man jumped up and fitted an arrow to his string. Drawing the string back, he barked, "That's far enough!"

Thunggg. Owen flinched, but the arrow never flew. The bow-string had snapped in two. The man dropped his bow in defeat.

"Wolf!" Gwynneth exclaimed.

Recognition flickered in the mutton-man's dark eyes. "So it was you riding those beasts!" he said, and his hand strayed toward the knife jammed in his belt. Then he sagged. "What's the use? My bowstring's broken and I'm outnumbered. The Deadwood has beaten me. I've failed to burn it, and I've failed to escape it. My men have deserted me. I have nothing left but a useless bow."

Gwynneth held out her hand to him. "Come with us, and we'll show you the way out of this place. We can take you home."

Wolf laughed bitterly. "Home? I have no home now but the accursed Deadwood. Here I shall die, and here my bones shall lie. At least the borwog holes have dried up. I was always afeared of falling into one. Then Dask would be standing here, not me."

"This forest is not accursed," Gwynneth said. "We don't belong here, that's all. Ride with us, and we will take you to the kingdom of the dremlens. Afterwards, you may stay or leave, as you wish."

"Maybe I will join you," said Wolf. "What have I got to lose?" Wearily dropping onto his stump, he asked, "First, do you have any grub? I haven't eaten a thing in days, and I'm famished."

"I might have some food," Owen offered. Opening his shepherd's purse, he found some crumbly bread and cheese. The borwog-cold had preserved the remnants of his simple Caerillion supper.

As he pulled out a chunk of cheese, a wiry tangle sprang out with it and slithered to the ground. It was the silver string Owen had salvaged from the waterfall-cave. He began untangling the cord.

"Where did you get that?" Wolf asked him with a keen gaze.

"I found it in a cave. It broke when I pulled on it. Here, have a look for yourself." Owen handed the sheepman the metal cord.

"This would make a fine bowstring," Wolf remarked. "Would you mind if I borrowed it until I can make another one of bark?"

"Not at all," Owen said. "I have no use for it now."

Wolf gruffly thanked him. Replacing his bow's broken string with Owen's silver one, he nocked an arrow against the braided cord and drew it back. Then he nodded and grunted in satisfaction.

"This will do," he decided. "I'll ride one of your winged lions to the dremlens' kingdom—but I'm bringing my bow and arrows!"

After devouring Owen's bread and cheese in a single gulp, Wolf hopped on Elwyn's mount, and the griffins took flight. It wasn't long before Wolf's complexion had turned a ghastly shade of green.

"That's what he gets for bolting his food," Melina told Owen.

The sun was shining high in Feirian's sky when the griffins alit in front of Mt. Morwynion. Dismounting, Owen and his companions marched up to the mountain's entrance. A great crowd of glynnies awaited. Armed with spears, Trellisant and a full complement of the Caerillion Guard stood at the forefront. Then their ranks parted for the Spirewalker, who stalked forward in a cloud of wrath.

"Why have you brought others of your kind to our home?" she demanded. "Have you already forgotten the Code of Caerillion?"

Working up his courage, Owen stepped out to meet Gisella. "Hail, Spirewalker of Feirian!" he said, bowing to her.

Gisella's face went whiter than frost, and she gasped, "Do the dead now walk the earth? Is it really you, Owen son of Tadwyn?"

"By Gaelathane's grace, it is," said Owen. "The shepherd's son has returned from the pit of death. You have met my friends."

"Not all of them," Gisella acidly observed with a scowl.

Owen explained, "Wolf has lived in your world for many years, but he is anxious to return home. As for this girl, do not judge her by her garments. She is not what she seems. You once knew her as my sparrow, but she has been restored to her glynnie form."

"Whatever she is, she does not belong here," the Spirewalker declared. She nodded at Trellisant, who drew Melina's hair back from one side of her comely head, exposing a misshapen ear.

"You see?" said Gisella triumphantly. "She has small ears."

"My father cut them that way," Melina said, flushing. "He wanted to make me look like the other villagers in Swyndon."

"Her ears are scarred, milady," Trellisant pointed out.

"What have her ears got to do with anything?" Owen asked.

Gisella lifted the hair away from her own ears. They tapered to a point at the top instead of rounding off. Like Melina, the glynnies wore their hair long, apparently to cover their ears.

Owen argued, "If Yannick hadn't cropped them short, her ears would have ended in pointy tips just like yours! Look at her face, her hands, her arms. She has 'glynnie' written all over her!"

"Nay, she has 'dust-girl' written all over her!" Gisella said. "Do not misunderstand me. We are most grateful for your selfless sacrifice. Nonetheless, we cannot allow these others into our city."

"And why not?" Wolf broke in. "I don't know who you are, but if you're in league with these slippery dremlens, you can lift the curse that imprisons my men and me in this miserable forest."

"Your plight does not concern me, sheepman," the Spirewalker coldly replied. "You and this girl are trespassers in our land."

To Owen's horror, Wolf rammed an arrow against his borrowed bowstring, drew the string taut and aimed at Gisella. "Tell me how to escape this dratted Deadwood, or I'll shoot you!" he growled.

Gwynneth cried, "No, Wolf! We already know the way out!"

Trellisant and his fellow guards lunged at the mutton-man, but they were too late. The bowstring twanged. As the arrow sped away, a diving wispwing knocked it off its course, and it twirled harmlessly into the ground. The slipwings were about to pounce on Wolf when they stopped short in confusion. The bowstring was still vibrating, setting the air, the rocks and the earth to thrumming.

Wolf threw down the bow as if it were a deadly serpent, and its string shattered. The thrumming stopped, giving way to a droning. A whirring golden cloud was descending like a locust swarm. It hovered briefly over the gathering before thinning and dispersing.

Like the smoke ascending from a funeral pyre, a keening wail rose from that vast multitude of glynnies. "What have you done, dust-man?" screamed Gisella. Snatching a spear from one of the guards, she strode toward Wolf with a murderous look in her flashing eyes. Just in time, Trellisant caught and held her back.

"It is forbidden, Spirewalker!" he cried. "It is forbidden for the People of the Glen to shed man's blood! Leave him be. He knew not what he was doing. Slipwings we have been, and slipwings we shall always be until the world is renewed in Gaelathane's time."

Gisella lowered the spear, but her eyes still blazed. "How dare you steal the Singing String to arm your bow, man of dust! The golden dragonflies you summoned with that cord would have restored our wings. Instead, you robbed us of our birthright!"

Unflinching, Wolf stood his ground. "I care not for your wings. The boy Owen gave me that bowstring. Ask him where he found the thing. I say good riddance to it and to all your accursed kind! Would that every one of you had perished in the fires I set."

"Guards!" Gisella screamed. "Slay this insolent dust-man; let his blood be upon my head. Obey me!" All the guards but Trellisant advanced upon Wolf with leveled spears, while the outringers drew their swords and nocked arrows to their bowstrings.

Quite unexpectedly, Owen heard himself say, "Please do not harm one another! Are we not all children of the King? Did He not die for men and glynnies alike? Wolf did not steal your 'Singing String.' I found it hanging at the back of a shallow cave."

Hundreds of pairs of hostile glynnie eyes turned on him as Gisella said, "What does it matter where you found the string, when this dust-fool has marred it beyond all hope of mending?"

"Why not let the boy have his say?" Trellisant suggested. "Surely we owe him and his friends that much for saving Feirian."

At Gisella's reluctant nod, Owen described his discovery of the golden cavern with its statuesque, nameless woman, whose perfectly preserved corpse he had envisioned being buried under flying nuggets. Doubt and wonder filled the slipwings' shining eyes.

"Those were not gold nuggets," Trellisant exclaimed. "Truly you have found the long-lost lair of the golden dragonflies!"

"And Starlyss's final resting place," added Gisella. "Sheltering Cave is well known to us, but we have never explored its depths thoroughly. None of us ever suspected another cavern lay hidden inside. Since the bite of golden dragonflies can heal more than withered wings, Starlyss must have spent her last days in the insects' den, hoping to prolong her life. Alas, death overtook her there, though the dragonflies did preserve her body from decay."

She knelt desolate among the shards of the shattered bowstring. "Starlyss evidently salvaged this string from her broken harp to hang outside the cavern as a signpost and door-opener. Now both cord and cave are forever lost to us—and I will be avenged!"

With a speed and strength belying her age, Gisella jumped to her feet and hurled her spear at Wolf. *Thunk!* The weapon sank deeply into flesh—but not Wolf's. Gaelathane had appeared in a splintered instant between the mutton-man and his assailant.

Gisella shrieked in horror and collapsed as the King drew the dripping lance from His side. Blood spurted from the gash, which rapidly closed up and healed, leaving a raised purple scar.

"This is a day of rejoicing and reconciliation, not of revenge," He said. "Vengeance belongs to Me. I am He Who raises up the humble and brings down the proud. I am also He Who breaks the bow and the spear!" The stringless bow leapt into His hands to join the bloody spear. He snapped both in twain like rotten twigs.

"Who *are* You?" Wolf said, cringing before the King's fury.

"I am the Shepherd of shepherds," Gaelathane replied. "Harwelf son of Andelf, no longer shall you hunt wild game with your bow and knife, but you shall care for the lost sheep of My flock."

"Harwelf!" Gwynneth snickered. "So that's where he got the name, 'Wolf.' I always thought it was because he never shaved."

"How do You know my real name?" Wolf sputtered.

"I know everything there is to know about you," Gaelathane told the shaggy hunter, who shrank back in red-faced shame.

"I—I killed a man, yet You saved my sorry life just now," Wolf hoarsely confessed to the King. "How can I ever repay You?"

"You cannot," Gaelathane replied. "I took the spear that was meant for you, just as I once died to take on Myself the punishment for all of men's misdeeds. Though you have killed no one, yet in My eyes, whosoever spills man's blood in anger is guilty of murder."

He laid His bloody hands upon Wolf's head, marking his forehead in red. "In My kingdom, there is no forgiveness of bloodguilt without the shedding of blood. You are pardoned; you shall not die for your offenses. I give you a new name: 'Maharen the Ram,' for you shall lead My flock into pastures of green. Will you follow Me and faithfully serve Me as your Shepherd, Maharen?"

Wolf raised his head, the light of hope kindling in his eyes. "I will. You just said I have killed no one. How can that be, when with my own eyes I saw Dask lying dead, pierced with my arrow?"

With the King's leave, Owen told Wolf of Dask's fate. When the mutton-man scoffed at Owen's story, Gaelathane said, "Come with Me, Maharen. Since you apparently must see in order to believe, I will show you the Tree of trees." The two went into the woods. Owen saw a burst of light, and Gaelathane returned alone.

"What happened to Wolf?" Gwynneth asked the King.

Picking up the top half of Gisella's broken lance, Gaelathane answered, "I took him to his home, where he shall serve Me."

"What are You going to do with that spear?" asked Rolin.

"I never waste any sacrifice in My kingdom," Gaelathane said, and with one swift thrust, He drove the lance into the ground.

To Owen's surprise, the spear started growing where it stood. First, the snapped-off wooden shaft lengthened and recurved on itself to form a graceful letter "D" shape. Then the buried metal blade sprouted long, wiry tendrils that curled around the top and bottom of the "D." Owen recognized the resulting instrument.

"Why, it's a harp!" Marlis exclaimed.

"In time, so shall I turn all that causes harm into healing," said Gaelathane. Handing the spear-harp to Gisella, He told her, "Play this instrument each year on the anniversary of this blessed day. The music will celebrate My goodness and renew your wings. You must also learn to forgive Wolf and others who have wronged you!"

Tentatively, the Spirewalker's fingers coaxed a world's worth of mingled joy and sorrow from the singing strings. Again the golden cloud gathered. This time, as the harp's piercing tones played on, the humming horde sank toward the breathless crowd below.

The wispwings scattered, while Gisella and her wingless companions bared their arms to the darting dragonflies. Settling on the slipwings, the insects nipped their naked skin, raising drops of ruby blood before flying away. In their pain, the faeries sang:

Dragonfly, dragonfly, so golden and swift,
Descend on us lightly to grant us your gift
Of the bite that brings blood but a blessing as well,
When the buds on our backs will awaken and swell!

Bare your skin to the sting; let all slipwings now sing!
After long yearning years we shall burst into wing!
Break forth into mirth, for the bite shall give birth
To the freedom of flitting high over the earth!

Dragonfly, dragonfly, so golden and swift,
Descend on us lightly to grant us your gift
Of the bite that brings blood but a blessing as well,
When the buds on our backs will awaken and swell!

No slipwings are we, when our wings shall break free,
And we soar through the sky to the King's own country!
To the heavens of light we shall soon take our flight;
We have broken our bonds all because of a bite!

Dragonfly, dragonfly, so golden and swift,
Descend on us lightly to grant us your gift
Of the bite that brings blood but a blessing as well,
When the buds on our backs will awaken and swell!

Meanwhile, a pair of bumps was sprouting from each slipwing's back, one on either side of the spine. The bulges grew until they split open, releasing tightly twisted, pink-and-white umbrellas. Like blossoming evening primroses, the "umbrellas" unfurled and fanned out, forming limp wings rosier than a summer's sunset.

"Ow!" cried Melina. "One of those bugs just bit me on the neck! I'm bleeding, too. And now my back itches where I can't scratch it." As she clawed at her shoulder blades, Owen used his knife to slice through the back of her blouse. Out popped two more unfolding umbrellas as shiny as new laurel leaves in spring.

"See? I told you!" he said smugly. "You really are a glynnie!"

"She must be," said Trellisant, wincing at the agony of his own emerging umbrellas. "Only glynnies sprout wings when bitten."

"It hurts!" Melina groaned, and she sagged into Owen's arms.

Through clenched teeth, Gisella told her, "You must remain standing upright. Otherwise, your wings won't grow properly."

After expanding to their full size, the glynnies' flaccid wings dried and hardened. Fluttering gracefully in the wind, they reflected the sunlight in rainbow hues. As if on unspoken command, the former slipwings tested their newfound wings and rose into the air, singing praises to Gaelathane. Melina eagerly joined them.

Wistfully gazing up at the glynnies, Owen felt a pang of envy. How he wished for his own wings! Still, he knew his weighty body would never take flight even if he could borrow a faery's wings.

Gaelathane took him aside and said, "In Gaelessa, you will fly with full-fledged wings as the angels do. For now, you must content yourself with riding griffins—and living a long, rewarding life."

The King whistled, and a golden dragonfly lightly alit on Owen's arm. He felt a sharp sting, and the insect darted off again, leaving a swelling drop of blood where its jaws had pierced flesh.

"Why did You let it bite me?" he cried. "I'm no glynnie!"

"And this one is no dust-girl!" announced Gisella, landing arm-in-arm with Melina. "Despite her clipped ears, she is a glynnie."

Owen sighed. "That's what I have been trying to tell you."

"She is not just any glynnie. Melina is my flesh and blood!"

Everyone turned toward the speaker. A stately slipwing was settling to earth beside Melina, his wings raising a cloud of dust.

"Who are you and how do you know this?" Gisella asked.

The slipwing gazed into Melina's eyes. "Don't you remember me?" She shook her head. "It has been many years," he said. "I recognized you from that small scar on your forehead. Wingless, you had fallen and gashed yourself on a stone. Later that day, I found you playing next to a slunge pit. You fell in before I could stop you. While trying to save you, I was pulled in, too. How cold it was! I remember only darkness until I awoke in another world."

Gisella frowned. "You make a bold claim, stranger. No man, beast or glynnie in Feirian or elsewhere has ever escaped the pits of death and returned to tell the tale, save Owen son of Tadwyn."

"I have," said a small voice. Melina repeated more loudly, "I have! When I fell into a pit, Gaelathane pulled me out and led me to the land of Clynnod to fulfill His prophecies. I had forgotten that terrible day until Owen and I met Gaelathane on the Downs."

Meanwhile, the slipwing had been examining Melina's ears. With a stunned look, he said, "Fy Melina, fy Melina, ble ydyn nhw eich clustiau, fy gwyddfid glynnwy-genethig? My honey-girl, my honey-girl, where are your ears, my honeysuckle glynnie-girl?"

"Papa?" Melina cried. "Papa!" She buried herself in his arms.

Gisella's hand flew to her mouth. "Blethryn? That is impossible! You vanished many years ago. How did you escape the slunge?"

"As I told Wolf," Owen reminded her, "Gaelathane and the Tree healed the dronzils. Blethryn must have been among them."

Gisella also fell into Blethryn's embrace. "My husband!" she cried. "My daughter Melina! Against all hope you have returned. Would that I could find mortal tears to pour out my happiness!"

The King wept. "Tears are both a blessing and a burden," He said. "Do not waste them on petty slights or annoyances!" Wiping His moist eyes with a forefinger, He dabbed His tears on Gisella's wondering eyes. Then He did the same to Blethryn and Melina.

A torrent of pent-up tears burst from the Spirewalker's eyes, then from Melina's and Blethryn's. Owen wept also as his friends patted their dripping faces and stared curiously at their damp hands.

"So this is what we have been missing," sniffled Gisella. "I feel like the forest after a refreshing spring rain." She knelt before the King. "Thank You for restoring my daughter and husband to me, and for giving us back our wings. For tears we are grateful, too."

"This gift is not for you three alone," the King told her. "As I have done to you, do also for all your people. But the time for tears has passed. A fresh chapter in Feirian's history has begun. The old things have passed away. Behold! I make all things new."

The King cupped His hands around Melina's ears. When He took away His hands, her ears were as tapered and shapely as Gisella's and Blethryn's. Melina touched herself and squealed with delight. Then she shot into the air and floated back to earth, spinning on her wings like a spiral of nested silken scarves.

I'll never have a better chance, Owen told himself. Kneeling before Blethryn and Gisella, he said, "Though I am not one of you, I am asking for Melina's hand in marriage. I wish to spend the rest of my life with her, however long or short that might be."

206

"It might be very short," Blethryn said. "Melina could live for a millennium, while you will be fortunate to see a century."

"Please, Father?" Melina begged Blethryn. "I do love him!"

Blethryn mused, "Though they are rare, such mixed marriages between man and glynnie have taken place before in Feirian."

"But they never turn out well!" Gisella wailed. The Spirewalker collapsed onto her leafy throne. "Oh dear, oh dear," she murmured, wiping away her tears. "Melina wishes to be wed to a *man*! No Spirewalker in our long history has ever married an outsider, let alone one of the dust-people. I cannot bear so much excitement in one day." She whimpered while Blethryn patted her shoulder.

"Have you forgotten the Royal Prophecy?" he reminded her.

When faery heir and mortal man
Shall meet amidst a meadowed land,
Then maid shall flee into the mist
With tree of passages to tryst.

The foreign feathers one shall wear
Will never warm the wintry lair,
That freezes flesh and swallows breath;
In dying, they shall conquer death.

At last, for life they shall be bound,
The first to govern glynnies' ground;
With singing wings they shall ascend
To myndyn worlds without an end.

"I never understood how either 'faery heir' or 'mortal man' could wear 'foreign feathers,'" said Gisella thoughtfully. "I still don't."

With a wink at Owen, Melina explained how she had become the "sparrow-that-was-not-a-sparrow." Gisella and Blethryn interrupted her tale several times with questions and exclamations.

"I have never heard of such trees," remarked Gisella when her daughter's story was done. "Those 'bird-myndyns' may well have been to blame for many unexplained glynnie disappearances."

"But why did Gaelathane say 'tree of *passages*'?" asked Elwyn.

"That's easy," said his sister, smirking. "Melina made double passage through her torsil—into the bird *world* and into bird *form*."

Gisella said glumly, "Then I suppose these two must be married, and Melina will be widowed untimely by her dust-boy."

"Be not dismayed at the briefer lifespan of Owen's kind," said Gaelathane. "Because he has tasted death's sting for the sake of the many, I have granted him to taste the dragonfly's sting as well. Though he grew no wings, his years shall now surpass those normally appointed to his race. Indeed, should the Tree tarry, he shall outlive many a myndyn and not a few stout glynnies, too."

A stunned look came over Gisella's face. "According to the Royal Prophecy, if Melina and Owen marry, that would make them—!"

"King and queen of Feirian," said Gaelathane. "Melina shall also succeed you as Spirewalker. You have served Me well, Gisella, but it is time you yielded your living throne to your daughter."

New tears sprang to Gisella's eyes. "Yet, without the Myndyn Hall's spires, how will Melina visit the worlds beyond Feirian?"

"There is more to being a Spirewalker than making a few rocks ring!" Gaelathane replied. He held out His hand to Owen and said, "I'll have that Clynnod-cone you've been keeping, please."

Puzzled, Owen handed the object to Him. After plucking one of His beard-hairs, the King tied it around the cone's stem. Suspending it by the hair, He offered the cone to the Spirewalker.

Gingerly, she grasped the hair. The cone spun freely this way and that, its splendor flashing from within like bottled lightning.

"Amazing!" Blethryn said. "The seeds inside shine as well."

"Now what shall I do with it?" Gisella asked.

"Tap it with your finger," Gaelathane instructed her, and the Spirewalker flicked the twisting cone with her fingernail. *Ting!* The cone responded with a high, piercing note. In a wispwing's blink, Gisella, Blethryn and the cone vanished without a sound.

CHAPTER 21

THE SPARROW AND THE BOY

Swyndon had scarcely recovered from Owen and Melina's reappearance—not to mention the Greatwood's return and Gaelathane's visit—when the village witnessed an event still retold in song. On a balmy June evening, the stars fell from the heavens, descending in glowing swarms upon the Downs.

Thinking someone had set the old torches afire to ward off some new foe, the villagers rushed out of their homes. However, the torches still lay neatly stacked in piles, ready to be burned up. Thoroughly alarmed, the townspeople retreated to their snug houses and hid behind locked doors and shuttered windows.

Then five winged figures bearing bright wands flew down into the village. Like tall lords they were, with sharp features and luminous garments, and the grasses barely bent beneath their feet.

"Hear ye! Hear ye!" they announced, with other such heraldic words. "All of Swyndon's inhabitants are invited to a great and grand celebration on the neighboring hill. Be not afraid, for this will be an occasion of blessing, rejoicing and honor for your people."

Curious, the townsfolk followed the stately heralds to Lone Oak Hill's summit, which was abuzz with fireflies. More winged people were milling about the hill in a state of high excitement.

Prowling through the crowd were several of the eagle-lions like the foul-tempered creature Percy and Mirrah had ridden into Swyndon. The villagers gave the outlandish beasts a wide berth.

High above the hill, Owen and Melina circled on Sharpears. Owen smiled to himself as he lowered Rolin's starglass from his eye. "Trellisant must have been very persuasive," he told Melina. "It appears the whole village has emptied. Now the real fun begins!"

"Only if someone brought fresh meat," muttered Sharpears.

After visiting Sweetspeech the amenthil, Gwynneth and Timothy's troth-tree, Melina and Owen had received the Gift of Understanding. Now the two were enjoying eavesdropping on their neighbors, thanks to Sharpears, who had been aptly named.

Descending in tightening spirals, they landed on the hilltop, creating quite a sensation among the assembled villagers. Yawning and stretching, Sharpears grunted, "I don't see what all the fuss is about. I've never been hungry enough to eat a stringy two-legs."

"Why, it's Owen and Melina!" several of the onlookers said.

"And Melina's got wings!" others exclaimed.

The villagers crowded around the couple, peppering them with questions. Then Owen's parents rushed up to embrace him. "Have you come back to stay?" Tadwyn anxiously asked his son. "The other day, a foppish flatlander showed up in Swyndon insisting he's a friend of yours. We have been letting him sleep in your room, but he doesn't know a sheep's head from its tail. I need you to help me with the flocks, especially now that those dratted trees have returned to reclaim so much of the best pastureland."

Owen was about to answer when Yannick and Mahilka plowed through the crowd. "What did I tell you?" Yannick said to his wife. "I knew they'd settle down here. Don't they make a handsome couple? I'll get right to work building them a house next to ours . . ." His voice trailed off as he noticed Melina's fluttering wings.

Tears filled Mahilka's eyes. "This is not their home now. Don't you see? Melina's folk have returned for her. She's going away!"

Yannick grunted. "At least that lass Mirrah knows a thing or two about sheep. It's a stroke of luck she blew into Swyndon when she did. I don't know what I would have done without her."

"Don't you care about anything besides those silly old sheep?" Mahilka scolded him. "You had better hope Melina's people don't become angry with you for what you did to her ears, my husband!"

Owen reached up along Melina's head and parted the hair around one ear. Stunned, Yannick and Mahilka stared at their daughter. Then they hugged her, weeping for wonder and for joy.

"Don't my ears look perfect now?" Melina asked them.

"Forgive us for trying to make you something you weren't," said Yannick, wiping his eyes. "We wanted to help you fit in better as a villager, but I see now you never really belonged here."

"Where *do* you belong, Daughter?" asked Mahilka softly.

Melina kissed her mother's forehead and pointed down the hill. "We belong with him," she said, her voice vibrant with joy.

A hush fell over the hilltop. Lightstaff in hand, the Gadabout was climbing the hill. Villagers and glynnies alike made way for him as he strode to the foot of the old oak tree. Then he faced the spectators. Raising his staff, he beckoned to Owen and Melina.

While the two approached, the Gadabout announced, "You Swyndonians have known Me as a roving shepherd, but you shall know Me thus no longer." Blazing light broke through His sheepskins, revealing Him as Tadwyn and Gyrta's supper guest.

"Who gives this woman to be wed to this man?" Gaelathane asked. Mahilka and Yannick came up to stand beside Melina.

"I love you, Mother and Father," she told them with tears in her eyes. "You raised me here in our village, and this will always be my home. Yet I once lived in a faraway land, where my birth parents took care of me during the years before you found me."

Melina lifted her hands to the singing stars. Blethryn and Gisella floated down to meet her. Having rung Owen's Clynnod-cone, they had learned that just as the Tree's every twig leads to a different land, so also does the cone that dangles from every twig's tip.

As the two sets of parents exchanged pleasantries, Owen read the silent words written in Melina's eyes. *I have always loved you,* those sparrow-eyes told him. *As a maiden I loved you, and I loved you even while a sparrow. Now I shall love you as your wife and queen until the day death parts us in this fleeting life. You are my heart!*

The Boy's shining eyes beamed back his reply: *Gaelathane has answered my prayers. My sparrow has returned to me at last!*

While Swyndon's shepherds played their panpipes, Gaelathane spoke of a love and faithfulness between man and maid that would last a lifetime of lifetimes. Tears flowed from faery eyes that had never known tears before. Then a thousand suns broke upon the hilltop as a great company of glynnies gathered overhead, their talisynds lighting up the night sky. Above the faeries, legions of bright angels flew betwixt the heavens and the earth.

After the ceremony, Owen greeted his new relatives. Embracing Yannick, he confessed to having let out his father-in-law's sheep.

The veins in Yannick's forehead swelled and throbbed. "You? That was you? I always suspected as much, but you cleverly covered your tracks." The veins stopped throbbing. "Still, what's done is done. There ain't no sense in crying over lost sheep, I always say. Thank you. It takes a real man to admit when he's done wrong."

Mahilka smiled. "What he means to say is, 'Welcome to our family!' Our sheep are your sheep now, and yours are ours."

Smiling back, Owen said, "I'm afraid Melina and I will be herding sheep of the two-legged, winged variety, not wooly ones!"

Yannick and Mahilka exchanged puzzled glances. Owen didn't expect the two to understand. Nobody in Swyndon could imagine the life he and his new bride were embarking upon as Feirian's first king and queen. Owen could hardly believe it himself. Kissing Melina's cheek, he said, "Shall we fly away now to Feirian?"

"We?" she impishly replied. "I'm the only one between us with wings!" To the onlookers' astonishment, she fluttered a few feet off the ground, where she hovered, thumbing her nose at Owen.

"We'll see about that!" Owen retorted, leaping onto Sharpears. He swept into the air, snatched up his bride and seated her before him on the griffin's back. Together, they soared heavenward.

As the newlyweds vanished among the moonlit clouds, Gisella's hand found Blethryn's. "'With singing wings they shall ascend to myndyn worlds without an end,'" she murmured to him.

"Now it is our turn!" Blethryn said, and fanning his wings, he set out with Gisella to seek the beaming face of the rising moon.

Gwynneth slipped away from the throng with Timothy. The night wind cut through her clothing, stirring up sharp twinges of the borwog-chill still lingering in her bones. She snuggled against her husband, who wrapped his flapping cloak around her.

"Is that better, my love?" he asked her. "The breezes blow briskly up here. Are you ready to pick up our lives where we left off?"

Smiling warmly into his eyes, Gwynneth nodded. "Another wedding awaits us in the Beechtown chapel," she said. "Thinbark the myndyn can take us to Thalmos." Hand in hand, she and Timothy left Lone Oak Hill and passed into the mists of Feirian.

EPILOGUE

As Feirian's king and queen, Owen and Melina enjoyed many adventures and reigned for years beyond reckoning, beloved by all their subjects. King Owen still flies about on Sharpears, whose friends and kin often bring along an outringer or two whenever they pop in for a visit. None of the Lucambrians has ventured to set foot in a faery ring since leaving Clynnod.

Melina became known as "the Bird Queen," for she grew very familiar with all of Feirian's feathered folk, but especially with the sparrow tribe. As Spirewalker, she spends much of her time inside Mt. Morwynion ringing the thousands of Tree-cones the glynnies have strung for her use in the City of Light. In altered form, this practice has passed into other worlds as well, where people hang shiny glass ornaments about their homes during Yuletide.

Owen and Melina often meet with Gaelathane in the Losswing Gardens, now known as the "Glorywing Gardens." That walled sanctuary is home to Gisella and Blethryn, who stand beside their fellow sleepwings dreaming of Gaelessa. The new queen and king still consult with the sleeping faeries on matters of importance.

As caretaker, Athyrea tends the gardens as well as the ferns and mosses that grace the encircling walls. Waterlilies and swans instead of cast-off wings now float upon the Wingwater Pool, though the melancholy faces of wispwings past still gaze out from its waters.

Dammed with rubble, the River Blynnys's underground waters rose to fill the hole resulting from the Glynnspire Cave's collapse. On moonlit evenings, one may still see stalactites and stalagmites littering the bottom of Blynnys Lake like broken statuary.

Melina and Owen often visit Swandel, as the village has been renamed. Many of the villagers now make their livelihood hunting, fishing or mushroom-picking in the Greatwood. Sheepshuns are no longer practiced in Swandel, since nobody disappears on the Downs these days except those who wish to. Most of the welving rings have faded away, although those mysterious circles still live on in the Welving Dance. One day each spring, Swandel's lads and lasses join hands and frolic in a circle around an unblemished lamb, commemorating Gaelathane's sacrifice for all of Clynnod.

The silver chalice remains among the rocks where it fell when Owen hurled it at the borwogs, and it has never since been empty. A crimson fountain bubbles from it, becoming a stream that flows through the Greatwood, down to the flatlands and thence to the Sea of Clynnod, healing and refreshing all who partake of its waters.

Having learned which end of a sheep is which, a humbler Percy wed Mirrah the following summer. Shortly thereafter, the two were crowned king and queen of Clynnod in the flatlands, where they ruled wisely and justly. To the end of his life, Percy bore a purple scar on his cheek, a memento of Dask's swordplay. The king still has a soft spot in his heart for shepherds. He lured some of Swandel's best away from their flocks to become his courtiers and advisors.

Timothy and Gwynneth often call on their friends in Feirian. They make passage through Thinbark, who escaped ax and fire to reach a ripe but talkative old age, even by tree standards.

After flying off to the Willowahs for their long-delayed honeymoon, the newlyweds returned to the Hallowfast. On rainy spring mornings, you might find them flinging oatmeal at Rolin and Marlis. Cook was always annoyed at this "waste of perfectly good mush." He also could not fathom why most of the royal family refused to eat mutton any longer—even as a savory stew.

Gwynneth never forgot the fireside sign language Mirrah had taught her. The pair remained fast friends and frequently visited. Signing proved handy for carrying on private conversations when husbands, children or servants were apt to eavesdrop.

Clynnod has a new Gadabout now. I still wear my sheepskin coat, but I carry a crooked lightstaff instead of a bow or knife. Wherever my men and I go, we speak of the King's love and mercy, for we recall our Deadwood days of hopeless misery.

Whenever I lie down to sleep under myndyn trees, I watch for lights dancing in the dusk, for the dremlens like to keep me company. We talk of singing strings, of wings and of worlds where the King's love is yet unknown. Before I climb the Tree, I do hope to spread the good news of the Shepherd in some of those lands.

Faeries and faery rings have become rather rare in these latter years. Men still fear the myndyns, which they cut down to make way for their farms and fields. Their axes have stranded many a faery far from Feirian and the Harp of Gaelathane. After losing their wings, most exiled slipwings have adopted the ways of men, wearing their hair long to hide their telltale ears. The exiles usually go by the surname, "Mendenhall," an echo of "Myndyn Hall," the lost cavern that once rang with the music of the stone spires.

As for the wispwings, if a sudden fog should overtake you, or if you glimpse a glimmering in the treetops at eventide, listen for the sound of singing. As everyone knows, fireflies can't sing.

217

Glossary and Pronunciation Guide

Athyr′ea. Glynnie character. (A fern-faery.) Sister of Osmund.
bay-bonnet. Type of mushroom that often grows in fairy rings.
Black Lake. Largest slunge pit in Feirian.
Bleth′ryn. Gisella's lost husband.
Blue Eye. Mirrah's nickname for Tabitha.
bolytarn (pr. bowl′-i-tarn). A type of edible wild mushroom.
bor′wogs. Black creatures of the night. See also *dronzils*.
Caerillion (pr. Sir-ill′-ee-on). Glynnie "City of Light."
camp′ion. "Mushroom" in the glynnie tongue.
Celembrose (pr. Sell-em′-brose). Owen's guardian angel.
Clynnod (pr. Klinn′-udd). Owen's home world.
Code of Caerillion. Glynnie codex of laws.
Crowlyn (pr. Krow′-linn). Elder of Swyndon.
Dask, Hammel, Pudger, Stubs, Wolf. Mutton-men.
Deadwood. Mutton-people's term for the Glynnion Wood.
Downs. Hilly grasslands where Greatwood formerly grew.
drem′lens. Mutton-people's name for glynnies.
dron′zils. Glynnie term for borwogs.
faery ring. Grassy ring supposedly made by dancing faeries.

Feeding Day. Day when sheep are sacrificed in Black Lake.
Feirian (pr. Fer´-ry-un). "Beautiful land" in the glynnie tongue.
firemaster. One responsible for tending fires in a firewatch.
firewatch. Clearing in Deadwood where campfire is maintained.
flatlanders. Inhabitants of the flatlands. (Southern lowlands.)
Gadabout. Old shepherd who walks the Downs.
Gaelessa (pr. Gale-es´-suh). Gaelathane's home.
Ghostwood. Name for any land beyond the myndyn trees.
Gisella (pr. Ji-sel´-la). Spirewalker of Feirian.
Glorywing Gardens. New name for Losswing Gardens.
glynniant (pr. glin´-nee-unt). Metal found in Mount Morwynion.
Glynniard-alffornion. Losswing Gardens.
glyn´nies. What faeries call themselves.
glynnion-daifalon. Faeries of the day.
glynnion-naifalon. Faeries of the night.
Glynnion Wood. Myndyn forest of Feirian. See also *Deadwood*.
Glynnspire Cave. Feirian grotto. Also known as *Myndyn Hall*.
Gray Death. Fog that flows from *Graylands* to cover the Downs.
Greatwood. Myndyn forest that once covered the Downs.
gwan´len. Glynnie term for veil between worlds.
Gyrta. Owen's mother.
Harwelf son of Andelf. Wolf's given name.
Landon Lake. Lake located near Swyndon.
Limbo. Netherworld that lies between torsil worlds.
Losswing. A wispwing that has just lost her wings.
Losswing Gardens. Gardens where wispwings shed their wings.
Melina daughter of Mahil´ka. Owen's shepherdess friend.
menes´tr. Ceremonial box-bearer in the rite of sheepshun.
Mirrah (pr. Meer´-uh). Mutton-girl and Gwynneth's friend.
Mount Crygmor. Mountain peak in Feirian.
Mount Morwynion (pr. More-win´-yun). Glynnies' home.
myndyn (pr. min´-din). Glynnie name for touch-torsil.
On´collon. King of the pit.
orella. Glynnie term for amenthil tree.
outringers. Owen's name for Rolin and company.
Owen son of Tadwyn. A young shepherd of Swyndon.

People of the Dust. Glynnie term for humans.
People of the Glen. Glynnies.
Plenion (pr. Plen´-yun). Gaelathane's prophecy of Feirian.
porthyl (pr. pore´-thill). "Portal" in the gwanlen.
Prince Percy. Heir to the throne of the Kingdom Clynnod.
River Blynnys (pr. Blinn´-iss). Feirian underground river.
Royal Prophecy. Prophecy of Feirian's future monarchy.
Sea of Thionne. Sea located in Feirian.
Sharpears. Owen's griffin.
sheepshun. Ritual intended to appease Swyndon's enemies.
sleepwing. Aged slipwing that has fallen into a trance.
slipwing. A mature, wingless glynnie.
slunge pit. Glynnie name for borwog hole.
Spirewalker. Feirian's chief glynnie.
Starlyss. The first Spirewalker.
Swandel. ("Dell of the Swans.") Former name of Swyndon.
Sweetspeech. Gwynneth and Timothy's amenthil troth-tree.
Swyndon. ("Deceiving Downs.") Owen's village.
Tabitha. Owen's lost sheep. (Blind in one eye.) See also *Blue Eye*.
Tadwyn son of Tarklin. Owen's father.
talisynd. Glynnie "wand" made of a Tree-twig.
teithlin (pr. tyth´-linn). "Taken" (on the Downs).
Teithliniau (pr. tyth-linn´-ee-eye). "The Taken Ones."
Thinbark. A myndyn tree leading to Thalmos.
touch-torsil. A smooth-barked torsil sensitive to touch.
Trellisant. Captain of the Caerillion Guard.
troth-tree. Tree uprooted and replanted by a betrothed couple.
tylwyth teg (pr. till-with tegg). Lucambrian name for faeries.
Valley of Glynnhaven. Feirian valley where glynnies live.
welving rings. Term for faery rings that grow on the Downs.
Wendell. The Hallowfast's wine steward.
Wesselwynd. Land where first myndyn was felled.
wingshed. When a wispwing loses her wings.
Wingwater Pool. Pond in Losswing Gardens.
wispwing. An immature, winged glynnie.
Yannick. Melina's adoptive father.